TALKER

Slowly, so as not to awaken Chris, Larsen slipped out of bed, tiptoed naked to the closed bedroom door, and pressed his ear against it. There was a sound, but he couldn't place it. Then he realized that his gun was in the living room with his clothes, and so was Chris's little automatic.

He opened the door a foot and looked into the living room, now lit by part of a moon. The room seemed empty. He stepped through the door, looking around him, ready to defend himself. His coat was on the coffee table, and the pistol was inside it, still in its holster . He freed the weapon and flipped off the safety, turning slowly around in the room, watching for any motion. He seemed to be alone.

He reached for a lamp on a small table and switched it on. The light illuminated the room sufficiently for him to notice the only thing that had changed. Near the door was a small chest of drawers with a mirror hanging above it. A tube of Chris's lipstick rested on the chest, and there was writing on the mirror in bright red.

YOU'LL NEVER GET AWAY FROM ME.
A.

Then he looked at the front door and saw that the chain was off the latch.

Books by Stuart Woods

Fiction:

*Imperfect Strangers**
*Dead Eyes**
*L.A. Times**
*Santa Fe Rules**
*New York Dead**
*Palindrome**
Grass Roots
White Cargo
Under the Lake
Deep Lie
Run Before the Wind
Chiefs

Travel:

*A Romantic's Guide to the Country Inns
of Britain & Ireland*

Memoir:

Blue Water, Green Skipper

*Available from HarperCollins*Publishers*

DEAD EYES

STUART WOODS

HarperPaperbacks
A Division of HarperCollins*Publishers*

HarperPaperbacks   *A Division of* HarperCollins*Publishers*
                   10 East 53rd Street, New York, N.Y. 10022

A hardcover edition of this book was published in 1994
by HarperCollins*Publishers.*

Cover illustration by Kirk Reinert

First HarperPaperbacks printing: October 1994

Printed in the United States of America

HarperPaperbacks and colophon are trademarks of
HarperCollins*Publishers*

❖ 10 9 8 7 6 5 4 3 2 1

This book is for Pegram and Ann Harrison.

ACKNOWLEDGMENTS

I am grateful to Detective Alejandro Valedez of the Threat Assessment Group of the Los Angeles Police Department, which is commanded by Captain Robert Martin and Lieutenant John Lane, for information about the stalker phenomenon; and to Dr. Robert Spector of Atlanta, Georgia, for information about trauma-induced blindness. If I got anything wrong, it is my fault, not theirs.

I am grateful to my editor, Gladys Justin Carr, HarperCollins Vice President and Associate Publisher, for her sharp eye and fine work on this manuscript, and to all the people at HarperCollins who helped publish the book.

Once again, I am grateful to my agent, Morton L. Janklow, his principal associate, Anne Sibbald, and to everyone at Janklow & Nesbit for their enthusiasm and hard work on behalf of my career.

CHAPTER

1

The first letter arrived on a Monday. Chris Callaway was annoyed when her secretary told her it had been in the mailbox. It was unstamped.

The tone was friendly, not too worshipful, not too familiar.

Dear Ms. Callaway,

Your work has given me such a lot of pleasure that I felt I had to write to you. Somehow I had missed your films until last week, when I saw Heart of Stone *on late-night television. I was so impressed that I saw* Valiant Days *in Westwood the following night. I have since rented the videos of* Mainline *and* Downer, *and I was impressed with your very high standard of work in all of them.*

Have you ever had the experience of meeting someone and feeling that you had known him for a long time? I have that feeling about you.

Thank you again for your fine work. You'll be hearing from me.

Admirer

When Chris had bought this house, she had taken a lot of trouble to keep the address strictly private. All her bills went to her manager's office, and when she found it necessary to give an address, she used a box number. Her friends sent their Christmas cards to the box, damn it, she thought, and now some *fan* had found her. She handed the letter back to Melanie, her secretary. "Answer it cordially, and refer him to the box number."

"There's no return address," Melanie said, turning over the envelope.

Chris felt oddly frustrated at not being able to reply to the writer. Many of the actors she knew didn't answer their fan mail at all or referred it to a service for handling, but she had always replied to everything, and it amounted to twenty or thirty letters a month, jumping to a hundred after the release of a new film. Melanie wrote the replies, and Chris signed them.

"Then call the security patrol and ask them to keep a watch on my mailbox."

Melanie gave her the "you-can't-be-serious" look. "Chris, don't you think you're overreacting? It's a letter, not a bomb."

Chris laughed. "You're right." Jesus, she thought, why am I letting a little thing like this get to me?

Melanie glanced at her watch. "You're due at Graham Hong's in twenty minutes for your class, and Danny's doing your hair here at one."

"Right, I'd better get going." Chris grabbed her duffel and entered the garage through the study door. A moment later, she was driving down Stone Canyon, past the Bel Air Hotel, toward Sunset in the Mercedes 500SL convertible. It amused her that in Bel Air and Beverly Hills, there were so many of the flashy little cars that she could think of hers as anonymous.

Graham Hong turned out to be big for an Asian— over six feet and well-muscled, yet lithe. He taught in his home and it was nothing like a gym, more of a teahouse. Hong greeted Chris with a cup of tea and asked her to sit down.

"Have you ever had any martial arts training?" he asked. His voice was accentless California; no trace of anything Asian.

"None," she replied.

He beamed at her. "I'm so glad."

"Why?" she asked.

"Any dance experience?"

"I started as a dancer, in New York."

"Very good. Do you work out with a trainer?"

"No, I have a little gym at home. I'm in good shape."

"Good, then you will not tire easily."

"Graham," she said, "if I tired easily I wouldn't be an actress."

He laughed appreciatively.

"Why is dance training better than martial arts?"

"I've read the script," he said. "What we want for

this picture is not anything ritualistic, but simply dirty fighting. Your dance experience will help greatly with your balance, and ultimately, it will make you more graceful." He stood. "If you've finished your tea, let's begin." He slid back a screen, revealing a good-sized room furnished only with a wall-to-wall mat and a canvas dummy. One wall was mirrored, with a ballet barre.

"First, some basics," Hong said. "Let's say that you find yourself in a fight—a fight with a man who is larger and heavier than you. How would you approach this fight?"

"I'd kick him in the crotch," Chris replied.

"Why?"

"Because I've been led to believe that would disable him."

"It might, if you caught him unawares. You might have more success kicking him in the shin, or better, the knee."

"Why there, instead of the crotch?"

"The idea is to inflict as much pain as possible with your first strike. It is the pain that is disabling. There is nothing in the testicles that is inherently disabling, except the pain caused when they are struck. If you are wearing hard shoes, you can inflict disabling—or at least, very distracting—pain in the shin. But if you kick in the knee, you can actually disable, even while barefoot or wearing soft shoes. The knee is a complex and vulnerable structure."

"Very interesting," Chris said.

"I would not recommend that, in a street scuffle, you kick someone in the knee, simply because you are likely to inflict such damage that lawsuits and serious medical expenses could result. However, if someone attacked you with a weapon or other deadly force, the knee would be an excellent choice." Hong took her by the shoulders and stood her in the center of the room. "Relaxed, weight on both feet, slightly forward, arms at the sides. This is the position from which to either attack or defend."

Chris held her hand up in a boxing stance. "Not like this?"

"That is a defensive stance," Hong said, "unless you are in a formal boxing match. In a street fight, you would only be telling your opponent that you were thinking of hitting him. If you, a woman, are up against a man, surprise must be your first weapon. Watch; this is slow motion." Hong stood facing her, lifted his left foot, and gently pushed against the inside of her right knee. It buckled, and she fell to that knee.

Hong helped her up. "Now you try, in slow motion. Simply put your left instep to the inside of my right knee."

Chris followed his instructions, and Hong fell to his knee.

"Now," he said from the floor. "This is what you have done. First, if you have kicked me really hard, you have damaged my knee, perhaps so badly that I cannot walk on it again without surgery. Second, because you have buckled the joint and made me fall, I am on one knee and vulnerable to further attack. Third, simply by falling with my weight on my knee, I may have damaged it even further. Someone with experience, when kicked in this manner, would avoid falling on his knee, then roll and come up with his weight on the other leg. Of course, if you have done your work well, he would have to stand on one leg only and would be very vulnerable indeed."

"Gotcha," Chris said.

"Now, can you kick above your head?" Hong asked.

Chris turned and did a high kick for him.

"Very good. What would work very well in your first fight scene would be simply to kick him in the face." He stood facing her and, again in slow motion, demonstrated.

"I can do that," Chris said.

"Then do it," Hong replied. "I want you to kick me in the face as quickly and as hard as you can. Leave it to me to protect myself."

Chris, who was standing ready, whipped out a leg and sent her instep at Hong's chin. To her astonishment, she connected solidly, and Hong flew backward. She rushed to his side. "Jesus, Graham, did I hurt you?"

Hong lifted his head and shook it. "I did not believe you could be so fast," he laughed, spitting out blood. "You are a ruthless woman, and I will not underestimate you again."

When Chris got home there was another unstamped letter in the mailbox.

CHAPTER

2

L ook at this," Chris said, handing Danny Devere the two letters. "Can you believe it?"

Danny was brushing Chris's thick brunette hair, shaping it around her shoulders. He put down his hair dryer and picked up a letter. "Well, Sweets," he said feigning a lisp, "looks like you got yourself a fella."

"Not that one," Chris said. "Read the second one."

Danny read the second letter and quoted, " 'You're certainly athletic. I'd hate to come up against you in a dark alley.' What the hell does that mean?"

"I just came back from Graham Hong's house; he's training me for the new film. We had this little session and I accidentally—well, not exactly accidentally—but inadvertently dumped him on his ass."

"*You* dumped *Graham Hong* on his ass?"

"He asked me to kick him in the face, and I did. He just didn't get out of the way fast enough."

Danny hooted with laughter. "God, I'd give anything to have seen that!"

"The point is, Danny, whoever wrote this letter saw it. The sonofabitch followed me this morning."

Danny read the letter again. "I think you're jumping to conclusions. This guy's just seen you in the movies. Remember when you hit the guy with the bottle in . . . what was it?"

Chris shook her head. "No, this guy was watching us."

Danny began to rub Chris's shoulders. "Relax, Sweets; you're making too much of this."

"That's what Melanie said this morning, when the first letter came. Neither of them was stamped; he put them in my mailbox. How the hell did he find out where I live?"

"Sweets, *anybody* can find out where *anybody* lives; don't you know that?"

"Danny, I *never* give this address to *anybody*. I get my *Christmas cards* through the P.O. box. The only mail I get here is catalogues, addressed to 'Resident.' "

"Look, I bet when you buy something at Saks or Neiman's you have it sent here, don't you?"

"No. I take it home; or, if something is being altered, Melanie picks it up. I *never* give anybody this address, unless they're coming to dinner or to play tennis. And *this* . . . " she held up the letter, ". . . did not come from somebody I'd invite to dinner. This is creepy. I'll tell you how this guy found out where I live; he followed me home, that's how."

Danny took her head in his hands and pointed it at the mirror. "Look at me," he said. "Don't do this to yourself. You're starting a new movie next Monday, and you can't get yourself all tensed up about something that you're probably imagining."

Chris slumped. "You're right, I guess; you always are."

"If you call the cops, they'll treat you like a nut case."

"I know, I know." She sighed. "The fame side of this business has never rested easy with me. I *hate* being recognized, having strangers come up to me and demand autographs or want their pictures taken with me."

"It's the price you pay, Sweets."

"It's too high a price. When I get the new house built and get some money in the bank, I'm going to back out of this business."

"Listen, you *love* what you do. You just have to come to terms with the fame thing. I know a good shrink."

She spun around in her chair and faced him. "You think this is *my* problem? You think I somehow *deserve* to have this creep following me around and leaving notes in my mailbox? This is not some fantasy, Danny; it's happening, and what can a shrink do about that?"

"She could help you figure out how to handle it, that's what."

Chris stood up and glanced at her hair in the mirror. "Enough of this; I've got to meet the security system guy at the new house in half an hour, and with traffic, I'll be lucky to make it."

"Boy, is that guy going to do a job on you today," Danny said. "You'll buy the biggest alarm system in the world; you won't be able to get into your own house."

"Oh, shut up," she said, grabbing his hand. "Come on, I'll walk you to your car." She led him out of the house to the little red Miata parked in her drive, then kissed him on the cheek. "Dinner this weekend?"

"I've got a hot new fella to see on Saturday," he said. "How about Sunday?"

"You're on. I'll take you out to Malibu and show you how the house is coming, then we'll have dinner at La Scala. Meet me here at seven?"

"Sounds good. You think you're going to feel any safer when you move to Malibu?"

"See you Sunday," she called over her shoulder. She got into the Mercedes and headed for the freeway.

She drove fast, her new hairdo blowing in the wind. She didn't care about that; she had great hair, and it would brush out. What was the point of having a convertible if you couldn't let your hair blow in the wind?

At twenty-two Chris had headed for New York, straight out of the University of Georgia, a B.A. with a double major in dance and drama tucked in her trunk. She got her first job a week later, in an off-Broadway musical, and she had hardly ever been out of work since. Sometimes the work had paid little or nothing, but she had never had to wait tables or do commercials to support her acting habit. She took classes at the Actors Studio, she took any part she could get in anything good, and turned down anything she'd be ashamed to have on her resume. During those years she turned down a lot that other actresses would have grabbed at—horror films, TV movies, a biggish part in a series, even. She had done two supporting roles in features before she'd even thought of leaving New York, and when she'd finally made the move to L.A., she'd had two offers in her pocket, a top agent, a business manager, and her moving expenses paid by Centurion Pictures.

There had been a two-year marriage to an actor, Brad Donner, and together they had scraped up a down payment on the Bel Air house. When the marriage failed, he did the gentlemanly thing and moved out, but she was uncomfortable living in the house, and she looked forward to selling it when her own house was finished, and splitting what should be a considerable profit with Brad.

Chris was not a bankable movie star—not yet, anyway; but she'd played featured parts in films with Gene Hackman, Dustin Hoffman, and Alec Baldwin, and two leads opposite slightly lesser stars. All she needed, she and her management felt, was one hot starring role in a film that she could carry herself—something like what Sally Field had found in *Norma Rae*. That one great part was her goal.

Not that she wasn't making a good living. Her price was half a million now, and a hot starring role would push it over the million mark. She was thirty-one—too old to be the kind of phenomenon Julia Roberts was, but she had a solid track record, and she was consistently considered for some of the best work in town.

As she left the Santa Monica Freeway and joined the Pacific Coast Highway, she reflected on her good fortune with this new house. It was at Big Rock, not necessarily the most fashionable part of Malibu, but the beach was great and the lot was good. An earlier house, damaged by mudslides and big waves, had finally burned down, and she had gotten the lot for a bargain price from a disgusted owner. Working with a good architect, she had built foundations that would withstand anything, even the violent vagaries of the Southern California climate. Let the Big One come, she thought; her new house would still be standing.

As she approached Big Rock she could see the

framing timbers of the roof above the construction fence. When the house was near completion, she would build a wall that would separate her from the Pacific Coast Highway traffic and from adoring nuts like her new letter writer.

As she parked, a van pulled up behind her, and a young man got out. "Miss Callaway," he said, "I'm Mel Parker—Keyhole Security."

"How do you do, Mel?" She shook his hand. He was nice-looking, she thought—blond, wiry, and athletic-looking. He had a scarred upper lip and hooded eyes, but the effect was not unattractive.

"I'm a real big fan of yours," Mel said. "I've seen everything you've done, and I can't wait for the next one."

"Thank you, Mel; I appreciate that."

He blushed. "Shall we take a walk around your place and see what you need in the way of a security system?"

"Sure."

He opened the plywood gate for her and they could see the house. That was how she thought of it now. At first, it had just been a burned-out wreck, then a hole in the ground, then a lot of steel and concrete. But now the house was framed, and she could see the shape that she had dreamed about, walk through the rooms and feel their size, pick her way among the timbers out onto what would be the deck and gaze at the blue Pacific. Just entering the gap where the front door would be gave her a thrill.

As she and Mel entered, another young man, a stranger, approached. He was wearing work clothes and carrying a clipboard. He stuck out his hand.

"Chris, I'm Bud Carson; I'm your framing contractor."

"Hi," she said, not put off by the use of her first name. The whole world seemed to have that privilege these days. Her general contractor, Mike Moscowitz, had introduced her to most of the subcontractors, but not to this one, who looked awfully young to be the boss of the framers. He also had an odd cast in his eyes that made it difficult to tell where he was looking when he spoke.

"How do you like the way the place is shaping up?" he asked.

"I'm thrilled. It's beginning to look the way I've imagined it would."

"Framing's the best part," Bud said. "That's when a project starts to be a house, and it happens fast. We'll have the house clad in another ten days, and the roof on a week after that."

"Great. You keep up the good work, hear? Now, if you'll excuse me, I've got to talk with this gentleman about the alarm system."

"By the way," Carson said, "I don't have any paper with me right now, but some other time when you're out here, do you think you could give me your autograph?"

"Sure, Bud, I'd be glad to." She turned to go.

"And can I get somebody to take your picture with me?"

This was the part of her life that drove her nuts; people seemed to think they had some sort of claim on her, just because they'd seen her in the movies. She tried to keep her voice pleasant. "If I have time. Now you're going to have to excuse me." She turned and walked away.

"Chris . . ." he called after her.

She ignored him and kept going. She spent an hour walking around the house with Mel, pointing out windows, deciding whether to have window or screen alarms, placing the keypads that would allow her to enter an entry code or push the panic button.

"How about video?" Mel asked when they were back at the front door.

"Video?"

"I can put a camera over there that will let you look at anybody who rings the bell from any TV set in the house. Then you can decide whether to open the door or talk to the caller on an intercom."

"That sounds good," she said, thinking about the two letters she had received that day.

"I think it's essential for a person in your position," Mel said. "I'm sure you get the odd unwelcome caller."

"Odd is the right word," she said. "Install the camera. What about one on the deck facing the ocean, too?"

"Good idea." He made some notes on the floor plan. "Listen," he said, "I want you to know that I'm going to give you the best possible security service. I've only had my own company for a year, but we're doing really well."

"You come well recommended," Chris said.

"I know it's a little strange for someone you don't really know to have your unlisted phone number and the keys to your house, but I want you to know that your privacy and security are my stock-in-trade, and that you can trust me and my people."

"Thank you, Mel, that's very reassuring."

"Anything at all happens, you hit any two buttons on the keypad, and we'll have a call in to the police within ten seconds. Response time out here is two minutes or less, usually. Of course, depending on what's happening in Malibu, it could take longer."

"Mel, I'm very protective of my privacy, and I don't want *anybody* in your firm to have my street address or phone number, unless it's absolutely necessary."

"I understand your concern," he replied, "but at any one moment, there are three operators sitting staring at computer screens at my office in Santa Monica. When an alarm goes off, if it's not a panic, the operator will immediately call your phone number. If there's no answer, he'll call the police; if you answer, he'll expect you to give him a verbal code, which you will select. If you don't give the code, or if you give the wrong code, he'll assume you're under duress, and he'll call the police."

"That sounds all right."

"My point is, all the operators on all the shifts will have your address and phone number right there in the computer. You should know, however, that I thoroughly investigate the background of every person I hire, and I don't take anybody with a criminal record or any kind of questionable past. Some of my people are former cops, and they know what to do in an emergency."

"Well," she sighed, "I guess I can't go through life without somebody knowing where to find me."

"That's right, but at least you can exercise some control over who knows."

I wish that were true, she thought to herself.

When she got back to the house there was another letter in her mailbox. That made three in one day.

"I can't seem to stop thinking about you," the last line read.

CHAPTER

3

O n Friday morning, Chris attended the first
reading of the final script of her new film,
Forsaken, her first western. This was not the
hot role she was looking for, but she was playing
opposite Jason Quinn, a rising young actor, and the
word was that this movie would make him a big
star. Once again, she was riding on somebody else's
coattails, but, although Quinn's role would domi-
nate the film, she had four very good scenes, including her fight.

The cast had been studying a draft of the screenplay, and this was the first time any of them would
see the final. Everyone was keyed up, but as they
settled around a long table, set up on an empty
soundstage, and began to read their parts, it was
clear to everybody that what they were reading
was a big improvement on what had come before.
Chris was delighted to find that her part had been

expanded, and she had a new scene with Quinn that was better than anything she had bargained for.

When they finished at lunchtime, Jason Quinn and the director, Brent Williams, took her aside, which made her nervous. Like any actor, Chris could be rattled by criticism, and she knew that if these two men didn't like what she was doing, she could be replaced on short notice.

"Chris," Brent began, "I want to tell you that this was the best first reading of a script that I have ever attended, and Jason and I think you are going to be brilliant in this film."

Quinn spoke up. "I can't think of any other actress who could do what you are doing with this part," he said. "And Graham Hong tells me that you are really going to look good wiping the floor with the bad guy."

"Well, thank you, Jason, Brent," Chris said, trying not to sound flustered at this unexpected praise. "I'm really looking forward to shooting."

"I know this is supposed to be the final screenplay," Brent said, "but there was a scene we cut out early on because we didn't think any actress could bring it off, and now Jason and I want to put it back in. Chris, I'm not exaggerating when I tell you that this is Academy Award material. The studio is very excited about this film; they loved your test for the part, and they're going to pump up the opening from eight hundred to twelve hundred screens—*if* they like the finished product."

"And they're going to love the finished product," Jason said, displaying a large amount of Beverly Hills dental work. "I think you and I are really going to work up some chemistry on this one."

Chris thanked them again, and Jason went back to his dressing room, leaving her alone with the director.

"I've talked to Jason about this," Brent said, "and I'm going to bump up your billing. You'll be above the title, single card, right after Jason."

"That's wonderful, Brent," Chris said, and she meant it. She had learned from experience not to get too excited about promises in Hollywood, but this time she couldn't help herself; her heart was thumping with joy.

"The changes in the script have made your role a real costarring one. Jason and I felt it was the least we could do." He gave her a hug and went off toward the studio commissary.

"Well," Chris said aloud to herself, "you could have given me costarring money." She had started back to her dressing room when she realized that no letters from Admirer had arrived today. She went off to her lunch date with a happy heart.

It was one of those brilliant L.A. days after a rain, when the smog had been swept away by a cold front and the sun lived up to its California promise. She met her agent, Ron Morrow, and her business manager, Jack Berman, at the Bistro Garden in Beverly Hills, and they lunched al fresco.

"I had a call from Brent," Ron said. "He told me the news; I think this is very good for you, Chris." Ron was not yet thirty-five, but he was the hottest young agent at CAA, Creative Artists Agency, the most powerful in town.

"Do you think you could pry more money out of them, Ron?"

Ron shook his head. "It would be a mistake to ask," he said. "If this picture does what I think it's going to do, we'll more than make it up on the next one. You'll have your pick of scripts, you wait and see."

"Ron is right," Jack said. "Let's not crowd the studio on this one. They're happy, and we want to keep them that way." Jack was in his mid-fifties, a veteran of the Hollywood game and business manager to a dozen big stars.

"If you guys say so. What are we getting in the way of offers?"

"Nothing good enough," Ron said. "But when this picture starts screening around town, they'll be flying in over the transom. Don't worry about it."

"I won't worry about a thing," Chris said, smiling.

"How's the house coming?" Jack asked.

"Beautifully. It's mostly framed, so I can see the shape of things. You'll both have to come out and see it."

"I drive past it every night on the way home," Ron said. "I can see the roof sticking up now."

Jack cleared his throat. "Chris, it's time you put the Bel Air house on the market."

"Not yet, Jack; we're another five months away from completion on the Malibu house—if we stay on schedule—and I don't want an endless procession of gawkers traipsing through the house while I'm living there."

"Five months is not too soon, believe me."

"Tell you what; we've got six weeks of interiors to shoot before we move to Monument Valley for the location work. When we leave town, you can put it on the market, okay?"

"Okay," Jack said resignedly, "but I worry about

it. You've insisted on paying cash for the new house, you won't let me get you a mortgage, and money is going to be tight for you."

"Jack, I don't spend much money when I'm shooting. There's just the mortgage payments on the Bel Air house, and my regular monthly nut . . . "

"Which is pretty big, sweetheart."

"Jack," Ron interjected. "Don't worry about it. When *Forsaken* is in the can, Chris's price is going to skyrocket. She'll be fine."

"I just don't like to see her cashing in her savings to build this place when I could get her a variable-rate mortgage right now at a terrific rate."

"Call me crazy," Chris said, "but I'm tired of debt."

Jack held up a hand. "We'll say no more about it."

They finished lunch in a haze of wine and camaraderie.

When Chris got home there were six dozen red roses waiting on her doorstep. They're from Jason and Brent, she said to herself as she gathered them up and struggled toward the kitchen with them. As she placed them in the sink and turned on the water, she noticed the card.

"You're wonderful," it said. It was signed "Admirer." She crumpled it in her hand and threw it at the trash bin.

CHAPTER

4

On Sunday night, Danny Devere showed up on
time. Danny, Chris reflected, was always on
time. It was reassuring to have someone in her
life who was entirely predictable.

When Chris had been married to Brad Donner,
most of their friends had seemed to be his, and since
the divorce she had been constantly working or
occupied with the house, so she hadn't seen much
of anybody. But Danny did her hair every day when
she was working and twice a week when she
wasn't, so, along with Melanie, her secretary, he
was a constant in her life, a fount of common sense
and good judgment. She'd want him at her back in a
fight, too, she thought.

Chris loved to drive, and they took her car.
"What a week!" she said to Danny. "The house
gets framed, and the new script turns out to be better than I thought it would be." She told him about

the first reading and what had happened afterward.

"Sweets," Danny said, "I'm forty, and I've been in this town since I was twenty-two, so I know what I'm talking about: you're headed for the big time, and nobody can stop you."

"I don't want to even think about that," Chris said over the wind noise as Sunset Boulevard ended and they turned onto the Pacific Coast Highway. "I mean, I dreamed about that when I was in New York, doing off-Broadway, but now that it seems to be within my grasp, it scares me a little. I know I put on a tough front, but inside, I'm as insecure as any actress in town, believe me."

"Listen, don't worry about it. You've already made most of the adjustments—you've moved to L.A., you're getting good parts, you're making money, you're building a house. You've got a *life* out here."

"Danny, is the fame thing going to get worse?"

"Not much; all you have to do is get used to it." Danny looked back. "Hey, wasn't that the house back there?"

"There's a full moon tonight, so I thought we'd have dinner first, then go back and wander around the house in the moonlight."

"Sounds good to me."

They dined at La Scala and talked the way old friends do. Chris hadn't been dating since the divorce, and she enjoyed the lack of complication in her friendship with Danny; she trusted him completely. Danny had had a rough time as a young man, she knew, but now he was established as one of the industry's leading hair stylists. He had two dozen films under his belt, working with the whole array of Hollywood's leading ladies, and Chris felt lucky that he always made time for her, both when she was working and when she was not.

"Listen, Chris," Danny said, "isn't it about time you started seeing some guys?"

"Oh, Danny, I just don't feel like it."

"Horseshit. You're a normal American girl; you've got hormones, just like everybody else. You can't spend all your time hanging out with a faggot like me."

"I'd rather spend time with you than anybody I know," she said.

"That's nice, but I'm just one of the girls. I know you, and you need something more than me."

"Maybe in time, but not now." She finished her coffee. "Come on, let's go see the house."

They drove back through Malibu to Big Rock, named for the geological formation that loomed over the highway. Chris parked at the gate and worked the combination lock that secured it, then they stepped past the fence and arrived at the front door. The full moon was high now, and everything appeared in sharp relief.

"Wow," Danny said reverently. "It's real, isn't it?"

"It's getting that way." Chris led him down the hallway that ran straight through the house, then to the right and into the living room, taking care not to trip over debris.

"A really nice-sized room," Danny said. "Are you going to buy a lot of new furniture?"

"Some. Brad said I could have whatever I wanted from the Bel Air house, and I like a lot of the pieces. I'll need new bedroom furniture, though." She led him through the living room to the kitchen. "It has its own little deck, for dining outside," she said, pointing it out, "and there's enough room for friends to sit around and talk to me while I'm cooking."

"I'll watch," said Danny, who was a lousy cook.

"It's going to be a great kitchen," Chris said. "Everything I've always wanted."

"There's a lot to be said for having everything you always wanted," Danny laughed.

"Come on, I'll show you the bedrooms." They walked down the arched hallway that led to a wide doorway, and Chris led him to the guest room. "This is where you can sleep when you're fighting with your boyfriends."

"Nice to have a bolt hole," Danny said. "A good room; I like it."

"Any time. Now, come and see my suite." She led him back to the wide doorway. "There'll be double doors here, and this is my bedroom. The big opening there will be French doors leading out to the deck." She led him across to another room. "This is my study, and it will have a little kitchenette concealed in a cupboard, so I can stay in this part of the house for days, if I feel like it."

"It's just wonderful, Chris," Danny enthused. "It has grace and charm and proportion. It has everything."

"Everything I need, anyway. Come on, you've got to see the view from the deck."

Chris led the way along a catwalk of planks.

"Be careful there," Danny shouted. "It's a long way down, and there are rocks at the bottom."

"Don't worry, I'm a regular tightrope walker," Chris called back. She pointed at the moon over the ocean. "Isn't that a gorgeous sight? I always wanted to live at the beach, but Brad didn't like it out here.

Now I've got just the right place." She jumped up and down on the plank, steadying herself against a two-by-four.

"Stop that, you're scaring me," Danny called.

Chris gave one last jump, and as she landed, she heard a sharp crack and felt the plank give way. She tightened her grip on the two-by-four and tried to turn and reach it with her other hand, but the plank had parted, and she was falling. She couldn't keep her grip.

Twenty feet separated her from the beach, and the fall seemed to be in slow motion. Her feet struck a supporting beam, and she began to turn sideways. Please, God, she was thinking, let there be sand below me.

She fell and fell, and when she struck the beach, only part of it was sand. She was lying on her back, and under her head were rocks. The pain was so intense that only unconsciousness could stop it.

As she passed out she heard Danny's voice from somewhere above her, frantic, calling her name.

CHAPTER

5

The pain had stopped, but it began again. Chris sucked in a deep breath, and when it escaped, an involuntary moan went with it.

From somewhere nearby there was a rustle and footsteps on a hard surface, then there was quiet. Chris was afraid to open her eyes for fear of making the pain worse. Most of her body ached, but her head hurt worst; she had never had such a headache.

A moment later there were more footsteps, this time two people.

"You're awake, are you?" a soft male voice said.

"I'm afraid to open my eyes," she said. "It hurts so."

"Your head?"

"Yes."

"Don't worry about it. Will you try something for me? You don't have to open your eyes."

"As long as it doesn't hurt too much."

A large hand took hers. "Will you wiggle your fingers?"

She wiggled them.

"Good." The hand took her other one. "Now this one."

She wiggled the other fingers.

The hand released hers, then two hands were resting on her feet. "Now wiggle your toes."

She wiggled them, then she heard a sigh.

"Good girl," the man said. "Wonderful girl. You had me worried for a while there."

"Worried about what?"

"I thought you might have been paralyzed in the fall."

"Fall?"

"You don't remember?"

"No."

"What was the last thing you remember?"

"Having dinner with Danny."

"Good. Not much memory loss. You'll be fine."

"Where is Danny?"

"He's been in and out of here since day before yesterday."

"What's today?"

"Tuesday."

"I remember Sunday; we had dinner on Sunday."

"Yes, then you went to see your house, and you fell from a deck to the beach."

Chris thought about that distance and shuddered, which made the pain worse.

"Lie still," he said. "I'll get you something for the pain."

Chris heard writing on a pad, and the other person, a nurse, she guessed, left the room and returned shortly. A hand pressed a pill to her lips, then a glass straw.

"Good. You'll feel better in a few minutes. Just rest and don't move around. I'll be right back." His footsteps left the room.

Chris tried to relax, tried to remember past Sunday dinner, but couldn't. Just as well, she thought. If she had fallen, she didn't want to remember it. She felt a little wave of something, something not unpleasant. The pain receded marginally.

Footsteps returned. "I've got someone with me," the man said. "Why don't you open your eyes?"

Chris felt sleepy, but she opened her eyes. The room was poorly lit; there was a dim light source somewhere to her left, but she could see only shapes. "Who is it?" she asked.

"It's me, Sweets," Danny's voice said. He took her hand. "I've been very worried about you; it's nice to have you back."

"I'm Paul Villiers," the other man said. "I'm a neurologist on staff at Cedars-Sinai. That's where you are."

"You sound like a nice man," Chris said. "Maybe if you opened the blinds I could get a look at you."

There was a long silence; everyone seemed frozen.

"Relax now," the doctor said. "I just want to have a look at your eyes."

Chris felt fingers at her eyelids, and from a great distance came a pinpoint of light. She heard the doctor sigh again.

"What is it?" she said.

"The blinds are open, Chris," Villiers said. "The room is filled with sunlight."

• • •

Chris sat up in bed and played at feeding herself. Why the hell did they serve peas to somebody who couldn't see them? Abandoning daintiness, she held the peas still with her fingers and stabbed at them with her fork.

"Why don't you let me do that?" Danny said. It was the following day, and he seemed never to have left her side.

"Because I'd rather do it myself," Chris said. Her head still hurt, but not as much. She had been allowed to sit up that morning.

Doctors and nurses had paraded through her room all the previous day, but no one had come today; not so far, anyway.

"Where is everybody?" she asked. "Have they given up on me?"

"I saw Dr. Villiers in the hall a few minutes ago. He said he'd be in to see you."

As if on cue, Villiers entered the room. "Good morning," he said. "How are you feeling today?"

"Better, but I still can't see anything," Chris replied.

He dragged up a chair. "I'm going to tell you all I know," he said. "I owe you that much."

"I'm blind? Is that it?" She held her breath and waited for the answer.

"Don't make it any worse than it is. The good news is that you can see some light, discern some shapes."

"What's the bad news?"

"That's the bad news, too. That's all you can see."

"Am I going to get any better?" She steeled herself for his reply, held her breath.

"I wish I could give you a definitive answer," he said, "but all I can promise you is that you have a very good chance of getting better."

Chris let out the breath. "Tell me about that."

"When you fell, you struck the back of your head on rock, damaging the occipital lobes of your brain. Those lie at the back of your skull. There was no fracture of the skull, and that's good; that gives us some indication of the extent of injury."

"And what is the extent of injury?"

"I wish I could tell you exactly, but I can't. Think of it this way: you've bruised a part of your brain, and all the pain you've felt has come from that. You're fortunate that the treatment policy of this hospital caused you to receive heavy doses of steroids when you were admitted to the emergency room. That's standard here since it was learned that in spinal injuries steroids can promote the regeneration of tissue, if they are applied immediately. As a result, the swelling in the back of your head has gone down considerably, and that's good."

"What's the prognosis?" She dreaded his answer.

"There's a wide range. Worst case is that you could remain as you are."

Chris gave an involuntary shudder. A death sentence could hardly have made her feel worse. What would she do? How could she work?

"But," he said hurriedly, "best case is that the injured area of your brain could regenerate completely, and your sight could be completely restored."

"What's your best guess?" she said, afraid to hope.

"Somewhere between the two extremes," he

replied. "Because of your treatment, I will hazard that you'll finish up nearer the good extreme than the bad."

"How long will it take?"

"It could take as long as eighteen months. That's a maximum."

"You mean that what sight I have after eighteen months is what I'll always have?"

"That's probable. I think you'll see improvement long before that, though. We'll certainly keep your treatment at an optimal level for the next few days. When the swelling has gone down and your pain is gone, then you can go home. We won't keep you here any longer than necessary."

"Dr. Villiers, thank you for being straight with me."

"That's how I try and do it. Now I have some rounds to make, and there are a couple of people here to see you."

Danny spoke up. "Ron Morrow and Jack Berman are here," Danny said. "I'll get them."

Chris tried hard to shift mental gears from fear of blindness to greeting guests.

The pleasantries and encouragement had passed; now everyone seemed at a loss for words.

"Let's talk about work," Chris said.

"Baby," Jack said, "you worry about getting well; Ron and I will worry about work."

"Ron, what have you told the studio?"

"That you'll be in the hospital for a few days. And laid up for a while."

"Do they know I'm blind?"

"You're *not* blind," Danny said.

"Let's call it what it is. I can't see much; I can't read a script; I can't work."

"No, they don't know that," Ron said. "Nobody does. But Chris, I have to tell you that they've replaced you on the film."

"When?"

"On Monday, right after they heard," the agent said. "That was to be expected. At that point, they didn't know if you'd ever regain consciousness, let alone if you could work anytime soon. They have a big investment to protect."

"I guess so," she said, then she laughed. "And Jason was just saying the other day that he couldn't imagine anybody else in the part."

"Sweetheart," Jack said. "Don't do this to yourself. This is only a setback. You'll be working again before you know it."

"What have you released to the press?"

"Just that you're recovering from injuries received in a fall, and that a complete recovery is anticipated. You made 'Entertainment Tonight' last night, and it was in the trades today."

"I've had a lot of calls," Ron said. "Everybody wishes you well."

"I've had a bunch, too," Jack said. "And look at all the flowers you got. Sorry, I mean . . . "

"Thanks, Jack, I know what you meant. I'd like all mention of my sight kept out of the papers."

"Of course."

"Listen, guys, I'm kind of tired. Why don't you go back to work, and I'll call you in a few days. Danny, you stay a minute, will you?"

"Sure," Jack said. "If there's anything at all you need—chocolate ice cream, cheesecake from New York—just call."

"Right," Ron said. "We'll be thinking about you. Let's have dinner as soon as you feel better."

The two men left, and Danny dragged his chair up to her bed.

"Tell me about the flowers," she said.

"They're from all over," Danny replied. "Some from the studio; some from Brent Williams and Jason Quinn; some from Brad. He's called a couple of times; he's on location in Spain. I've handled all the calls."

"You're a treasure, Danny. Who else?"

"Well, there are a lot of roses from somebody— six dozen. No card."

Chris began to laugh.

"What?" Danny said, laughing with her. "Oh, shit, it's not him, is it?"

"It's him," Chris said.

Later, when Danny had gone and she was alone, Chris began to cry. She had never been so frightened in her life.

CHAPTER

6

As soon as Chris and Danny pulled to a stop in her driveway, Chris was out of the car, striding up the front walk, determined not to feel blind in this place she knew so well. She ran up the stairs, put her key expertly into the front door lock, opened the door, and fell flat on her face in the entrance hall.

Danny was right behind her. "Oh, shit!" he moaned. "The maid left the vacuum cleaner right in front of the door. And I asked her to have the place perfect for you."

Chris untangled her feet from the machine and stood up. Suddenly she was dizzy and disoriented, and she reached out for Danny. She began to cry. "I'm crying because I'm mad," she said.

"Just hold on to me, Sweets," he said, taking her hand. "Come on, let's find your bedroom."

"Wait," she said, wiping her eyes with the back of

her hand like a little girl. "Are there any other unusual obstacles?"

Danny looked around. "Nope."

"Any of the furniture been rearranged?"

"Nope."

"Then I'd better start getting used to doing this myself," she said, and set off for her bedroom, Danny in her wake with her hospital suitcase. She crossed the living room and turned down the hall, and, occasionally feeling for the wall with the backs of her hands, found her bedroom. What light she could see had barely illuminated the objects in the room; they were just smudges, seemingly arranged at random.

Chris sat down on the bed and wrinkled her nose. "Do I smell roses?"

"Afraid so," Danny said. "The usual six dozen; the maid must have put them in a vase."

"Would you please get them out of here, Danny?" she pleaded. "I don't think I'll ever feel the same about roses again."

"Sure," he said, and she could hear him bustling about, wrapping the flowers in newspaper.

"Was there a card?" she asked.

"Pretty much the same," Danny replied. " 'Get well soon, Admirer.' "

"Throw them out," she said, and fell back on the bed, already tired. She felt sick with dread; what was going to happen to her?

Danny was back in a minute. "Listen to me, kiddo, and don't argue. I'm moving into the guest room."

She didn't move. "I can manage, Danny," she said. "I'll just . . ."

"The hell you can," Danny replied in a tone that

brooked no argument. "This house is going to seem different to you until you get used to it again, and I'm not having you here alone at night with Admirer lurking somewhere nearby. You'll be okay when Melanie is here in the daytime, but not at night."

"Oh, all right," Chris sighed. "I'm too tired to fight you. The guest room is yours; go home and get your things."

"My things are already here and unpacked," Danny said.

The first morning back in the house Danny tried to bring her breakfast in bed, but she wouldn't have it. She insisted on making it herself, and under Danny's watchful gaze, she fumbled around the kitchen, burning herself on the toaster and spilling orange juice, until she had breakfast for both of them on the table.

"Baby," Danny said quietly after they had eaten, "I think you ought to get some temporary professional help."

"Danny, I keep telling you, I don't need a shrink. My head is on perfectly straight."

"Not that profession," he replied. "I mean somebody . . . who's worked with people . . . who have trouble seeing."

"*What?*"

"Approach it the way you would research a new role," Danny said. "Learn how to be blind."

"You mean, get one of those telescopic white canes and tap my way around the neighborhood? Are you crazy?"

"No, no, I mean that . . . there have to be some

shortcuts to learning to deal with this, and there are people out there who can teach you."

"Danny, I know you mean well, but I have to tell you that I think part of getting over this is to *believe* that I'm going to get over it. I think it's important what you *think* when you're sick. If I start learning to be blind, that means that I've accepted being blind, and I'll be damned if I'll accept that. I'm not going to let anybody teach me to be blind; I'm going to teach myself to see again." She paused. "Does that sound crazy?"

Danny laughed. "No, baby, it sounds like *you*. If stubbornness can make you well, then you'll see again in no time."

"The first thing I'm going to do is learn to be in this house again, and I don't want you following me around picking up the pieces, do you hear?"

"I hear Melanie's car in the driveway," Danny said, "and that means I'm out of here. I'll see you tonight." He pecked her on the cheek and ran.

Chris spent a few minutes letting Melanie know that she was not going to be treated like a blind person; then she got herself dressed, choosing her clothes by their feel, brushed her hair, and began blundering from room to room, knocking things over, righting them, and memorizing where they were. By the time Melanie had left for the day there was a new map of her residence imprinted on Chris's brain, and she was moving about with new confidence. She had an hour before Danny would arrive home from work, and she resolved to use it to become perfect in her movements.

She walked about the house, first slowly, then quickly; she backtracked, circled, and sometimes spun her body to disorient herself. She was getting good at this.

She was walking from the living room, across the entrance hall toward the dining room, when she stopped. There was something different in the way the entrance hall sounded when her heels struck the marble; less of an echo, or something. Then she had the oddest feeling on one side of her body, the side nearest the door; it was as if someone were passing a hand near her skin, but not touching her. Suddenly she was certain there was another person in the house, only a few feet away from her, standing near the front door.

Chris froze for a moment, then turned and went back into the living room, trying to stop trembling. There was a vase of dried flowers on a table to her right; she picked it up and started back toward the dining room, as if she were simply moving the vase. Then, when knew she was in the middle of the entrance hall, she drew back and threw the vase of flowers at the front door as hard as she could. Then she ran.

Behind her, she thought she heard the front door open and close, but she didn't stop running. In a moment, with her newfound sense of the house, she was in the bedroom, locking the door, then dialing 911, shaking, feeling helpless and afraid.

CHAPTER

7

By the time the Beverly Hills police arrived, Chris had recovered herself sufficiently to insist on making the two patrolmen coffee. She was very careful not to spill a drop.

When she began to tell her story, one of them asked to use the telephone.

"It's nice of you to make coffee, Miss Callaway," said the older of the two, judging from the sound of his voice.

"It gave me something to do rather than just feel nervous," Chris replied.

The other officer rejoined them. "There's somebody coming from the station house I think you should talk to," the officer said.

"Who?"

"His name is Larsen; he's a detective. He specializes in cases like this."

"There can't possibly be any other cases like this," Chris said ruefully.

"I mean about the letters and flowers," the officer said. "Are you sure you're all right, ma'am?"

"I really am."

"You just seemed a little clumsy with the coffee cups; I wondered if you were having some sort of delayed reaction."

"Oh, I'm always clumsy; especially when I'm nervous."

"I see."

Chris heard the front door open, and a minute later, Danny rushed into the room, breathless. "What is it?" he demanded. "What are the cops doing here? Are you all right, Chris?"

"Take it easy, Danny; everything's fine." She introduced him to the two policemen.

"Well," the older voice said, "if your friend is here, and you're all right, we'd better get back on patrol. Larsen will be here shortly."

Chris stood up. "Thank you both for coming. I feel a lot better just knowing you're in the neighborhood."

"I'll show them to the door," Danny said.

Chris sat back down and thought about the reaction of the two policemen to her. When Danny returned, she told him what had happened.

"You're sure somebody was in the house?"

"Yes, I am. Danny, I don't think those two cops knew that I'm blind."

"Didn't they?"

"No, I don't think so. One of them remarked that I seemed a little clumsy with the coffee cups, but I don't think he caught on. I could tell by his voice."

The doorbell rang; Danny went to answer it and came back with another man.

"Chris, this is Detective Larsen," he said.

"How do you do, Detective?" Chris asked, not

extending a hand. She wasn't quite sure where he was. "Would you like some coffee? There's some made."

"Thank you, yes," Larsen said.

Chris heard him drag a chair up to the kitchen table. He sounded nice, maybe in his mid-thirties. She treated the cup carefully this time and got it onto the table without spilling it.

"I'm sorry you have to go over this twice," Larsen said.

"Actually, the two patrolmen seemed not to want to hear the whole story."

"That's because they have standing orders to refer a case like this to me," Larsen said.

"I was . . . in the house alone," Chris began, "and I . . . felt that someone was in the house with me. Standing near the front door. I picked up a vase of dried flowers, chucked it at the door, and ran like hell to my bedroom. Then I locked myself in and called 911."

Larsen was silent for a moment. "I don't quite understand," he said finally. "You *felt* there was someone in the house?"

"That's right."

"Do you have psychic tendencies, Miss Callaway?"

"No, no. I just meant I didn't actually see him."

"You threw a vase of flowers at someone you couldn't see?"

"Yes, I suppose I did."

"Miss Callaway, is your vision impaired in any way?"

Chris sighed. "I had hoped you couldn't tell. Your two policemen seemed not to notice."

"Most people wouldn't have," Larsen said. "I have a younger sister who was blinded in an accident when she was nineteen. She fools people all the time."

"Oh. Well, I'm not completely blind," Chris said.

"But enough so that you wouldn't know if some-one were standing by your front door."

She nodded. "I'm afraid so."

"I'm aware that you're an actress, Miss Callaway; I've seen a couple of your movies, and I think you're very good."

"Thank you."

"And I knew about your accident; saw it on 'Entertainment Tonight.' I just didn't know you had been blinded."

Danny spoke up for the first time. "Neither does anybody else. Hardly anybody."

"I see," Larsen said. "Please don't worry; I'll respect your wishes in that respect."

"Thank you," Chris replied.

"Now, let's begin at the beginning," Larsen said.

When Chris had finished, Larsen sipped at his cof-fee and didn't say anything.

"Well?" Danny said. "What do you think?"

"Well, your case is not . . . unusual," Larsen said.

Danny spoke up. "You mean this happens all the time?"

"Not all the time," Larsen replied, "but it happens. I run . . . rather, I *am* the threat management unit on our force; I deal all the time with something called the stalker phenomenon, people who obsessively fol-low or contact other people—sometimes men stalk-ing women, but sometimes the other way around."

"Like the David Letterman thing," Danny said.

"That's right."

"Who are these people that do this?" Chris asked.

"All sorts," Larsen replied. "Sometimes they work in the same office or go to the same school. These guys can make life a living hell for their victims, and they don't bother to conceal their identities. They usually sign the mail or find some way to let the victim know who they are. They *want* their victims to know who they are. It's part of the satisfaction they get from these acts. They have this warped conviction that their victims *like* the attention. They're usually bright, otherwise well-adjusted people who have careers, even families. They just sort of flip out over one person."

"And you think 'Admirer' isn't like that?"

"Well, he's been very carefully anonymous. In roughly half of our cases the stalker tries to keep his identity secret."

"And what do you think that means?" Chris asked.

"It's hard to say, but of course the first thing we want to do in an active case is to identify the stalker. I'm sorry you didn't keep the letters; we might have tried handwriting analysis."

"The letters were all very neatly typed," Chris said. "The ones I was able to see, anyway."

Danny broke in. "Come to think of it, they were so neatly done, I think they were probably written on a computer and a laser printer."

"Lots of people have those," Larsen said. "Your man is probably affluent, or at least has a good job. He owns a computer, and his habit of sending six dozen roses at a time is an expensive one."

"I'll bet he's got a car, too," Danny said. "Anybody on foot in Bel Air would be noticed immediately by the security patrol."

Chris laughed. "Oh, Danny, *everybody* in L.A. drives a car."

"There's something encouraging about all this," Larsen said.

"What's that?" Chris asked.

"From your recollection, the notes have all been very benign, even respectful. A stalker is often vulgar or obscene. Has he made any demands?"

"What sort of demands?" Chris asked.

"Has he asked you to mail him your dirty underwear, or to meet him at some secluded place?"

"No, nothing like that. He often promises to stay in touch, says I'll hear from him again."

"And you probably will. He's never given you a mailing address—a box number or mail drop?"

"No."

"Then he doesn't really anticipate a reply. Maybe he doesn't even want one."

"A wanker," Danny said.

"Beg pardon?" Larsen replied.

"He'd rather do it with himself than with Chris."

"Oh, yes. Maybe he's just shy."

"Let's hope he stays that way," Chris said.

"So what steps are you going to take, Detective?" Danny asked.

"None, at least at this point. If you knew him you might be able to go to a judge and get a restraining order to keep him from contacting you, but it's not a crime to write to somebody or send her flowers; he's made no demands or threats; he hasn't tried to harm you. We do have a stalker law in California, since '91, and that law comes into effect if he commits a crime."

"What about breaking and entering?" Danny said.

"I'm afraid we have no hard evidence of that," Larsen said, almost apologetically. "Miss Callaway, when Marie—that's my sister—lost her sight, she often thought people were standing closer to her than they were; she even thought, once or twice, that someone was standing in the room with her, but refusing to speak. You may just have experienced some sort of neurological phenomenon associated with the damage to your vision."

"Maybe," Chris said, "but I don't think so. He was here."

"He could have been here today," Larsen said. "I don't disbelieve you."

"What should we do, then?" Danny asked. "What steps should we take?"

"First of all, Miss Callaway . . . "

"Please call me Chris; the whole world does."

"Thank you. I think it would be a good idea if you weren't left alone for a while; at least, until we see how this situation develops."

"You think it will develop?" Chris asked.

"I don't know. I think it's probable that your 'Admirer' will keep writing. I'd like to hear about it if there's any change in the tone of the letters, or if he starts sending something besides flowers. Also, if he should telephone you, try not to aggravate him. Don't yell at him or demand that he stop writing. You can try to accomplish that politely—just tell him that you appreciate his interest in your career, but you'd prefer not to hear from him again. Be nice, and don't try to find out who he is or anything about him; he could get paranoid if you start asking questions. He may volunteer information about himself or even his identity; if that happens, then I can have a little talk with him." Larsen rose to go.

Chris rose with him. "I don't think he'll telephone; I have a private number."

"Well," Larsen said, shaking both their hands, "you thought you had a private address, too."

8

L ight on the makeup," Chris said. Danny had
done her hair and was applying powder with
a brush.

"Yes, dear," Danny said archly.

"Danny, the first two cops didn't notice that I was
blind, and Larsen said most people wouldn't."

"So?"

"I wonder if I could get away with it."

"Get away with what?"

"I wonder if I could keep people from finding out
that I'm blind."

"For how long?"

"Until I can see again."

"Are you talking about working?"

"Yes."

"I don't know, babe. That's a tall order. What if
someone asks you to read a few lines of a script at a
meeting?"

"I don't think I could convince people that my sight is perfectly normal; just poor, but getting better."

"Why don't you just take it easy for a while and not worry about working?"

"Because if I'm marked as an invalid, nobody will even consider hiring me, except out of charity. I've got to be seen as healthy, even if I don't work for a while."

"I see your point. It's like actors with AIDS; people who are still healthy enough to work, but nobody will hire them once the news is out."

"Exactly. It's not enough to keep it a secret that I can't see; I have to make people believe that I can."

"Okay, how do we start?"

"I think Sunday lunch at the Bistro Garden would be the perfect place."

"That's tomorrow; there'll be a dozen people you know there."

"I know. Maybe we'd better have a dry run today. How about the promenade in Santa Monica?"

"I'm free all day," Danny replied.

The city of Santa Monica had closed several blocks of Third Street to traffic and created a pedestrian promenade. The area, once seedy, was making a comeback now, and on a Saturday afternoon the street was crowded. Chris, in jeans and a sweatshirt, with her hair in a ponytail and wearing big sunglasses, knew she was unlikely to be recognized by the filmgoing public; informality was her disguise, and it nearly always worked. The sun was a relatively bright spot in the upper left-hand corner of her vision and the people were no more than a jumble of dark shapes.

"How about a little window-shopping?" Danny asked.

Chris laughed. "Perfect."

"There's a little shop with some cute stuff in the window, coming up on your right, maybe six steps."

Chris counted and stopped. "I like that little number," she said, pointing.

"It isn't you," Danny said, "but you're pointing to the right place. How about some lunch?"

"Sounds good."

"There's a little sidewalk place on the next block."

"Good."

They strolled on to the restaurant and Danny found them a table.

"Order a sandwich," he said quietly as Chris pretended to peruse the menu. "That way you won't have to hunt your food with a fork. The Reuben is good here."

The waiter came, and Chris ordered the sandwich.

Danny made a little grunting noise.

"What's wrong?" she asked.

"Just a little cramp; I ate some suspect shrimp last night, and I've had a tiny case of the trots. Will you be all right for a few minutes?"

"Sure, go ahead."

Danny left the table, and Chris turned her face to the sunshine, tilted her head back, and closed her eyes. Might as well work on the tan, she thought.

There was a tiny scraping sound from across the table, and, just as she had the day before, Chris knew someone was present. She didn't move, didn't look at him; waited for him to speak. When he didn't, she turned slightly toward where she felt he was sitting. If she had to confront this guy she was happy it was in such a public place.

"Thank you for the roses," she said. "They were lovely."

There was no response.

"They brightened my stay in the hospital; it was very thoughtful of you."

Still no reply. Chris was becoming annoyed.

"However, I have to say that if the only way you feel you can contact me is through anonymous letters and flowers, I'd rather not hear from you again. I prefer people in my life who are more straightforward and who don't play games."

There was still no response.

Chris closed her eyes and turned toward the sun again. If the bastard was going to clam up, then she would, too. Then she heard the little scrape again as a chair was pushed back, and a moment later she was startled by the sudden sensation of body heat near her cheek. It took all her willpower not to flinch.

The voice came in a tiny whisper. "This is not a game," it said. And then the visitor was gone.

Chris made a point of not moving until Danny returned a minute or two later.

"Everything okay?" he asked.

Chris sat up. "Danny, did you see anybody leave the table when you were coming back?"

"No, why?"

"He was here."

"Who was here?"

"Admirer."

"What did he say?"

"Nothing, at first. Then I tried to talk to him, but he wouldn't answer. I told him I didn't like people who played games, and he leaned near me and whispered, 'This is not a game.' "

Chris heard Danny rummaging in the canvas shoulder bag he carried everywhere. "What are you doing?"

"I'm looking for my phone," Danny said. "I'm calling Larsen."

Danny went nowhere without the little pocket cellular phone, and this time she was glad he had it.

She told Larsen what had happened.

"This is no game," Larsen repeated.

"That's what he said."

"He knows you can't see him," Larsen said. "He'd never have done this otherwise."

"I suppose you're right," she replied.

"I don't think you should interpret this as ominous," the detective said, "not unless he makes some specific threat."

"This sounded like a threat to me," Chris said.

"I think that, in your present frame of mind, it certainly would sound that way. But to Admirer, it may just have been some sort of personal declaration that he feels seriously about you."

"I suppose you could interpret it that way," Chris admitted.

"I think we should interpret it that way for the present," Larsen said.

Danny, who was listening, turned the phone toward him. "Listen, Mr. Larsen, how long are you going to wait until you do something about this guy?"

"What do you suggest I do?" Larsen asked pleasantly, as if he really wanted to know.

"How about some protection for the girl?"

"We can't be in the bodyguard business," Larsen

said. "Not unless some serious threat has been made."

"Swell," Danny said. "You mean this guy has to take a shot at Chris, or something like that?"

"Mr. Devere," Larsen said, "my department requires me to act on my experience and judgment. At this stage of this stalking I cannot conclude that a real threat to Chris exists. However, if Chris feels that one exists, in spite of my judgment, then she is perfectly free to hire private protection. Frankly, I think it would be a waste of good money at this time, but if it would make her feel better, then maybe she should take that course."

"It would not make me feel better," Chris said. "Somehow, after today's experience, I feel I can handle this guy."

"Don't become overconfident," Larsen said. "You have a fine line to walk between too much and too little caution. And please keep me posted on any other events. The moment this man crosses the line of criminality, I can act, and believe me, I will."

"Thank you, Detective," Chris said.

"Please call me Jon." He spelled it for her.

"Thank you, Jon," she said, and hung up.

"Danny," she said, "what does Detective Larsen look like?"

"Late thirties, six two, a hundred and eighty, blond in a Scandinavian sort of way—the whitest white man you ever saw." Danny paused. "I wondered when you'd get around to asking."

"Stop smirking," Chris said.

CHAPTER

9

They parked in back of the restaurant and went in through the rear door. The Bistro Garden had been one of Chris's favorite restaurants ever since she had come to L.A. Her agent had first taken her there, introducing her to the owner and headwaiter and showing her off to his friends and other clients, and she had loved every minute of it.

The tables in the garden were arranged in rows, with umbrellas where necessary, and Danny pushed her ahead of him as they had planned. "Charlton Heston at one o'clock and five yards, speak *now*," he whispered.

"Chuck, how are you?" she beamed into space.

The large actor loomed before her, a shadow that shut out all light. "How are you, Chris?" He kissed her on the cheek. "I heard about your fall."

"Much better, Chuck," she said. "How's Lydia?"

"Very well. Will you come up to the house for some tennis soon?"

"Very soon. Give Lydia my best."

Danny steered her onward toward the front wall of the garden. "Your agent is at ten o'clock, two rows over. Smile and wave."

Chris obeyed, and they reached their table. Danny got her seated without seeming to steer her, and Chris began to relax.

"Here comes Ron," Danny whispered. "Three, two, one, *now*."

"Ron, hello!" Chris called to the approaching blob.

Ron kissed her hand. "My darling, you look *wonderful*."

"I'm feeling pretty good, too. Ready to work."

"I'll get on it," Ron said, then his voice fell to a whisper. "How are your eyes?"

"Coming along, Ron, coming along."

"I'll call you tomorrow," he said, and kissed her good-bye.

"Uh, oh," Danny whispered, "here comes your late leading man, Mr. Quinn."

"Chris!" Jason Quinn practically yelled as he approached the table. "How in the world are you?"

Chris held out a hand. "Very well, thank you, Jason." She could not help being cool. The sound of a chair being dragged up reached her ears. "Do you know my good friend Danny Devere?"

"Hi," Quinn said. "Listen, Chris, I want you to know that I fought to have you kept on the film, I really did. So did Brent Williams. It was the front-office boys that shot us down."

"It's all right, Jason, I understand," Chris replied, more warmly than she felt.

"Brent and I had already revised the schedule to

shoot around you for twelve days in the hope that you'd make it back."

"That was kind of you, Jason. Will you thank Brent for me?"

"Sally Woodson came in and has mostly made a hash of a great part," he said conspiratorially. "Just between you and me."

"You're sweet, Jason."

"I hope we can find something else to work on real soon," he said. "Can I send you a script sometime?"

"Of course, send it to Ron." She heard him rise.

"Let's have lunch and talk about it when I'm through with this shoot."

"Sure, call me."

The actor beat his retreat, and Danny gave a sigh of relief.

"Did he notice?" she asked.

"Not for a second," Danny said. "There were moments when you weren't looking directly at him, but they were the *right* moments, when you were being a little bitchy anyway." Danny sucked in a deep breath suddenly.

"Danny, what's the matter?" Chris asked.

"Nothing to worry about," Danny replied.

"Danny, *tell* me."

"Oh, all right. I just looked up and saw roses coming."

"Oh, shit."

"Don't worry, I waved the waiter off."

"Danny, do me a favor: talk to the front desk and see if you can find out what florist they came from."

"As soon as we order," he said. "Here comes our waiter."

They ordered and Danny left the table. He was

back in a moment. "They were from the florist at the Beverly Hills Hotel," he said.

"Good God! You don't think he's staying at the Beverly Hills!"

"I doubt it. The florist is right next to the drugstore; anybody could order them. I know a front-desk man at the hotel; I'll call him tomorrow and get him to check it out."

"Thank you." Chris knew well that Danny had a huge network of gay friends scattered all over Southern California.

Their food came, and Chris began to relax. It was no different from two dozen other Sunday lunches she'd had here, except that she couldn't surreptitiously case the crowd the way she usually did. Today, Danny did it for her, chatting animatedly and cracking her up with his bitchy comments about the stars and hangers-on at the other tables.

As Danny asked for the bill, the headwaiter approached. "Excuse me, Miss Callaway, your car is here; he's waiting out front."

"I didn't order a car," Chris said. "Send him away."

"Wait," Danny said, "let me do it." He got up from the table and left the restaurant.

He was back in a moment. "I talked to the driver: somebody sent cash and directions to the car service. I asked where he was supposed to deliver you, and he said home; that you'd give him directions."

"The nerve of the bastard," Chris said. "He's really starting to get on my nerves." She threw down her napkin. "Let's get out of here."

They left the restaurant and exited through the rear door to the parking lot. When they reached Danny's car, two of its tires were flat.

10

On Monday morning, Chris made Danny's breakfast, as she always insisted on doing, and Danny read her excerpts from the papers while they waited for Melanie's arrival.

A few minutes later Chris asked, "What time is it?"

Danny glanced at his watch. "Jesus, it's twenty past nine. I'm due in Burbank at nine-thirty."

"Why don't you go ahead," Chris said. "Melanie is never late; there must have been unusually heavy traffic coming in from the Valley."

"I hate to leave you alone," Danny replied, "but I can't be late for this. They're doing hair tests for a film this afternoon, and I have three heads to do."

"Go on; Melanie will be here any minute."

Danny pecked her on the cheek and rushed from the house. Chris busied herself with getting the breakfast dishes into the dishwasher, then went into her study and switched on the television to CNN. It annoyed her in the extreme that she couldn't read, and she kept the news on all day just to stay abreast of events.

The phone rang.

"Hello?"

"I'm afraid Melanie is going to be late today," a voice said in a whisper.

Chris struggled to hear. "What? What are you talking about?"

"You don't really need all these people around you," the voice whispered. "I'm perfectly capable of meeting your needs—and I mean *all* your needs."

"What did you say about Melanie?"

"She's going to be late."

"How do you know?"

"I know. I wouldn't lie to you. I'd never lie to you, Chris."

"What have you done to Melanie?"

"Done? I haven't done anything to her. It's time you fired her, though. There's nothing she can do for you that I can't do."

"Listen to me very carefully," Chris said. "I don't want to hear from you again; I don't want to receive letters or flowers from you, or telephone calls; I'm giving you fair warning, because if I do hear from you again—for *any* reason—I'll go to the police, and I don't think you'd want that."

There was a soft chuckle from the other end of the line. "The *police*? What on earth do I have to fear from the police? I'm a law-abiding citizen; they wouldn't *dare* touch me. What would they charge me with? Sending you flowers? Writing you adoring letters? Put the police out of your mind, Chris; they're oafs; they're helpless in dealing with somebody of my caliber."

"Go away," Chris said stubbornly. "Do you understand those words? Do you grasp their meaning? *Go away*!"

"You don't mean that," the voice whispered.

"You love my little expressions of affection; you wouldn't know what to do without me. Very soon now, I will be your life."

The line went dead.

Chris hung up the phone. Where the hell was Melanie? The woman knew she shouldn't be alone in the house.

The phone rang again, and Chris snatched it up. "Hello?"

"Chris, it's Melanie. I'm awfully sorry to be late, but I've had an accident."

"What sort of an accident? Are you all right?"

"I'm okay. Some son of a bitch ran me off the road, coming down Beverly Glen; I had to walk to a phone. Don't worry, the wrecker's on its way, and the car doesn't seem to be much damaged. It just has two wheels in a ditch."

"I'm all right, Melanie; just come as soon as you can."

"Is Danny still there?"

"No, he had to go to work."

"Well, try not to worry; I'll be there within the hour."

Chris sat for a moment, frightened, trying to figure out what to do. Then she picked up the phone, dialed the Beverly Hills Police Department, and asked for Jon Larsen.

"Hello?"

"It's Chris Callaway. Admirer has forced my secretary off the road in her car, and Danny has already gone to work. I've had my first phone call from this guy, and I'm scared."

"I'll be there in fifteen minutes," Larsen said. "If you're really worried I can get a patrol car there in a couple of minutes."

"I'll be all right until you get here," she said.

She hung up the phone and listened. Was that a noise? Was somebody outside the window? She struggled into a back hall where she kept wine in racks and retrieved a bottle, then returned to the study and sat down with the wine bottle in her lap. At least she'd have a club.

" 'I will be your life.' Is that what he said?" Larsen was writing all this down.

"Yes."

"Did he have any sort of recognizable accent?"

Chris tried to remember the voice. "I'm not sure; he was whispering, and that made it hard to tell, but I don't think so. I think the accent was pure, unaccented Californian."

"Melanie is your secretary? What was it he said about her?"

"He said she would be late; then Melanie called a minute later and said somebody had run her off the road up Beverly Glen somewhere."

"How long ago was that?"

"Maybe twenty minutes. I can't see my watch."

"Was she hurt?"

"No, she said she was all right." Chris heard the front door open and Melanie's footsteps on the marble floor.

"Well," Melanie said as she walked into the study. "That was some experience. Oh, I'm sorry, I didn't realize you had a visitor."

"Melanie, this is Detective Larsen. Are you sure you're all right?"

"I'm fine, just annoyed as hell."

"Please sit down," Larsen said. "Tell me what happened."

"I was driving in from the Valley, coming down Beverly Glen, and this guy pulled up next to me and forced me off the road into a ditch."

"Did you see his face?"

"No, just the van."

"He was driving a van?"

"Yes, one of those windowless kind, sort of industrial-looking."

"Do you know what kind?"

"I'm afraid not. I wouldn't know a Ford from a Toyota."

"What color?"

"Sort of a grayish green—I think."

"New? Old?"

"Newish. It was clean, anyway, and I don't remember any dents or rust."

"Did you get a look at the license plate?"

"Just long enough to see that it was a California plate. I was too busy driving to get the number."

"That's understandable in the circumstances. Is there anything else you can tell me?"

"Nothing. He came out of nowhere; I never even saw him in my rearview mirror."

Larsen turned back to Chris. "And what was it Admirer said?"

"That Melanie would be late."

"He didn't say why?"

"No. Just what I told you."

Melanie stood up. "If you don't have any more questions for me, I've got work to do."

"No," Larsen said, "thanks for your help."

Melanie left the room, walking toward the little room off the kitchen that was her office.

"Jon, isn't there anything you can do?" Chris asked.

"I've waited this long because I needed some criminal act to get you onto the active list."

"Active list?"

"I handle about four hundred stalker cases a year—that's the number of calls we get. Most of them are disgruntled boyfriends, that sort of thing; I only seriously investigate about twenty to twenty-five cases—there's no manpower for more. My chief doesn't allow me to get involved until there's at least the threat of a criminal act. Now, I can't actually prove that Admirer is responsible for Melanie's accident, so I'm going to stretch a point and use that incident to get you on the active list. What I'll do is park a patrol car outside your house for twenty-four hours. This man seems to keep very close tabs on you, so he's bound to see it, and that may be enough to scare him off."

"Not a chance," Chris said. "When I said I would call the police he was contemptuous; he said the police couldn't touch him. In fact, he said they were oafs and wouldn't dare mess with someone of his 'caliber.'"

"I see," Larsen said. "In that case you're probably right; the patrol car wouldn't help. What we need to do is leapfrog him, get ahead of his thought process."

"How do you mean?"

"Well, I think he'd expect something like the patrol car, to start with. Maybe what we need to do is give him something he doesn't expect."

"Such as?"

"Instead of scaring him off, let's try to catch him."

CHAPTER

11

M elanie came into the study where Chris was sitting disconsolately, listening to CNN.

"Chris, did you call a plumber?"

Chris started. "No. Why?"

"Because a plumber's truck just pulled into the driveway."

"Christ, you don't think it's Admirer, do you?"

"Who knows?"

"Keep the chain on when you answer the door."

"Right." Melanie left the room. A moment later she was back, introducing two men to Chris. "These gentlemen are the fuzz," she said. "Come to do something to your phone."

"I'm not a cop," one man said. "I'm from the phone company, but the cops made me come in their van."

The other man spoke up. "I'm the cop; Detective

·

62

Larsen thought you might like a new line in the house, in addition to the old one, a number that your stalker doesn't have."

"What a good idea," Chris said.

"We're also going to install a phone company service called Caller ID."

"I've read about it; it gives the name and number of anyone calling?"

"Right. The name and number appear on a little screen."

"I'm afraid I can't see the screen," she said. "I'm having some trouble with my eyes."

"That's okay. The number will appear simultaneously on another screen down at the department."

"So you'll know when he calls?"

"Not unless you call on the new line and tell us, but there'll be a recorder on the line, so at least we'll be able to tape his voice. Sorry we can't have somebody listening all the time, but we just don't have the manpower."

The two men did the work in less than an hour, and the cop told Chris her new number. "I'm going to give the number to Larsen, but he has asked that, for the time being, you not give it to anyone else, not even your secretary or your housemate."

"All right," Chris said. She repeated the number aloud a few times to imprint it on her brain.

"If he calls, keep him talking as long as you can, and we might be able to track him down and grab him."

"I'll do that," she said.

When the cop and the telephone man had left, and Melanie was back in her office working, Chris turned off the television and sat, thinking how stuck she was. She couldn't call a friend for lunch, or go out without Danny, not if she wanted to maintain the illusion that she could see. She couldn't go out to Malibu and check on the house or take a walk on the beach; she couldn't read a book or a new script. She had never realized how alone blindness could make a person. Feeling sorry for herself, she dozed.

The phone startled her wide-awake. She turned toward the instrument—the two instruments, now that she had a second line—and felt for the one on the left, her old number.

"Hello?"

"So," the voice whispered, "how is your day going?"

"Why would you care?" she asked.

"Oh, I care. I care more deeply than anyone has ever cared for you. In fact, you're about to receive a little token of my caring."

The doorbell rang. Chris remained where she was, knowing that Melanie would answer it.

"That was the doorbell," she said into the telephone. "Is that something from you?"

"Wait and see," the voice whispered.

Suddenly, she was frightened. "Melanie!" she called out, "watch yourself!"

"You don't have to shout, I'm right here," Melanie said.

"Who was at the door?"

"A deliveryman with the biggest box of chocolates you've ever seen; must be ten pounds!"

"I can't eat chocolate," Chris lied into the phone. "It makes my skin break out, and I gain weight."

"Go ahead and gain weight," the voice said. "You won't need to be slim for the screen anymore."

"What do you mean?" Chris asked, alarmed.

"I mean that I'll take care of you from now on; you won't have to work."

"I really am having a hard time understanding you," Chris said. "Why would you force all this attention on someone who hasn't the slightest interest in you? Why on earth do you think I'd give up working so that someone I am growing to despise could support me?"

"You don't really feel that way," the voice whispered smoothly. "At least, you won't for long. I'll grow on you."

The line went dead. Chris put down the phone and reached for the new line. She felt for the keypad and dialed Larsen's direct line. "It's Chris," she said when he answered.

"It was a pay phone on Wilshire Boulevard," Larsen said. "A unit is on the way; they just might snag him."

"He sent a huge box of chocolates."

Larsen chuckled. "At this rate, with the flowers and limousines, you'll break the guy. That ought to give you some satisfaction."

Chris laughed in spite of herself.

"Nice to hear you laugh," Larsen said.

"God," she said, "I can't remember the last time."

"Hang on, I'll see if Dispatch has any news." He put her on hold.

Chris waited, realizing that talking to this faceless policeman was becoming the high point of each day.

"I'm back," Larsen said. "The car found an empty booth. They figure they missed him by less than half a minute."

"Oh," she said, disappointed, but not surprised.

"Don't worry; we'll have other chances. Next time he calls maybe we'll get lucky."

"He's had all the luck so far," she said glumly.

"Our turn will come," Larsen said. "Do you mind if I drop by a little later this afternoon? There's something I'd like to give you."

"I'll be here all day," she said. "See you later." She hung up and sighed. Who would have thought she would look forward so much to a visit from a policeman?

The phone rang.

She felt for the instrument on the left and picked it up. "Hello?" She was greeted with a dial tone.

The phone rang again.

It was the new line; Jon must be calling back. She picked it up. "Don't tell me you're breaking our date," she laughed.

"We don't have a date yet," the voice whispered, "but we will. You've been a bad girl." He hung up.

Chris continued to hold the receiver, stunned. She had had the new line for only a few hours, and Admirer already knew the number.

CHAPTER

12

M elanie showed Larsen to Chris's study. "Chris," she said, "if Detective Larsen is going to be here for a while, do you mind if I go home early? Danny will be home soon."

Chris turned to Larsen. "Jon, can you wait until Danny comes?"

"My pleasure," Larsen replied.

"Sure, Melanie, go on home," Chris said.

"See you tomorrow." Melanie called from the front door.

When they were alone, Chris found her chair and sat down. "Bad news," she said.

"What's that?"

She told him about the call from Admirer on the new line.

"I don't believe it," Larsen said, astonished. "Who did you give the number to?"

"Nobody."

"Chris, come on, there must have been some-body."

"I swear, I gave it to absolutely no one."

Larsen sank into a chair and seemed to think for a moment. "Either he works for the phone company, or he's got a contact there; it's the only possible way he could have gotten the number."

"Swell," she said.

"How are you feeling?" he asked.

"Depressed. I'm glad you could come over." It was worse than depressed, she admitted to herself; it was very nearly desperate.

"It's a beautiful day outside. Does this house have a back garden?"

"Yes, quite a nice one; would you like to see it?"

"I'd love to; here, take my arm."

"I'll lead you," she said. "I know the way."

He followed her through the kitchen and out the back door. They emerged onto a terrace overlooking planted gardens, a pool, and a tennis court.

"Like it?" she asked.

"It's beautiful, but I didn't get you out here to look at the garden."

"What do you mean?"

He led her to a chair. "I want you to sit down and wait here for a few minutes. I'm going back inside."

"Wait a minute; what's going on?"

"I'll explain when I get back. Just relax and enjoy the sun." He turned and walked very quietly back into the house.

Chris sat in the sun, immobile, helpless, entirely dependent on this policeman, Melanie, and Danny. It was infuriating.

• • •

In the kitchen Larsen removed his shoes and padded into Chris's study. He went to the telephone on the desk and, while holding down the flasher button, removed the receiver from its cradle and unscrewed the mouthpiece. He looked inside, screwed the cap back on, then conducted a thorough inspection of the study, the living room, the kitchen, and Chris's bedroom before he returned to the rear terrace.

"What have you been doing?" she asked. "It's been at least half an hour."

"I'm not quite finished," he said. "Do you know where the central telephone box for your house is?"

"In the basement, I think."

"Where's that?"

"There's an outside entrance around the corner of the house to your left," she said. She dug into a pocket and handed him her keys. "It's the silvery one."

"I'll be right back." Larsen walked around the house and found the door, down a short flight of steps. He opened it, found the light switch, and walked into a large cellar room. There was a musty smell, and everything was covered in dust. The telephone box was on the opposite wall; he walked across the concrete floor and opened the box. He inspected the insides carefully and, at first, found nothing amiss. There was a flashlight on a shelf next to the box, and he switched it on and inspected the wiring again. The batteries were weak, but there was enough light to reveal a small wire running from a terminal, through a drilled hole, out of the box, and up to a brick ledge.

Larsen felt along the ledge, following the wire until it ran down the wall and behind some empty cardboard boxes. He moved the boxes and used the flashlight to follow the wire to its end. It was connected to a small plastic box, and a telescopic antenna about three feet in length was attached to that. He held the flashlight close to the plastic case but could not see any trace of fingerprints. Admirer was a very neat fellow. Larsen carefully replaced the boxes, then found a broom and scattered dust behind him as he walked to the door.

Back on the rear terrace he pulled a chair up next to Chris's and sat down.

"Now, tell me what the hell you've been doing," she said.

"I've been thoroughly searching your house."

"Rummaging in my underwear drawer?"

"Not that thoroughly," he said. "I'm afraid your Admirer has bugged your house."

"*What?*"

"He has placed electronic bugs in all your telephones—the kind that pick up any conversation whether the telephone is in use or not. Then he wired a small transmitter to your central telephone box. He probably did this when you were in the hospital; was there anyone here during the evenings?"

"No. Melanie leaves in the late afternoon, and Danny wasn't staying here then."

"It's not a very big transmitter, but it may have a range of a mile or two. He either lives nearby, or he has some sort of base in the neighborhood; he probably has attached a tape recorder to his receiver when he can't tend it, then he listens to the recordings later."

Chris was stunned. "You mean he's been listening to everything that goes on in my home?"

"I'm afraid so. That's how he got the new telephone number; when the phone company man told you what it was, he heard it, too."

"The rotten little son of a bitch. I hope you ripped out his handiwork."

"No, I left it in place."

"Why? I don't want him listening to my life."

"If I take it out, he'll find another way. Admirer is a very clever fellow. At least this way we can control what he hears, and we'll be able to use his system against him."

"I see," Chris said. "At least, I think I see."

Danny stuck his head out the back door. "Jesus," he said, "you scared me to death. I couldn't find Chris anywhere."

"Come on out, Danny, and join us," Larsen said.

Danny dragged up a chair and sat down. "So," he said, "what's happening?"

Larsen told him.

"This guy is really determined," Danny said when Larsen had finished.

"Not only that, he's mad," Chris said.

"What?" Larsen asked.

"On the phone, he said I had been a bad girl; it was as if he were going to punish me."

"I don't like the sound of that," said Danny.

"It may not mean anything," Larsen said. "Did he actually *say* he was going to punish you?"

"No."

"There's no threat, then."

The three of them sat there for a minute or two without speaking.

"Okay," Larsen said finally, "here's what we do. We walk back into the house and chat for a few minutes, and I'll take my leave. Then, Danny, you and Chris sit down in the study—we know he can listen well in that room—and you tell Chris that you've got to go out tonight."

"I can't leave her alone," Danny said.

"Don't worry," Larsen said, "she won't be alone. You leave at, say, seven. It'll be dark then, and I'll enter the house through the back door. Be sure to leave it open."

"Then what?" Chris asked.

"The last time you were alone in the house Admirer paid you a visit, remember?"

"I remember."

"Well, he might not be able to pass up another opportunity—especially if he wants to punish you."

"I see," Chris said unenthusiastically.

"Oh, I almost forgot," Larsen said. "I have something for you; let's go back into the house."

They went back into the study, and Larsen picked up a box he had left there. He took a wristwatch out of the box and handed it to Chris. "My sister sent you this," he said.

"That was kind of her, but I can't use a watch," she said.

"You can use this one." He guided her fingers. "Press this button, and the crystal opens; then you can feel the hour and minute hand. Try it."

Chris felt the face of the watch. "It works! It's five-thirty!"

"She also sent you some recorded books—novels, mostly. Do you have a cassette player?"

"Yes," she said, "right there on the desk."

"Good," Larsen said. "Why don't you listen to one tonight?"

CHAPTER

13

Chris sat in her study and listened to Danny's car pulling out of the driveway. She had always enjoyed solitude, had treasured an evening with nothing to do but read a novel, but not tonight. She had been unable to get used to the idea that whatever she said, someone outside the house could hear her, follow her movements, destroy her privacy. She felt locked in the black box of her blindness, and someone was watching her through a peephole. And listening.

Now she walked a fine line between fear and anger, and tonight she did what she could to get closer to her anger and farther from her fear. The windows were open and she could hear the loud chirp of crickets that started with dusk. Automatically she reached for the lamp switch above her head, then stopped herself. Jon had told her not to turn on any lights; it wouldn't be the natural thing for a blind person, he had said. It made her uncomfortable, knowing that she sat in the dark, even though the light would have made little difference to her.

She sat, listening to the little noises an old house makes, breathing more rapidly than she usually did. She hated waiting for something to happen. Finally, she groped for the box of tapes that Jon had left and chose one at random. Her fingers felt the bumps of the Braille label, which she could not read; she got up, found the tape machine, inserted the cassette, and sat down again. She instantly recognized the voice of Hal Holbrook; she had worked with him once, in a production of *King Lear* in New York.

> *But the basin of the Mississippi is the Body of the Nation. All the other parts are but members, important in themselves, yet more important in their relations to this. Exclusive of the Lake basin and of 300,000 square miles in Texas and New Mexico, which in many aspects form a part of it, this basin contains about 1,250,000 square miles.*

What was this? A geography course? Never mind, listen.

> *In extent it is the second great valley of the world, being exceeded only by that of the Amazon. The valley of the frozen Obi approaches it in extent; that of the La Plata comes in next in space, and probably in habitable capacity, having about eight-ninths of its area; then comes that of the Yenisei, with about seven-ninths; the Lena, Amoor, Hang-ho, Yang-tse-kiang, and Nile, five-ninths; the Ganges, less than one-half; the Indus, less than one-third; the Euphrates, one-fifth; the Rhine, one-fifteenth. It*

*exceeds in extent the whole of Europe, exclusive of
Russia, Norway, and Sweden. It would contain
Austria four times, Germany or Spain five times,
France six times, the British Islands or Italy ten
times.*

Chris tried to imagine the Mississippi Valley set
down in Europe; she sighed and began to relax a
little.

*Conceptions formed from the river-basins of
Western Europe are rudely shocked when we consider the extent of the valley of the Mississippi; nor
are those formed from the sterile basins of the great
rivers of Siberia, the lofty plateaus of Central Asia,
or the mighty sweep of the swampy Amazon more
adequate. Latitude, elevation, and rainfall all com-
bine to render every part of the Mississippi Valley
capable of supporting a dense population. As a
dwelling-place for civilized man it is by far the first
upon our globe.*

She had it now: Mark Twain—*Life on the
Mississippi*. She dozed.

Larsen had stayed at the station house long enough
to speak to the new watch, with the watch
sergeant's permission. He had fidgeted while the
sergeant had read lists of stolen cars, given the
descriptions of two muggers on Sunset, and had
generally exhorted his watch to vigilance. Finally,
the sergeant nodded to Larsen.

"I need your help on a stalker," Larsen said to
them. "The victim is up Stone Canyon, here . . . " he

pointed to the place on the neighborhood map ". . . and we think he may come calling tonight. I don't think he'll come right up the street, so don't make any special passes there. But stop and question any male on foot—don't forget to get his ID—and any lone male apparently cruising the neighborhood in a car or even a bicycle. We don't have a make on the guy, and we need one. Questions?"

"You have a profile on the guy?" a policewoman in the front row asked.

"Nothing. He could be anybody."

She nodded, and there were no other questions.

Larsen hurried from the station and drove up Sunset to Stone Canyon. He parked his car in the parking lot of the Bel Air Hotel, crossed the street, and continued on foot. He couldn't just drive up to Chris's house, but he had found he could get there by way of an unused bridle path. He entered a wooded area, making his way slowly through the overgrowth, trying not to use his pocket flashlight.

The moment we were under way I began to prowl about the great steamer and fill myself with joy. She was as clean and as dainty as a drawing-room; when I looked down her long, gilded saloon it was like gazing through a splendid tunnel; she had an oil-picture, by some gifted sign-painter, on every stateroom door; she glittered with no end of prism-fringed chandeliers; the clerk's office was elegant, the bar was marvelous, and the barkeeper had been barbered and upholstered at incredible cost.

Someone switched off the cassette player.

The going was easier for Larsen now. He turned down his handheld police radio, so that transmissions would not give away his presence, and walked faster. He was less than a hundred yards from the back garden of the house when, perhaps thirty yards ahead, a man came from out of the woods and onto the bridle path. Larsen began to run.

Chris didn't move, didn't let an eyelid flutter. Something had wakened her, not a noise, but a feeling. She sat upright in the wing chair, her head resting lightly against the tweed upholstery, and tried not to scream. After a moment's silence, she heard someone sit down in the other wing chair, opposite her. She still did not move.

Larsen hit the astonished man low, the way he had not done since high-school football. Then they were on the ground and struggling. The man had recovered from his surprise now and was fighting for all he was worth. It was dark in the woods, but Larsen managed to get his left forearm across his opponent's throat, and his gun into his right hand. He pressed it to the man's temple.

"Freeze! Police!" Larsen shouted, and the man suddenly stopped struggling.

The whisper began, low and sibilant: "Chrissychrissychrissychrissychrissy." It grew louder, then stopped.

Chris raised her head and opened her eyes. "Who are you and what do you want?" was all she could think of to say.

"I want everyone to know you're mine," the voice whispered.

She started to rise, but she was pushed back into the chair by a heavy weight, and her left wrist was seized in an incredibly strong grip. He was sitting on her, pressing her back into the upholstery, and there was a buzzing noise in the room. Now there was a stinging sensation on the back of her left hand, which did not go away. Chris struggled to hit at him with her right hand, but she could move her arm very little because of the weight pinning her. She tried to scream, but his back was pushed into her face, and when she turned her head, the upholstery muffled the sound.

They were locked together for several minutes, it seemed to her; then, suddenly, she was released.

Larsen handcuffed the man, then dragged him to his feet and, holding on to the cuffs, marched him toward Chris's house. With his free hand he found the little radio. "Officer needs assistance, suspect in custody. This is Larsen; I need a squad car at the Stone Canyon house."

"Now you are mine, and everyone will know it," the voice whispered. "Start getting rid of all these people in your life—the queer, the secretary, the cop. You won't need them anymore."

Chris bolted. Secure in her knowledge of her house, she sprang from the chair and sprinted toward the front door. She had it open and was down the steps and running down the long lawn to the road before she tripped and fell headlong down the hill.

Larsen shoved his suspect through the back door of the house and found the study. "Chris?" he called. Then he heard the siren as the squad car approached. "Come on, buddy," he said, shoving the man before him toward the front door.

When they were on the front steps, he looked down the lawn and saw Chris, on her feet, swinging wildly at the cop and his woman partner, who were trying to calm her.

CHAPTER

14

I want to know what this is about," the man said angrily. He was sitting in one of the two wing chairs in Chris's study, rubbing his wrists. It was the first time he had spoken.

Chris was sitting in the chair opposite; she recognized his voice. "Detective Larsen will explain everything," she said shakily. "Jon, this is Warren Perle; he's a neighbor of mine. I'm sure he has nothing to do with this."

"Mr. Perle, I'm sorry for the inconvenience," Larsen said.

"*Inconvenience!*" the man sputtered. "You attacked me and handcuffed me like I was a criminal or something! You pointed a *gun* at me!"

"Can you tell me what you were doing on the old bridle path?" Larsen asked.

"I was taking a goddamned walk, that's what I was doing! Is that against the goddamned law?"

"Mr. Perle, please let me explain. Miss Callaway has been the victim of a stalker, someone who has lavished unwanted attention on her. We expected someone to try and enter her house tonight, and I mistook you for that person."

"Oh," Perle said, a little deflated. "Chris, I'm awfully sorry you're having this problem. Is there anything I can do?"

Chris tried to speak and failed. Her heart was still pounding, and her breathing was shallow.

"You can let me know if you see anyone in the neighborhood who looks out of place," Larsen said, handing Perle his card.

"Of course, I'll be glad to," Perle replied accepting the card.

"I'm very sorry for the case of mistaken identity this evening," Larsen said. "I'll have someone drive you home in a squad car."

"Oh, Christ, no!" Perle said. "If the old lady across the street saw me getting out of a police car I'd never hear the end of it."

"Would you please walk along the street, instead of the back way?" Larsen asked. "My people are still searching the woods."

"Of course," Perle said, rising.

"If anyone stops you just refer them to me," Larsen said, offering the man his hand.

"Thank you," Perle said. He shook Larsen's hand, then left.

Larsen sat down across from Chris. "Are you all right?" he asked.

Chris took a deep breath. "I think so; but he sure scared the hell out of me." She felt drained, listless; she hurt all over.

"I'm sorry. I was delayed in getting here, and

then I ran into Warren Perle in the woods. Are you sure he could have nothing to do with this?"

"He has a production deal at Warner Brothers; he wouldn't have the time or the inclination."

"Tell me exactly what happened tonight," Larsen said.

Calming herself, Chris related the events of a few minutes before.

"He *sat* on you?" Larsen asked.

"Yes. He seemed to want my left hand. It stung for a while; in fact, it still stings." She felt Larsen take her hand.

He made a small noise of disgust.

"What's the matter?" Chris asked, alarmed. "What did he do to my hand?"

Larsen sighed. "He . . . " He rubbed the back of her hand. "It looks as though he made a sort of crude tattoo on it."

Chris snatched back her hand and held it to her breast. "What? What kind of a tattoo?"

"It's a little crude, but it appears to be a rose."

"He's tattooed a rose on my hand? Will it come off?"

"Tell me, did you hear anything while he was doing this?"

"Yes, there was a kind of buzzing noise."

"I think you'll probably have to see a dermatologist to have it removed," Larsen said. "Admirer apparently used an electric tattoo needle."

Chris began to cry, moved by anger and shame. Branded, she had been branded by this bastard, as if she were an animal.

"Please don't," Larsen said, putting his hand on hers. "You're not hurt, and the tattoo will come off. I'll find somebody to do it for you, if you like."

"I'm just so . . . *mad*!" she said. "Why is he doing this to me? Have I done something to deserve this?"

"Don't blame yourself," Larsen said. "It's not your fault; it's nothing to do with you, really; it's his obsession, not yours. You were just unlucky enough to come to his attention at the wrong moment, and he's latched on to you."

"Well, I want him to *unlatch*. I don't think I can take any more of this."

"I want you to know I'll do everything I can to stop him."

"Well, that's not a hell of a lot, is it?" she said bitterly.

"I'm sorry about tonight."

"I'm sorry, too; I know it's not your fault."

"Chris, I have to ask you something."

"Okay, ask."

"Do you own a gun?"

"No, I don't.

"Good."

"Why good?"

"Because it's a dangerous thing to have around; you'd be as likely to hurt yourself as someone else."

"Thanks for the vote of confidence."

"It has nothing to do with a lack of confidence in you, believe me."

Danny burst into the room "Are you all right? What happened?"

Larsen patiently took him through the events of the evening, then took his leave. "I don't think you'll have any more problems tonight, now that Danny's here," he said, "and I've removed the telephone taps."

"Thank you, Jon," Chris replied. "I appreciate everything you did tonight, and I'm sure I'll be all right now."

When the police had cleared out, Danny made them a cup of tea, and they sat in the study together.

Suddenly, Chris began to cry. She wept as she had not done since she was a child, and she couldn't seem to stop.

Danny took her in his arms and stroked her hair. "You go right ahead, baby," he said. "Get it all out."

Finally, when she was able to get control of herself, she looked up at her friend. "Danny," she said, "I want you to do something for me."

"Sure, Sweets, anything," Danny said.

"I want you to buy me a gun."

CHAPTER

15

L arsen found the note on his desk when he
arrived for work. "See me." It was signed in
the familiar scrawl of Bob Herrera, Chief of
Detectives. Larsen didn't like seeing Herrera, and he
didn't hurry to respond to the note. The two men
had been rookie detectives together, and they had
once served on a homicide task force together.
Larsen had made the bust—a famous one—and
Herrera had never forgiven him for it. But Herrera
was the better politician and had climbed the department ladder faster.

He checked through his messages to make sure
there was nothing from Chris Callaway, then he
trudged down the hall to the corner office. Herrera was
reading something; he motioned Larsen to a chair and
took his time finishing. Finally, he looked up.

"Tell me about this brouhaha on Stone Canyon
yesterday."

"One of my stalker cases," Larsen answered. It wasn't good enough.

"Go on," Herrera said irritably.

"I had a chance for a setup on the guy; he got there before I was ready."

"And you tackled some citizen in the process?"

Larsen reddened. "He was in the wrong place at the wrong time. I extended my apologies, and he seemed to understand."

"This is an active case?" Herrera asked.

Herrera had imposed strict terms on what could and could not be on the active list. Larsen was well aware that his chief thought of stalker cases as nothing but a nuisance—that the only reason he was assigned to the task was just in case one resulted in a murder; then the chief's ass would be covered. "I put it on the active list yesterday," Larsen said.

"If it's so important, why the delay?"

"I've been waiting for a criminal act, as you've specified."

"And what act has this stalker committed?"

"Illegal wiretap, for a start." Larsen told him about the bugs in the Callaway house.

"Sounds like the tabloids to me. Can you connect the taps to the stalker with something material?"

"He knew the unlisted number of a new line I had installed within hours."

"Come on, Larsen, hundreds of people in this town can get hold of an unlisted number. Hell, there are services selling that information. What else have you got on the guy?"

"Aggravated battery."

"Has he harmed her?"

"Not exactly."

"Now what the fuck does *that* mean?"

Larsen told him about the tattoo.

Herrera convulsed with laughter.

Larsen tried not to sound angry. "He sat on her, held her down, and tattooed the back of her hand with an electric needle."

"Aggravated battery with a tattoo needle," Herrera chuckled. "It's original, I'll give you that. Can she identify him?"

"She's . . . Her vision is impaired."

"How impaired?"

"Better than ninety percent," Larsen admitted.

"Any other way to identify him? Prints on the scene?"

"Nothing; he's slick."

"What about the computer profile on stalkers?"

"We have no information for the profile; there are twenty-four questions on the list, and we can't answer a single one."

"That's just terrific, Larsen. How much time have you spent on this one?"

"A few hours."

"How many hours?"

"Twelve, fifteen."

"Are you sure he exists?"

"What?"

"Maybe he's a figment of Ms. Callaway's imagination."

"She's blind and hardly capable of rigging all this."

"Cute?"

"She's a well-known actress." That should help; Herrera was a sucker for movie stars.

"A star?"

"Not quite; she's getting there."

"What does that mean?"

"She's had a number of featured roles and gotten good reviews. She was supposed to star with Jason Quinn in a big one at Centurion, but she lost her sight in a fall. She wants to keep her blindness quiet."

"You think she's in any danger?"

Larsen hesitated. "This guy worries me."

Now it was Herrera's turn to hesitate. Larsen knew he was weighing the embarrassment of the girl getting hurt against the pleasure of yanking him off the assignment.

"Give it a few days," Herrera said finally. "Then, unless you can demonstrate a clear and present danger, she goes back on the inactive list."

Larsen rose without speaking.

"Do you read me, Larsen?"

"Yes, chief." He hated knuckling under to the man.

"Good. Now get out of here."

Larsen trudged back to his desk, his ears burning, like a schoolboy scolded by his principal. He sank into his chair and reviewed his position. It was not good. So far, Admirer was ahead of him all the way. Larsen didn't like playing catch-up.

CHAPTER

16

When the phone rang Chris forced herself to answer it. Admirer had been calling daily and she was sick of him, but she wouldn't hide from him. It was Sunday.

"Hello?"

"It's Jon. How are you?"

She breathed a sigh of relief. "Annoyed," she said. "He's been calling every day, and I've talked to him the way you suggested."

"Have you learned any more about him?"

"No, and it's maddening. He knows *everything* about me."

"What sort of things?"

"Where I shop, restaurants I like, that sort of thing; not to mention every biographical detail."

"He can get that in a library."

"I know. I wish I'd never had an entry in *Who's Who*."

"So what are you doing on a Sunday afternoon?"

"Listening to one of your sister's tapes," she replied. "They've been wonderful, and so has the watch; will you thank her for me?"

"Sure I will. Listen, I thought you might like to get out of the house this afternoon."

"I'd love to, and I'm sure Danny would like an afternoon off. He's been stuck here with me all this time."

"Can I pick you up in about an hour?"

"All right, but I get to choose what we do."

"Okay by me."

"Promise? No arguments?"

"Okay, I promise."

"See you in an hour." She hung up. "Danny!" she yelled.

"What?" he called back from the living room.

"I've got a date! You get the afternoon off."

Danny came into the study. "I'll bet it's with the cop."

She felt herself blushing. "Well, I'll feel safe, anyway."

"And I get to have a sex life again!" Danny crowed. He picked up the phone and started dialing.

Larsen helped her into the car.

"What is it?" she asked, feeling the dash.

"It's an old MG TF 1500," he said, walking around the little car. "Built in 1954; the last of the classic MGs." He got in beside her. "I spent two years restoring it."

"What color is it?"

"A silver gray, with a white top, which is down at the moment. Mind getting your hair blown?"

"Not a bit."

"Good; it's a little claustrophobic with the top up. Now, I said I'd take you anywhere you want to go. What'll it be?"

"I want you to take me to a particular place, and when we get there I'll tell you more."

"All right; where to?"

"Do you know where the other end of Mulholland Drive is?"

"You mean way the hell out there, almost to Malibu?"

"Yes. It starts there and runs all the way to Beverly Hills."

"We used to go out there and neck in high school," Larsen laughed. "It's been that long since I was there." He started the car and drove off.

"Let's take Sunset down to Pacific Coast Highway," she said. "You can enjoy all the curves."

"My thought exactly," Larsen said. He turned right on Sunset and accelerated.

"I love it!" she cried.

"I love a girl who loves it," Larsen replied. She was easy and natural for an actress, he thought.

"Are you an L.A. native?" she asked as they crossed over the freeway. She wanted to know more about him.

"Yep. Born and raised in Santa Monica. Went to UCLA, both undergraduate and law school."

"You're a lawyer?"

"Passed the bar, never practiced."

"Why not?"

"My father was a lawyer; I think that's why I went to law school. I had graduated before I found out how he really felt about practicing law."

"How did he feel?"

"He hated it. He was a partner in a little firm in Santa Monica, did general work, and as the years wore on, he hated the work more and more. He found it boring and repetitive, and he hated being at the beck and call of clients, hated listening to them whining about their problems, hated dealing with the courts."

"Most of the lawyers I've known felt that way by the time they were forty," she said. "Except the entertainment lawyers—they're making too much money to care."

"Pity I didn't think of that," he said. "Maybe I wouldn't have become a cop."

"Why did you become a cop?" He seemed too polished, too smart to be a cop; she thought of cops as cruder, somehow.

"I had a criminal law instructor who was a cop; I liked him a lot, and he made the work seem interesting, took me on patrols, let me look over his shoulder."

"Has the work been interesting?" she asked.

"Oh, yes. Cops get hooked on their work; not many I've known have dropped out."

"Not much money, though."

"You're right about that. I managed to stay single, though, so I've done okay. My tastes are simple."

"My tastes were simple, until I started to make money," she said. "Funny how sophisticated they can become in a very short time."

"You mean you think that if I had more money I'd consume more champagne and caviar?"

"Metaphorically speaking, yes."

"I don't think I would."

"Let me ask you something," she said. "If you could have any car in the world, free, what would you choose?"

"That's easy: a Porsche Cabriolet."

"Aha!" she crowed. "Not such simple tastes after all."

He laughed.

"Let's say you suddenly started practicing law," she said, "and suddenly, you could afford the Porsche. You know what would happen then?"

"What?"

"You live in an apartment or a house?"

"An apartment."

"Well, one day you'd come home from work, and you'd notice that, somehow, your apartment house didn't exactly go with the Porsche. So you'd move into a classier place, and then you'd notice that your furniture didn't quite go with the new apartment, and when you got new furniture, your clothes wouldn't quite go with that, and so on."

"I see your point," he admitted.

"Being rich is all about keeping up with yourself, not the Joneses."

"Has that happened to you?"

"Of course it has. Now I'm trying to level off and let the money catch up with my tastes."

"Sounds like a good idea."

"That's what my manager keeps telling me."

They had reached the coast now, and soon he turned right and started uphill. "We're headed up into the mountains," he said. "We'll be on Mulholland in a few minutes."

"Good. I'll bet you can't guess what I want to do when we get there."

"You want to neck," he said.

"Nice try."

"That's what all the other girls I took up here wanted to do."

"I'm not surprised," she laughed. "Danny says you're good-looking, and he's a pretty good judge of beefcake."

Larsen hooted with laughter. "Well, I'm glad *somebody* finds me attractive these days." He drove around a series of curves, then turned right. "It's going to get bumpy," he said.

Mulholland Drive was nothing but a dirt track at this end, the province of teenage lovers and dirt bikers. Larsen drove slowly, taking care of his little car. "Any particular place you want to go?" he asked.

"When you start to be afraid for your car and nobody else is around, you can pull over."

"We're there," he said, pulling off the road onto the grassy shoulder. "Now what?"

Chris reached into her handbag and pulled out a small automatic pistol. "I want you to teach me to use this," she said.

17

The day was warm, and a breeze stirred the grass at their feet. The coast was a dim outline through the smog.

"I thought you told me you weren't going to buy a gun," he said.

"Nope; *you* told *me*. I'm afraid I ignored your advice; as soon as you left, I asked Danny to buy one for me."

Larsen picked up the little pistol and looked at it. "You realize that by having this in your bag you were carrying a concealed weapon?"

"Sue me."

He laughed and examined the pistol. "Italian, .22 caliber." He slid the clip out. "Takes six or seven cartridges. Did Danny buy ammunition, too?"

Chris took a box from her purse and handed it to him.

"Hollowpoints," he said.

"What are hollowpoints?"

He removed a cartridge from the box and held her finger to the tip. "Feel that? Each lead slug has been hollowed out. That means that when the bullet strikes its target, it will penetrate, then spread out, like a mushroom. A .22 is a small caliber, but this slug will do a lot of damage; it's the sort of thing that Mafia hit men put into people's heads."

"Good."

He was surprised. "Do you think you could kill another person?"

Chris did not hesitate. "I could kill Admirer, if I were ever in the same room with him again."

"Would you just point at his voice and pull the trigger, or would you wait until he did something to you?"

"I'm not sure I could answer that, in the circumstances."

"Does Danny know anything about guns?"

"He had never even held one, until he bought this for me."

"Well, I guess I'd better show you how to use it; otherwise you'd end up shooting yourself with the damned thing."

"That occurred to me," she said.

"Danny got some good advice," he said. "This is the right sort of weapon for the circumstances. It's for close work; you'd never hit anything with it beyond about ten feet. It's small; you can put it in the pocket of your jeans." He shoved the pistol into her pocket. "Those jeans are pretty tight; see if you can get it out in a hurry."

Chris reached into her pocket and yanked on the gun. It caught on her pocket and she had to struggle with it.

"You'll have to practice that," he said, taking the weapon back. He removed the clip and put it in her hand, then put a cartridge in her other hand. "Feel this; you point the bullet in this direction and push down and back. It's spring-loaded."

Chris dropped the bullet.

"Try again," he said, dusting the cartridge off and handing it back to her.

This time she managed it.

"Now, let's see how many it will hold." He fed her more ammunition. "Good, seven; remember that number. Now, take hold of the pistol here—feel the rough place in the metal—pull the slide back and release it."

Chris followed instructions.

"Now there's a bullet in the chamber. Feel this little protrusion? That's the safety; it's on when it's up and off when you push it down."

Chris pushed the safety down with her thumb.

"Hang on, point it away before you do that."

"I *am* sorry," she said.

He walked her a few feet and faced her toward an embankment. "Now, right in front of you is a bank of earth about a foot taller than you are. I want you to hold the pistol out in front of you and fire one round."

Chris did as she was told, and a popping sound was heard.

"Congratulations, you hit the bank."

"I thought it would make more noise," she said.

"It's a little gun; it makes a little noise."

"Oh."

He picked up some pebbles. "Listen, now, shoot at the sound." He tossed a pebble toward the bank, to her right.

Chris turned and fired in the direction of the sound.

"You missed it by about two feet, but that's not bad at the distance. Here's another."

Chris fired again and came close.

Larsen continued with the exercise until the clip was exhausted. He took the pistol from her, removed the clip, and worked the action. "Now you're *sure* the pistol is unloaded," he said, putting it back into her hand. He put his hands on her shoulders and turned her toward him. "Shoot me," he said.

"You're sure it's unloaded?"

"I'm sure."

She pulled the trigger, but nothing happened.

"You have to work the slide, and then take the safety off."

She did as he told her, then pointed the gun at him and pulled the trigger. A sharp click was heard.

"Do it again, but this time, get close to me and put the gun to my heart."

She moved in close and pressed the gun to his body.

"Go on."

She pulled the trigger again.

He took her gun hand and pressed it to his chest. "This is my heart, right here, just left of center." He took her free hand and placed it on his neck. "Now you know where my head is; you can press the gun up under my jaw and shoot there."

She felt her way and pulled the trigger again.

"Once you're close to him and know where you're shooting, keep pulling the trigger; it may take more than one to do the job. The trick is not to panic and start shooting too soon."

She nodded. "I don't like pointing the gun at you."

"I'm glad to hear it," he laughed.

"I mean, I don't think I'd have any trouble emptying it into Admirer, but . . ."

"I appreciate the thought. Not wanting to kill me could be the basis of a . . . friendship."

She laughed. "It could, at that."

He loaded the pistol for her, put the safety on, and placed it in her hand again. "You've done enough shooting. Now the gun is ready to use; all you have to do is work the action, take the safety off, and pull the trigger. If you think you might have to use it, work the action before you put it in your pocket, but be absolutely sure the safety is on."

"I understand," she said.

"I hope you do," he replied. "And for God's sake, don't ever tell anybody who taught you to use it. The department frowns on that sort of thing."

"I won't. I'm grateful for your help."

Larsen took her arm and steered her back toward the little MG. As he opened the door, he looked up and, in the distance, shimmering a little in the smog, he saw a man on a motorcycle, stopped in the road half a mile behind them. As he closed the door he reached into the glove compartment and retrieved a pair of small eight-power binoculars and raised them to his eyes. When he focused he saw things more clearly.

The motorcycle was red, and the rider was dressed in black leather and a black helmet. His face was obscured by a pair of binoculars. He was looking at Larsen and Chris.

"What is it?" Chris asked. "What are you doing?"

"Just tucking in my shirttail," Larsen said. He went around to the other side of the car and got in.

Driving back to Bel Air, he occasionally caught sight of the motorcyclist in his rearview mirror, far behind them in traffic.

They had a bite to eat, and by the time they got back to the house it was getting dark and Danny was waiting for them. Larsen said his good night, and as he started to leave, Danny waved at him and mouthed the word "wait."

Larsen left the house, but waited outside. A moment later, the front porch light went on and Danny came outside.

"Thanks for waiting," he said. "I wanted to show you something, and I didn't want Chris to know about it."

"What is it?" Larsen asked.

Danny pulled an envelope from his pocket. "This was in the mailbox when I got home."

Larsen opened the envelope and carefully removed a Polaroid photograph. He held it up to the porch light and looked closely at the image. "Jesus Christ," he said.

CHAPTER

18

Larsen sat at his desk and looked at the photograph again, this time through a clear plastic evidence bag. He had looked at it over and over during the past fifteen hours, but it still made him feel ill.

Feeling at a loss for something to do, he switched on his computer and gazed blankly at the screen while the program was loaded into memory.

STALKER PROFILE
Prepared for the Threat Management Unit
of the Los Angeles Police Department
by C. E. Ripley, M.D.
This program is confidential
and use by unauthorized persons is prohibited.

The profile was useless, because he had no personal information about Admirer. Suddenly he focused on the screen. He reached into a bottom desk drawer, found a phone book, looked up the number, and dialed.

"Dr. Ripley's office," a woman's voice said.

"Good morning, this is Detective Jon Larsen of the Beverly Hills Police Department. May I speak with Dr. Ripley, please?"

"He's with a patient at the moment. May I take a message?"

Larsen hesitated. "Would it be possible for me to see Dr. Ripley sometime today? It's in connection with a computer program he prepared for the LAPD."

"Let me see," she said.

Larsen could hear pages turning.

"He's had a cancellation later this morning; could you be here at eleven?"

"Yes, I certainly can," Larsen said. He thanked her and hung up. He was grasping at straws, but straws were all he had left.

"I'm Chuck Ripley," the doctor said. He was tall, stout, and balding.

"Jon Larsen, Dr. Ripley," Larsen said, shaking hands. "Thank you for seeing me."

"Call me Chuck," Ripley said. "I've always got time for the LAPD."

"It's Beverly Hills PD," Larsen said.

"Oh; I heard they loaned you the program."

"Yes, our threat unit is a long way behind theirs, but your profile has helped us a lot."

"Good. What can I do for you?"

"I'm investigating a stalker, and in spite of our best efforts, we've been unable to ID him, so the profile hasn't been of any help in this case."

"Yes, that would pose a problem," Ripley said drily. "No ID, no profile."

"Exactly. It occurs to me that the profile represents only a fraction of what you must know about the stalker phenomenon."

"I think it's fair to say that," Ripley agreed. "I first got interested in the phenomenon when I was the staff psychiatrist at San Quentin, and that was fifteen years ago, long before there was any public awareness of stalkers, not to mention police awareness."

"Then you must have studied a large number of cases over the years."

"About three thousand, at last count."

"What I'd like to do is to tell you about this particular stalker—we call him 'Admirer'—and I'd like to see what conclusions, if any, you can draw about him."

"Shoot."

Reading from his notes, Larsen reconstructed each incidence in which Admirer had contacted Chris Callaway. "On one occasion, he assaulted her," Larsen said, and told the doctor about the tattooing.

"That's very interesting," Ripley said. "Go on, tell me everything, and then I'll respond."

Larsen took him through each event, up through the motorcyclist of the previous day.

"Is that everything?" Ripley asked.

"No, there is one further incident, but it is so different from the others that I'd like to wait until after your initial response before we discuss it."

"All right," Ripley said. "Let's see; there are many characteristics of this man that are common to stalkers: the degree of obsession; the regularity, nay—*infallibility*—of his attention; the gifts; the admiring letters; the veiled threats; his following her about; his contention that she needs no one but him. None of these things distinguishes him from other stalkers for purposes of identity.

"Some useful information you have already gleaned: he seems affluent; he has some technical competence; he is highly intelligent."

Larsen nodded. "I'm assuming, of course, that Admirer is, in fact, responsible for each of these incidents, and that Miss Callaway's perceptions of his presence are correct."

"I think we have to assume that," Ripley agreed. "Some random thoughts: I think he either has private means or is self-employed—he seems to have a lot of personal freedom. I am inclined toward self-employment of a technical bent—computers, electronics, some sort of consulting, or he may have employees who carry on his business without his constant supervision. His lack of fear, his *contempt* of the police is interesting. There is a touch of megalomania there—any reasonable person, even a practiced criminal, fears the police. I think it is remotely possible, but not likely, that he has spent time in prison. More likely, he has a long-standing record of unlawful behavior without getting caught. He sees himself beyond the reach of the law, because of his intelligence and ingenuity, and not without some justification. He will not be easy to identify or apprehend.

"Certainly, he has problems establishing close relationships with women, and probably with men as well. He's a loner, but superficially, at least, is personable in his dealings with others. His reluctance to meet his victim face-to-face could indicate some physical deformity, real or imagined—anything from dwarfism to acne—that he feels he must conceal until his prey gets to know and love him." Ripley paused. "Has his use of language been syntactical and grammatical?"

"Yes, as a matter of fact. Miss Callaway noticed that. She thought he seemed educated."

"Not beyond high school or technical training, I would wager. From what we know of his possessions—a van, a motorcycle; of his skills—electronics and tattooing; and his rather mundane choice of gifts—roses and chocolates—I'd place him in a lower socioeconomic background. These are not things that someone from an upper-class milieu would spend his money on; there's an element of the *nouveau riche* here. I think his language skills have been picked up from watching television or movies—or, less likely, from reading." Ripley shrugged. "I know I'm pontificating here, but I'm just giving you my immediate impressions. I couldn't substantiate any of this, of course."

"I understand," Larsen said, "and this is very helpful."

Ripley sighed. "What else? His running the secretary off the road doesn't necessarily show a tendency to violence; it may well be that he holds a sort of comic-book attitude toward that kind of action, something acquired from too much TV or movies. I doubt that he seriously considered that he might have killed the woman. His lack of appreciation of the consequences of his actions, however, could make him *inadvertently* dangerous." Ripley massaged the bridge of his nose. "I must say, I find the forced tattooing much more disturbing. It shows a willingness to physically coerce in order to get his way."

Larsen spoke up. "As I'm sure you know, Chuck,

there have been incidents in the past when stalkers have harmed, even murdered their prey, but these are rare. There was a murder some years ago, but in the time since the LAPD Threat Management Unit was established, they haven't had a case of a stalker physically harming his victim, and in our shorter experience, neither have we."

"I wouldn't take a great deal of comfort from statistics," Ripley said, shaking his head. "Each of these stalkers is an individual, with his own psychological problems, even psychoses, and you can never predict with any degree of accuracy when one of them will become violent. However, in the case of Admirer, I feel quite certain that he believes completely that if he should wish to harm Miss Callaway, the police could never apprehend him."

Larsen greeted this opinion with silence.

"I think that's about all I can suggest," Ripley said, "until I know about the most recent incident, the one you've been reluctant to tell me about."

Larsen nodded and placed the Polaroid photograph on the desk between them. The two men looked at it together. It was a picture of another photograph from an open book, lying on a corner of a rug. A wooden floor was revealed in a corner of the picture.

"Mmmm," Ripley mused. "It seems to be from a book of medical photographs; you wouldn't ordinarily see a shot of an open chest in a consumer magazine or book. The sight of stainless-steel retractors pushing apart the rib cage might cause a lot of suburban housewives to faint."

"Notice the printed caption," Larsen said. "It appears to have been done on an electronic labeling machine. You see them in mail-order catalogues for around a hundred and fifty dollars."

"'One of my favorite pastimes,'" Ripley read aloud. "And have you noticed that the torso is that of a woman?"

"I noticed," Larsen said.

"Does Miss Callaway know about this?" Ripley asked.

"No. I didn't think it would be helpful."

"Quite right."

"What do you think of the arrival of this photograph?" Larsen asked.

"Rather a jarring note, isn't it?" Ripley replied.

"It certainly jarred me."

"I think the photograph means that Admirer has moved the game to a new level. There seems to be little doubt, in light of this message, that he could very well become violent. In fact, I would regard the photograph as a promise."

"I was afraid you'd say something like that," Larsen said.

"You may have something else to be afraid of," Dr. Ripley said.

"What do you mean?"

"Tell me, has Admirer had an opportunity to observe you and Miss Callaway together in circumstances that he might construe as romantic?"

Larsen thought about their drive up to Mulholland Drive in his car. "Yes, he has."

"Then I should think you have at least as much to fear from him as does the young lady."

CHAPTER

19

B ack in his car, Larsen took the Polaroid photograph from his pocket and stared at it again, willing it to yield more information. Suddenly it did. He held it as close to his eyes as he could and still focus, wishing he had a magnifying glass. He didn't know much about these things, but he had a strong urge to talk to somebody who did.

He started the car and began driving. There was an expensive-looking shop on Melrose that dealt in such things; he had passed it a dozen times and had meant to go in and browse but never had. Now was the time.

He invented a parking place on a yellow line, flipped down the sun visor with the police ID, and jaywalked across the street to the shop, which was called Westward Ho! There was a display of Indian pots in the window, and some of them looked very old. Inside, he waited while the only person in attendance, a small man in his early fifties, carried on a lengthy conversation with a young couple about the rising value of beaded clothing of the Plains Indians. Finally the couple took their leave, and the man turned his attention to Larsen.

"I'm terribly sorry to keep you waiting," he said. "May I show you something or answer a question?"

"Thank you, yes," Larsen said, producing the photograph. "I know there's not much of it visible, but I wonder if you could tell me anything about this."

The man looked at the photograph. "Ooooh, yuck," he said.

"I'm sorry about the nature of the photograph," Larsen said. "It's the rug under it that interests me."

"Oh, yes," the man said, looking at the photograph closely.

"I thought it looked like something that might be found in a shop such as yours. Can you tell me anything about it?"

"How large a rug were you interested in?" the man asked.

"Forgive me, I'm not shopping for a rug," Larsen said. "I just want to know as much as possible about this particular rug."

The man looked at him. "Why?" he demanded.

Larsen produced his badge. "I'm with the Beverly Hills Police Department; this photograph is evidence in a case, and I hope the rug might tell me something about the person who took the picture."

"I see," the man replied, but he did not seem enthusiastic about speaking with a policeman.

Larsen stuck out his hand. "I'm Jon Larsen."

The man shook hands. "Jason Willoughby." He glanced at the photograph. "Well, Officer, the rug is unquestionably Navajo—a chief's blanket; I would place it in the mid–nineteen twenties."

"You can tell that much about it from just the corner visible in the picture?"

"Not everyone could," Willoughby said. "*I* can."

"That's remarkable," Larsen said admiringly. "Can you show me what about the rug gives you that information?"

"Of course. The design is Navajo, for a start, and although the Zapotec Indians in Mexico regularly copy Navajo designs, they use different wools and dyes. This rug is thicker and softer than a Zapotec knockoff. Also, the stitching on the edge here . . . " Willoughby stopped talking and stared at the photograph.

"What sort of value would you place on a Navajo rug like this?" Larsen asked, anxious to keep the man talking.

Willoughby didn't speak for a moment, then he looked up at Larsen. "I can tell you exactly what it would have sold for a couple of years ago," he said. "Eighteen thousand dollars."

"And what would it be worth today?" Larsen asked.

"I could get twenty-five thousand from the right buyer," Willoughby replied. "It's not the rarest sort of Navajo, but it's a very good one. I found it in an estate sale."

Larsen blinked. "Do I understand you to say that you sold this same rug?"

"That's right; two years ago, give or take."

This was too good to be true. "Are you certain?"

"Let's see," Willoughby said. He walked to a card file in a corner of the gallery, opened a drawer, and began flipping through cards. He kept looking for a good two minutes while Larsen waited nervously. "Aha!" he said, and extracted an index card from the file, handing it to Larsen.

There was a photograph of the rug stapled to the card. Larsen compared it with his Polaroid shot; they were identical. He grinned. "That's extraordinary," he said. "You keep very good records."

"Well, it pays. You see, I could have a customer walk in here and ask for something in particular. If I've sold something similar, I can always call the client and ask if he's willing to part with it. I've made many sales that way."

"And do you have a record of who you sold it to?"

"On the back of the index card."

Larsen flipped over the card. "Bennett Millman," he read aloud.

"Ah, yes, Millman. The rug was the second piece he bought from me."

The address was on Copa de Oro, in Bel Air, not half a mile from Chris Callaway's house. "Do you know if Mr. Millman is still at this address?"

"No; I haven't seen him since he bought the rug."

"Thank you very much, Mr. Willoughby; you've been very helpful."

"Not at all," Willoughby replied. "Do you know the most extraordinary thing about that rug?"

"What?"

"It's on the floor. A knowledgeable collector would hang a textile of that quality, not walk on it. Mr. Millman is awfully cavalier with his possessions. Makes me wonder what he did with the pot I sold him." Willoughby shook his head sadly.

Larsen sprinted for his car. As he drove toward Bel Air, it occurred to him that he might not want to face Millman alone, especially since the man knew what he looked like. He picked up the microphone and radioed for a squad car to meet him at the Copa de Oro address.

There was a wrought-iron gate at the entrance to the property, but it was open. Larsen waited a couple of minutes for the squad car to show up, and when it did, he got out and spoke to the two uniformed cops inside.

"I don't expect to kick down the door," he said, "so you guys sort of hang back. Don't get involved unless there's trouble."

The cops nodded, and Larsen got back into his car. The driveway was curving and short, and it ended in a circle of European-style cobblestones. Larsen parked his car and got out. The place was beautifully landscaped and manicured, as was most of the property in such an expensive neighborhood. He reckoned the house was worth four or five million.

Larsen walked to the door and rang the bell. He expected a servant to answer, but no one came. Larsen was about to walk around to the rear of the house when a car, a white Cadillac, pulled into the driveway and three people got out—an attractive young woman and a middle-aged couple. The young woman approached him.

"Can I help you?" she asked.

"I'm looking for Mr. Millman," Larsen said.

She looked at him oddly. "May I ask what for?"

"I'm Detective Larsen, Beverly Hills PD. I need to speak to Mr. Millman."

"I'm afraid that's impossible," the woman said. "Mr. Millman died nearly three months ago."

"What?"

"I'm a real-estate agent; I'm here to show the house."

"I see," Larsen said. "Tell me, are the furnishings still in the house?"

"No. Mrs. Millman held an auction a couple of weeks ago and sold everything, right to the walls."

"Can you tell me who the auctioneer was?" Auctioneers kept careful records of sales; he could trace the rug.

"Mrs. Millman was. She didn't want to pay an auctioneer, so she put an ad in the *Times* and sold it all herself, cash only. She wouldn't even take a check. Tell you the truth, I've never seen anybody so tight with a buck; I think she wanted to hide the proceeds from the IRS."

"Were you at the auction, by any chance?" He was grasping at straws again.

"Yes, I bought two chairs—got them for half what I'd have paid in a shop. Tell you the truth, I think she'd have done better with a professional auctioneer, somebody who knew the value of things, who'd have advertised the sale properly."

"Do you, by any chance, recall the sale of a Navajo rug?"

"Mr. Millman had a number of Indian rugs and pots, a very nice collection, but that wasn't where my interest lay, so I didn't pay much attention."

"You don't remember who might have bought the rug?"

"I'm afraid not." She leaned in closer. "Listen, I don't want to scare my clients off, having the cops here. If there's nothing else, would you and your buddies mind leaving?"

"Sure," Larsen said wearily. "There's nothing else

for us here. Tell me, where can I get in touch with Mrs. Millman?"

"She's living in Palm Springs." The woman produced her business card. "If you'll call my office, they'll give you her address."

"Thanks, I'll do that."

Back in the car, Larsen laid his head against the headrest and sighed. His hot lead was getting colder by the minute.

CHAPTER

20

C hris blinked. The light hurt her eyes. It hurt
her eyes! How grateful she was for the
pain!

"Tell me how it happened." Dr. Villiers said.

"I woke up this morning, and I was lying on my
side, facing the windows in my bedroom, and I had
to put my hand over my eyes. It took me a minute
to realize that I was seeing something new—bright
light!"

"I'm very pleased about this," Villiers said. "It
means you're responding to treatment. Can you
make out people or shapes?"

"Just barely. I mean, I could look at Melanie when
she was talking to me, instead of having to guess
where she was by the sound of her voice, but she
was still just a blob. When will I be able to see
again?" she asked.

"Hold on, now; you're going to have to be patient.

It's taken all this time for you to perceive light well, and it's going to take a while longer before we'll know just how much of your vision is going to be regenerated."

"Could this be it?" Chris asked. "Could this be all I'll ever see? I'd like to know the worst."

"I think that's unlikely in the extreme," Villiers replied. "What's happened is only the first step. I can't guarantee you that you'll end up with the eyesight of an eagle, but the prognosis is very good."

"I've never been very good at being patient," Chris said.

Villiers chuckled. "Sometimes Nature forces it on us. Just be sure that when this is over, you don't forget the lesson."

"I'll try and remember that."

"We've got some good people here who could offer you therapy while you're waiting," Villiers said. "Why don't I make an appointment for you?"

Chris shook her head. "Thank you, no. If I thought my condition were permanent, I'd jump at the chance for therapy, but I'm finding my own ways to live with this, with the help of some friends. I don't want to get used to being a blind lady."

"As you wish," Villiers said. He touched the back of her hand. "What's this? It wasn't there before."

Chris recoiled and covered her left hand with her right. "It's a sort of tattoo. I'm going to have it removed."

"Why don't I take you down to the dermatology department, and we'll get it looked at."

"Yes, I'd like that," Chris said enthusiastically.

"Take my arm," he said.

Villiers steered her down the hall to the elevator and pressed the call button. "Are you getting out of the house at all?" he asked.

"Yes, from time to time. I'm certainly spending more time at home than I used to, but I don't feel comfortable going out unless I'm with someone I trust, someone who understands my condition. You see, I've sort of kept it a secret."

"I see," Villiers said, leading her onto the elevator. He waited until they had exited on a higher floor to speak again. "I hope you're not cutting yourself off from your friends."

"You have to understand, Dr. Villiers . . . "

"Paul; please call me Paul."

"Paul, in my business to be disabled is not to work again. You remember how quickly I was dropped from a film when I was injured?"

"Yes, that made me very angry."

"I was angry too at first, but then I had to look at it professionally. When a film starts principal photography it's on a very tight schedule, and every hour of work counts. A studio or a producer can't hire a cast with thirty speaking parts and maybe a hundred extras, plus a director and crew, and then leave them idle while one person recovers from an injury. In retrospect, they were right. If they'd waited for me they'd have lost a lot of money."

"I see. Here's Dermatology."

A young man in a white coat looked up from some paperwork. "Hi, Paul."

"Hi, Jerry. Let me introduce my patient, Chris Callaway. Chris, this is Dr. Jerry Stein."

Stein stood up. "Hello, I know your work, and I've enjoyed it."

"Thank you," Chris said.

"Jerry," Villiers said, "Chris has acquired a tattoo that she'd like to get rid of. Can you help her?"

Chris held out her hand.

Stein pulled her closer to his desk light and looked carefully at the tattoo. "Amateurish," he said. "This is the sort of thing people get drunk and do to themselves."

"That wasn't the case," Chris said.

"I'm sorry, I didn't mean to imply that it was. You're lucky, though; it's one color, red, so the q-switched yag will take care of it."

"The what?"

"There are two FDA-approved lasers for removing tattoos, the q-switched ruby and the q-switched yag. The first removes blue and black pigments, and neither one does very well with greens, but the q-switched yag is the only one that gets the red out. Nothing works on yellow."

"What's involved?" Chris asked.

"You won't even need local anesthesia," Stein said. "The lasers pulsate in short bursts—only one forty-billionth of a second; that heats up only the tattoo pigment and fragments it, then the surrounding tissue eats up the ink and either carries it away or pushes it up through the skin. Normally it would take half a dozen treatments, but your tattoo is so lightly applied that I suspect we can do it in one."

"Let's get on with it," Chris said.

Back in the car with Danny, Chris rubbed the back of her hand.

"Don't do that," Danny admonished. "You'll just get it infected."

"How does it look?" she asked.

"Pretty red."

"The dermatologist said it would heal just like sunburn."

"It's not going to be a problem, Sweets; don't worry about it."

"Danny, is anybody following us?"

"Not that I can see. Come on, now, don't get paranoid on me."

"When they were removing the tattoo, all I could think about was the bastard who did that to me."

"Easy, now. Anger isn't going to help."

"Oh, yes, it does help. I think I feel best these days when I allow myself to think about killing Admirer."

"Sweets, I know I got you the gun, but that doesn't mean you get to hunt the guy down. It's for self-defense in an extreme situation."

"You know I can't hunt him down."

"I was speaking figuratively."

"I know how a deer in the forest must feel," she said. "Just waiting for the hunter to step out from behind a tree and blast away. I don't like being the prey."

"I know you don't, and I wish I could do something to change it."

"There is something you can do for me, Danny," she said.

"Anything."

"Start watching your back. I'm going to tell Melanie the same thing."

"What are you talking about?" Danny asked, sounding worried.

"I'm going to stop being the prey," Chris said.

"What do you mean?"

"I'm going to start putting Admirer on the defensive every chance I get."

"Sweets, that could be dangerous. Remember, Jon told you not to get him riled."

"*I'm* riled; why shouldn't *he* be?"

"Because he has you at a big disadvantage."

"I've got some advantages, too. I have you and Melanie and Jon. Admirer doesn't have any friends to help him. He's all alone, and I'm going to find a way to exploit that."

"Chris . . ."

"Just start looking out for yourself, Danny. I don't want him to take out his anger on you."

"Chris . . ."

"Just watch your back."

"Chris, be reasonable."

"And Danny, I want to see Graham Hong."

"What for?"

"Will you call him and ask him to come to the house?"

"Sure."

"And Danny?"

"Yes?"

"Maybe you should get a gun for yourself, too."

CHAPTER

21

A call to Palm Springs information produced only one Millman, and the number was unlisted. Larsen asked for a supervisor, gave her his name, grade, and badge number, and got the number and address.

"Hello?"

"Mrs. Millman?"

"No, this is the maid."

"May I speak to Mrs. Millman?" he asked.

"Mrs. Millman doesn't speak on the telephone."

"Beg pardon?"

"She doesn't talk on the phone."

"To anybody?"

"Not unless she calls them."

"Would you tell her it's the Beverly Hills police calling?"

"Wouldn't do any good. She wouldn't talk."

"This a matter of some urgency."

"Sorry." The woman hung up.

Larsen had never before encountered anyone who refused to use the telephone, not in L.A. anyway. The whole of L.A. lived and died in cars and on the phone, often both. Bennett Millman's widow was an eccentric.

Annoyed, he dialed the number again. It rang fifteen times; no answer. He looked at his watch. Nine o'clock straight up. He dialed Chris Callaway's number.

"Hello?" Her voice was tense, challenging.

"Hi, it's Jon. Is everything all right?"

"Oh, hi." The voice relaxed; she sounded glad to hear from him. "Yes, everything's all right."

"Listen, I've got to drive down to Palm Springs this morning, on business. I know it's short notice, but I just found out; would you like a drive in the sun? Have some lunch, then come back?"

"Boy, would I! I'm starting to get cabin fever."

"Has Danny left the house for the day?"

"No, he has to be somewhere later this morning, though."

"Can I speak with him?"

Danny came on the line. "Hi, copper."

"Hi. Listen, I'm going to drive Chris down to Palm Springs for the day, and I don't want to take a chance on Admirer following us. You up to a little subterfuge?"

"Always," Danny said, laughing.

"Will you drive Chris away from the house and meet me?"

"Sure. Where?"

"Drive her into Beverly Hills and park in the lot behind Neiman-Marcus; then walk her through the store, and I'll be waiting out front."

"Okay; what time?"

"In an hour?"

"See you there."

"Let me speak to Chris again."

She came back on the line, "Hi."

"Hi. Danny's going to drive you to Neiman's, and I'll meet you there in an hour, all right?"

"Are we eluding somebody?"

"That we are."

"Sounds like fun. I'll see you in an hour."

When Chris came out of Neiman's Larsen thought she had never looked so good. She was wearing yellow slacks and a white cotton sweater that made her breasts look inviting, plus a head scarf and sunglasses.

"Good morning," he called.

"Hi. We made it."

"Danny, did you notice anybody following you?"

Danny shook his head. "I checked the rearview mirror a couple of times, but I didn't notice anybody."

Chris got into the little MG, and Larsen helped her with her seat belt. "Ready?"

"Ready!"

"Thanks for your help, Danny," Larsen said. "I'll have her back by dinnertime."

"Keep her as long as you like," Danny called as they drove away.

"Free at last!" Chris cried as the car picked up speed.

"I'm glad you feel that way."

"Tell me, is this car going to break down somewhere, and then we have to send to England for parts? Is that part of your plan?"

"Sounds good to me," Larsen laughed. "Trouble is, the boot's full of spare parts. It's the sort of thing you learn driving a classic car."

"Poor planning," she said. "So what are you doing in Palm Springs today?"

"I have to interview a lady."

"Couldn't do it on the phone?"

"She doesn't talk on the phone," Larsen replied. He told her about his conversation with the maid.

"Sounds crazy to me."

"I hope not too crazy."

"Is this something to do with Admirer?" she asked.

Larsen hesitated. He didn't want to tell her about the Polaroid photograph. "No," he said. "Another case."

As he got on the freeway he checked the ramp behind him in the rearview mirror. Only one car, a red Japanese number. Relieved, he merged with the traffic and picked up speed.

When he checked the mirror again, he saw a van a couple of cars back, then it seemed to go away. He checked another two or three times, then forgot about it.

22

Larsen found the Millman house in Palm Springs and parked the MG in the shade of a palm tree. "I'm not sure I could explain the presence of a beautiful woman at this interview," he said to Chris. "Do you mind waiting here?"

"This is fine," Chris replied. "I'm enjoying the weather."

He left the radio on for her and approached the house. A low hedge separated a lushly planted front yard from the sidewalk; four sprinklers worked at keeping the grass an emerald green. He didn't wonder that Southern California had perpetual water problems. He rang the bell.

A small Hispanic woman answered the door. "Yes?"

Larsen didn't waste time with pleasantries; he showed her the badge, the sight of which seemed to rattle the woman. "I'm the police; we talked this morning. I want to see Mrs. Millman now."

The woman quickly let him in, no doubt with

visions of the Immigration Service dancing in her head, he thought. She led the way through the house and out into a larger and even more densely landscaped garden surrounding a kidney-shaped swimming pool. "Please wait here," she said, and shuffled toward a woman in a lounge chair. The two exchanged a few words, and the maid waved Larsen over, then fled back into the house.

Larsen approached the poolside, and he discovered that whatever mental image he had formed of Mrs. Millman was incorrect. The widow, who he guessed was an extraordinarily well-preserved forty, was clad in the smallest bikini he had ever seen; her skin was tanned, her flesh firm, and her hair and makeup perfectly arranged.

"Good day," Larsen said, showing his badge again. "I am Detective Jon Larsen of the Beverly Hills Police Department."

"How do you do, Detective?" she said, rising. "Let's find some shade." She walked ahead of him toward a cabana a few yards away.

Larsen followed, entertained by the movement of her hips, the back of the bikini being nothing more than a string that passed between her cheeks. The woman was a living monument to the wonders of Beverly Hills cosmetic surgery.

That done, Mrs. Millman turned, leaned over the bar, and exhibited her ill-concealed breasts. "Can I get you something to drink?" she asked.

"Some fizzy water would be nice," Larsen replied, trying to keep his gaze fixed above her neck.

She uncapped a large bottle of San Pellegrino, filled a glass with tiny ice cubes, and poured the water. Then she mixed herself a very light gin and tonic. "What can I do for you?" she asked.

Larsen listened for innuendo but never heard it. The woman, in spite of her state of dress—or undress—was all business. He produced Jason Willoughby's photograph of the rug. "Do you recognize this?" he asked.

"Yes, it belonged to my husband," she said.

"Did you recently sell it at auction?"

"I did."

"Do you, by any chance, recall to whom you sold it?" He tried not to hold his breath.

"Of course," she said. "He paid thirty-five hundred dollars for it."

A bargain, Larsen thought. Willoughby had said he could get twenty-five thousand for it. "Do you recall the buyer's name?"

"Of course; it was James."

"His last name?"

"Oh, I don't know; I never called him anything but James."

"You knew him before the auction?"

"Why, yes; he lived in our guest house, acted as sort of a house sitter when we were down here or in New York."

"He lived on your property, and you never knew his last name?"

"Oh, Bennett knew it, I suppose; after all, he dealt with the fellow. I never saw him, except from a distance. He went to work early in the morning and was rarely home before dark."

"How did you know when he left and returned?"

"Well, either the van or the motorcycle would be gone, and then it would be back under the guest-house carport."

"He drove a van and a motorcycle?"

"That's right."

"Do you know what kind of van or motorcycle?"

"The van was a sort of grayish green, and the motorcycle was red."

"I meant, did you ever notice the manufacturers' names?"

"No."

"Where did James work?"

"He apparently had some sort of business, but I never knew what. He was very handy; he'd sometimes repair things around the house."

"What sort of things could he repair?"

"Anything—the air-conditioning, the plumbing, the cars. He was very useful."

"Can you describe James, in as much detail as possible, please?"

Chris sat in the MG, her head against the back of the seat, half dozing. She felt happy to be away from the house, out of L.A. and with Jon Larsen. She felt the face of her wristwatch; he had been gone for twenty minutes.

A car pulled up next to the MG and stopped. Chris turned her head toward it. A gray shape; bigger than a car; noisier, too. It sat there, idling. She heard the door open, and suddenly she was alert; an all-too-familiar smell had reached her—the scent of roses.

Chris acted without thinking. She tore open the door of the little sports car and scrambled out, tripping on the curb and falling onto grass. She rolled to her feet, feeling the edge of the sidewalk. Which way had Jon gone? She picked right and began running down the sidewalk; she had no idea where she was going, but there were rapid footsteps behind her.

"James was, I don't know, medium," Mrs. Millman was saying. "Medium height, medium weight, medium hair."

"Eyes?"

"I never looked into them."

"Any distinguishing marks or scars?"

"Bennett said he had a tattoo. It worried him at first because he associated tattoos with convicts, but James won him over quickly. He was very honest; paid his rent on time; took care of the furniture; lived quietly. He never seemed to have people over or play loud music."

"Do you know where on his body the tattoo was?"

"I'm afraid not."

"Can you remember anything else about him?"

She shrugged. "He always wore a baseball cap. At least, whenever I saw him he wore one. Except on the motorcycle; then he wore a helmet."

"What color helmet?"

"Black. He dressed in black when he rode the motorcycle."

"You said he was a house sitter, but that he paid rent."

"My husband was very good with money; no one ever got anything free from him. James paid a couple of hundred a month, I think; it would have been a great deal more if he hadn't rendered some services."

"Did he ever give your husband a check for the rent?"

"I don't think so. Bennett liked to deal in cash."

"Did you ever have a conversation with James? About anything—the weather?"

"No."

"Did you ever speak to him on the phone?"

"Not exactly. When we were going out of town one of us would call him to let him know our schedule. I called once or twice, and his answering machine always picked up."

"Do you recall what the announcement on the machine was?"

"Very brief; terse, you might say. 'Hi, leave a message, I'll get back to you.' Something like that."

"Can you describe his voice?"

"Sort of a medium voice, I guess. Not deep, not high-pitched. Pleasant enough."

"Did he have any sort of accent?"

"Not that I recall. Sounded pure Californian."

"When did James move out of the guest house?"

"Well, now that you mention it, I'm not sure that he has. His rent was paid until the end of this month. He put it in the mailbox, along with a neatly typed note of condolence; said he was looking for another place. I've been down here at the Springs for nearly two weeks. He might have moved; he might not have."

Larsen's heart leapt. "You said there was a telephone in the guest house. Was it in his name or yours?"

"Ours."

"Is there anything else you can remember about him? Anything at all?"

"I'm afraid not. Is James in some sort of trouble?"

"Not exactly. I'd just like to speak to him."

"I'd hate to think that some sort of criminal had been living in my guest house."

"As far as I know, he's never been arrested," Larsen said, putting the best possible face on his reply. "Thank you for the mineral water. I'd better be going."

She walked with him as far as her chaise longue. "Can you find your way?" she asked, stretching out her lithe body on the lounge again.

"Of course. Thanks for your help."

She gave a little wave, then closed her eyes.

Larsen could not resist taking a moment to look her over again.

Mrs. Millman opened her eyes and smiled slightly. "Thank you, Detective," she said.

Larsen fled the scene.

When he returned to the car, Chris was not in it. Alarmed, he looked up and down the street. She was nowhere to be seen. The radio was still playing.

CHAPTER

23

Larsen jumped into the MG, got it started, and drove off down the street, forcing himself to drive slowly, to look in every driveway and front lawn. He turned right and kept looking.

What had happened? Surely she wouldn't have left the car, not unless she was enticed or forced to do so. He came to a driveway that disappeared behind a hedge; he turned in and drove a few yards until he could see the rest of the property. Nothing. He turned another corner. Why this route? Why not? He had no way of telling which way she might have gone. He made two more right turns and was back on Mrs. Millman's block.

Suddenly there she was, sitting at a wrought-iron table on a side patio, chatting with an elderly woman. The house was two down from the Millmans'. He stopped and jumped out of the car. "Hello there," he called out as he approached. His heart was banging around inside his chest. Chris turned toward him and stood up. "Are you all right?" he asked as he took her hand.

She squeezed his hand. "I'm fine. Jon, this is Mrs. Burgess; she was kind enough to come to my rescue."

"Rescue?"

"I was waiting for you when some sort of large vehicle pulled up beside the car, and someone got out. I smelled roses."

"I see."

"I got out of the car and ran, ran right into Mrs. Burgess, in fact; nearly knocked her down."

Mrs. Burgess spoke up. "The man appeared to be hurrying after her," she said. "When he saw me, he ran back to his car—or rather, it was a van."

"Did you see his face, Mrs. Burgess?" Larsen asked.

"Not really. He turned around quite quickly."

"Can you describe the man?"

"Oh, I don't know; he was not too tall, nicely dressed, I suppose; he wore a baseball cap."

"Did you think to get the license number of the van?"

"Yes, but too late; he was already down the block, and my eyesight isn't what it once was. It was a California plate, though; I'm sure of that."

"Thank you, that's very helpful."

"The very idea of someone frightening a blind girl like that!" the woman said indignantly. "I wish I'd had time to go and get my pistol!"

Larsen laughed in spite of himself, and so did Chris. Was everybody in this country armed, even old ladies? "Thank you, ma'am," he said. "I'll take Chris off your hands."

Chris shook hands with the woman. "Thank you for rescuing me," she said.

"Any time," Mrs. Burgess replied. "Next time, I'll blow him away!"

When they were back in the car Larsen heaved a sigh of relief. "I should never have left you alone," he said.

"Nonsense; who would have thought he could find us in Palm Springs?" She laughed. "I'm like Mrs. Burgess; I wish I'd had my pistol."

"I'm glad you didn't; I wouldn't want you to blow away the UPS man, or somebody like that."

"You promised me lunch," she said.

"I did."

"Can I suggest a place?"

"Sure."

"There's a hotel here someplace called the Racket Club; it's an old-time Hollywood hangout."

"We passed it on the way in," he said. "We'll be there in five minutes."

The Racket Club was not busy, but it was cool and dark, and Larsen wasn't looking for a crowd anyway. From behind the bar, movie stars of another day smiled down on them—Clark Gable, Lana Turner, and Rita Hayworth mugged for the camera beside the pool.

"Can we lunch outside?" Larsen asked.

"Sure," the bartender replied. "Pick a table, and I'll send a waitress out."

They found a table under a tree near the pool, and a waitress took their orders.

"This place was owned by Charlie Farrell, who was a big-time agent, and the actor Ralph Bellamy," Chris said. "It was *the* place to be seen in the old days. I sometimes wish I had been in Hollywood during the thirties. I think I'd have liked being cossetted by MGM, having all my decisions made for me. The money's better these days, but I think it must be a lot harder than it was."

"My favorite movies were made then," Larsen said. "Fred Astaire and Ginger Rogers, Gable, Jimmy Stewart, Cary Grant, Katharine Hepburn, Spencer Tracy."

"I'd give anything to have worked with Spencer Tracy," she said. "He may be the best actor the movies ever produced."

"I can't disagree."

She was quiet for a moment. "The visit to Palm Springs was to do with Admirer after all, wasn't it?"

"Yes, it was. I didn't want you to know, unless I found out something."

"And did you?"

"I know his first name—James—and I know where he lives," Larsen said.

"Where?"

"Not half a mile from you, in a guest house."

"Is somebody arresting him?"

"Not yet. He apparently works all day, comes home late. I'll pay a call on him this evening."

"At last," Chris sighed.

Their food arrived, and they ate and chatted until mid-afternoon. "Well," Larsen said, "I promised Danny I'd have you home in time for dinner."

"Then we'd better go, or Danny will yell at me."

"He sounds like a father," Larsen said, taking her arm.

"More like a mother," Chris replied.

They left the hotel and crossed the pavement to

where Larsen had parked the MG. He stopped short of the car.

"What's the matter?" she asked.

"Wait here for just a moment," he said. "I'll only be a few yards away, and I won't let you out of my sight."

"All right, but hurry."

He walked to the car and surveyed the damage. The windshield was smashed, and the paint on the hood and front fenders was marred by deep scratches. But that wasn't the only gift. The interior of the little car was practically filled with dead roses. He cleaned them out, being careful of the thorns, then went back for Chris.

"It's okay," he said. "We can go now."

As he walked her to the car he began looking forward to calling on Admirer that evening.

CHAPTER

24

Larsen pulled into Chris's driveway, and Danny met them at the door.

"Another half hour and you'd have been grounded, young lady," he said, wagging a finger at her. He looked at the car. "What happened?"

"Don't ask," Larsen replied.

"Oh, Danny, Jon has found out something about Admirer. He lives near here, and his first name is James."

"Good news," Danny said. "Are you going to bust him?"

"You bet," Jon said, "if I can get my hands on him." He looked at his watch. "I'm going over there now and have a look around, and then I'll wait for him to come home from work."

"You be careful," Chris said, reaching out for him and finding his hand. "You're going to have back-up, aren't you?"

"Police jargon from a nice young lady like you!" Larsen laughed.

"Well, I had a featured role on 'Hill Street Blues' once," she replied. "I'll bet I can talk cop just as good as you—mug shot, a.k.a., murder one, freeze, dogbreath! See?"

"We could use you on the force," Larsen said. "Do you mind if I leave my car here for a while?"

"Of course not; what are you up to?"

"I'm going over to the Millman place on foot. I don't want my car visible on the street, since Admirer knows it all too well."

"What about your backup?"

"I have a handheld radio in the car. You go on in, and I'll get it." He went back to the car, sat down in the passenger seat, and unlocked the glove box. The radio was there, charging, and so was his personal weapon, a 9mm Glock automatic, in a soft leather holster. He clipped it onto his belt, pocketed an extra clip, and retrieved a hooded windbreaker from behind the seat. Concealing the pistol and radio with the jacket, he walked back into the house. He didn't think he was being watched, but he had learned, somewhat late in the game, not to underestimate Admirer.

"Would you like something to eat before you go?" Chris asked.

"I'd better get over there now," he said. "There's not that much time left before dark."

"Be careful, and call me when it's over," she said. She reached up, found his face, and pulled him down to her for a kiss.

It was the first real affection that had passed between them, and it surprised him. The line between cop and victim had been crossed. "See you later," he said.

Larsen went to the back door, looked carefully around, then let himself out and headed for the old bridle path. Once there he flipped up the hood on his jacket and with his khaki trousers and sneakers, he was just another neighborhood jogger. He briefly considered asking for backup, but he now had a strong desire to meet Admirer face-to-face—just the two of them.

He loped down the path and emerged onto a street, then followed it toward Sunset for a few blocks. When he met Copa de Oro, he turned left and jogged slowly up the hill toward the Millman house, doing an all-too-credible imitation of a jogger whose legs were slowing him down. He was not a regular runner, and he had underestimated the distance to the house.

Finally, in front of the house, he leaned against a tree, wiped his face with his sleeve, and tried to catch his breath, all the time stealing glances at the Millman driveway. The guest house was out of sight down the drive, so he couldn't tell whether anybody was home.

His breathing and heart rate having returned to something like normal, he jogged on past the house, looked around to be sure he couldn't be seen, then dashed into the woods. From there he worked his way around to the back of the Millman property, where he ran up against a rusted chain-link fence. At least there was no barbed wire at the top, he thought. He took a running start, planted a foot as far up the fence as he could, grabbed the top railing, and flung himself over, landing heavily, then rolling.

He found himself behind the swimming pool, and he worked his way to the left through the dense undergrowth, avoiding a walk across the exposed lawn. He was making a lot of noise, but it didn't seem to matter. The sun streaked through the trees, low in the sky and red as blood through the L.A. haze.

He came to the end of the undergrowth and saw that he was another ten yards from the back of the guest house, across a patch of lawn. A light burned at the back of the little house. Larsen looked around carefully, then sprinted across the lawn to the rear wall of the building. He stopped there and caught his breath again.

He put an ear to the wall to see if he could hear anyone inside. Nothing, but the wall had to be at least six inches thick. He flipped back the hood of his jacket and looked carefully through a corner of the window into a kitchen. The light was on, but there was no one in the room. In the corner nearest him was a steel workbench bolted to the wall, and on the bench was a large open briefcase containing an extensive tool kit. Some sort of circuit board lay next to the briefcase, and a soldering iron lay beside that in its cradle. Larsen couldn't tell if it was hot.

He worked his way around to the side of the house, away from the driveway, and looked through another window. A bedroom, but in the bad light he couldn't see much, except an open suitcase on the bed. A dim light showed from the next room. He moved farther along the side of the house and tried still another window.

The living room. A small lamp was on next to the sofa, and beyond that Larsen could see several card-board boxes, apparently full and sealed with silver duct tape. It looked as though Admirer had packed for his move and planned to come back for his belongings. Larsen peeked around the house at the open carport. He could see the front fender of a red motorcycle around the far corner of the house, but not well enough to judge its make. The van was nowhere to be seen.

How long before Admirer returned? Was he still in Palm Springs, or on the way back from his new residence? Five minutes, Larsen thought; surely he had that long. He went back to the kitchen door and carefully tried the knob. Locked. From his wallet Larsen took something thoroughly illegal, something that no police officer should have in his possession, although many did. Two small pieces of metal, milled from a hacksaw blade by a friend, came into his hand, and went into the lock on the kitchen door. Half a minute later, the door was unlocked.

Larsen turned the knob very slowly and opened the door two inches. He moved an ear to the opening and listened hard. Not a sound from the house. He stood up and opened the door.

The kitchen was small and equipped only on one side of the room. The other side was taken up by a stackable washer and dryer and the workbench. He eased the door shut behind him and walked softly to the workbench. He picked up the circuit board: it was about two by three inches and had a connecting edge on one side, but he couldn't tell what equipment it might be a part of. He put down the circuit board and looked at the briefcase to see if there might be a nametag. Nothing.

The tools seemed to cover almost any sort of work—not just electronics but automotive and light carpentry. There was a set of socket wrenches, a small scroll saw, and a voltage meter. Nothing here that would help with an identity.

He turned and moved to the living-room door.

Across the room near the little lamp was a stack of magazines, and on top was a *Popular Mechanics*. But what fixed his gaze was the white address label stuck to the magazine cover. It contained all the information he wanted.

Larsen stepped into the living room, and as he did, a shadow moved on the wall to his left. He started to turn toward it, and as he did, he was struck hard on the back of the neck. Emitting a cry of pain, he fell to one knee, but managed to grab the arm of a chair, steadying himself and hanging on to consciousness. He began to rise, and as he came up something came down to meet him. This time he pitched forward onto his face and blacked out.

CHAPTER

25

Chris jerked awake. She was sitting in a wing chair in her study, and she had been asleep. She could hear Danny's regular breathing from the sofa. She felt for the face of her wristwatch; just after midnight. Why hadn't Jon called?

She picked up the phone and called Jon's direct line at police headquarters.

"Detective Larsen's office, Officer Burns speaking."

"Officer, my name is Chris Callaway; I'm looking for Detective Larsen. Is he in?"

"No, ma'am, he's not due until nine tomorrow morning."

"Have you heard from him at all this evening?"

"No, ma'am. Can I take a message?"

"Thanks, I'll call again tomorrow." She hung up, and she was frightened. "Danny, wake up!"

"Huh?" Danny rubbed his eyes and sat up. "What's up? Did Jon call?"

"No, and I'm worried. There's a phone book in the bottom desk drawer; see if there's a Millman listed on Copa de Oro."

She heard the desk drawer open and close and pages ruffled.

"Yeah, there is."

"Remember the address; we've got to go over there."

"Are you sure that's a good idea, Chris? Jon didn't ask us to do that, and we don't want to get in his way."

"He said that Admirer came home from work after dark, and it's been dark for hours, and he didn't call for backup; I checked." She got up. "I'll be right with you." She walked quickly to her bedroom, opened the drawer of the bedside table, and took out the little automatic Danny had bought for her. She shoved it into the pocket of her jeans, grabbed a sweater, and went back to the front of the house. "Come on," she said, holding out a hand for Danny, "let's get moving."

Larsen moved his head, and the effort hurt; he couldn't seem to move anything else. He tried to roll over onto his back, and that didn't work, either; something was in his way. His hands and feet were bound, and there was tape over his mouth and eyes. He didn't know where he was. He was fully conscious now, and he thought it wise to listen for a while before trying to move again. Silence. Where the hell was he, and why was he bound and gagged? He struggled to remember what had happened to him.

·   ·   ·

Danny stopped the car in front of the Millman house.

"Can you see the guest house?" Chris asked.

"No, just the main house; it must be down the driveway."

"Then drive down there."

"Chris, we don't know what's going on here."

"Just put your lights on bright so that anybody can see we're coming, and drive straight to the guest house."

"Chris . . ."

"I know this is the right thing to do, Danny."

Danny turned the car into the driveway, put his headlights on bright, and began driving. The guest house came into view dead ahead; no lights were on, and no car was in the carport. "It looks deserted," he said.

"Pull up to the house and leave your headlights on," she said.

Danny did as he was told.

"Now see if you can get into the place."

"Okay, if you say so."

"Wait a minute." She retrieved her pistol and pressed it into his hand.

"Listen, I don't know anything about guns."

"Take it; just press down this safety, and it's ready to fire."

"I think we ought to go home and call the police, Chris."

"Danny, *please*. Do this for me."

Danny got out of the car and approached the house. He peered in through the window, but saw nothing but furniture. "It still looks deserted," he called to Chris.

Chris opened the car door and got out. "Try the front door," she called.

Danny turned the knob and pushed; the door opened easily. "The door is open."

"See if you can find a light." Chris was walking gingerly toward Danny's voice.

"There's no switch, but I can see a lamp by the sofa." Danny walked into the room toward the lamp and suddenly pitched forward onto the floor, crying out in surprise.

"What's wrong, Danny?" Chris yelled, waving her hands before her, trying to find her way.

"I'm okay," he called back. "I just tripped. There, the light's on. Holy shit!"

Chris found the front door and stepped into the room. "What is it? What's the matter?"

Danny leaped back and looked at the struggling heap on the floor in front of him. "Shit, it's Jon!"

"Is he hurt?"

"I don't know; wait a minute." Danny grappled with the tape over Larsen's eyes, and finally yanked it away. Larsen blinked in the light. Danny ripped off the tape over his mouth.

"Thanks very much, Danny," Larsen said. "Now do you think you could get my hands free?"

It took him a couple of minutes, but Danny finally was able to unwind the duct tape. Larsen sat up and began working on the tape around his ankles.

"Jon, you tell me this minute, are you all right?" Chris demanded.

"I've got one hell of a headache," Larsen replied, "but I'm all right." The last of the tape came free, and, steadying himself on the arm of the sofa, Larsen struggled to his feet. He sat down immediately. "Jesus, I'm a little woozy, and I feel nauseated."

Danny sat Chris down next to the policeman. "You take care of him; I'll see if I can find something to help." Danny went into the kitchen, found a dish-cloth, wet it, and brought it back to Larsen.

Larsen held the cloth to his face and then the back of his neck.

"Jon, can you tell us what happened?"

"Tell me where I am, and I'll try to figure it out."

"You're in the Millman guest house."

"Oh, Jesus, now I remember; I picked the lock and got inside. I thought it was deserted; I guess I was wrong."

"I think we should get you to an emergency room and make sure you're all right," Chris said.

"She's right, Jon," Danny agreed.

"No, I'm feeling better now. You sure got here fast."

"Not really," Chris replied. "It's after midnight."

"Oh," Larsen groaned. "Then I've been out for hours."

"So were we," Chris said. "Danny and I both fell asleep, waiting for you to call."

"I'm glad you came," Larsen said, looking around. "Well, he's gone. There was still a lot of his stuff here when I got into the house. There was a suitcase in the bedroom, and some boxes and some magazines. I think I was about to read his name on a magazine address label when the sonofabitch hit me."

Danny went and looked in the bedroom and kitchen, then returned. "Looks like he left nothing," he said.

Jon carefully picked up the phone on the table by the sofa and dialed a number. "This is Larsen," he said. "I want a fingerprint team right now." He gave the address and hung up. "Let's find out if Admirer is as smart as he thinks he is."

Two hours later, the detectives were still combing the guest house.

"Looks like he wiped everything down," one of them said.

"Not everything," replied the other, pointing at the bottom of the telephone. "I've got a good print right here; male, left hand, second finger, I'd say. He held the phone in his left hand and made a call with his right."

"Good," Larsen said. "Let's get back to the office and run it. I want to know who this bastard is."

CHAPTER

26

Larsen tried not to look at the chief of detectives. His head and neck hurt so much he could hardly turn his head, and Herrera was sitting with his back to the window. The light hurt Larsen's eyes, and Herrera was not happy.

"Let's see," Herrera said, while counting on his fingers, "you attempted to apprehend a potentially dangerous suspect without calling for backup; you illegally entered a premises; you allowed the suspect to overpower you and take your weapon and your police radio; you sustained a head injury sufficient to cause unconsciousness and did not seek a medical evaluation; and you have apparently become personally involved with a crime victim in an active case. And then you waste a fingerprint team on a sweep that takes three hours and turns up nothing. Does that about cover it?"

Larsen nodded.

"Speak up, I didn't hear that."

"Yessir, that about covers it. I would like to point out that I had Mrs. Millman's permission to enter her guest house." This was a lie, but just let Herrera try to get the woman on the phone to prove it. It was the only one of his actions that constituted a crime, and he didn't want his chief to have that to hold over him; it was grounds for outright dismissal from the force.

"Swell," Herrera said.

Larsen knew he should leave well enough alone, but he couldn't. "I'd also like to point out that we did find a print, and that there's nothing in police regulations that bars me from being friends with a crime victim."

"You're fucking her, aren't you?"

Larsen was on his feet. "Why don't you bring me before a review board, and we'll call her as a witness and find out!"

Herrera stood up, too, and leaned across his desk. "I'm not going to take insubordination from you, Larsen."

Suddenly all the impotence and repressed anger that had lurked in Larsen's mind came out. "And I'm not going to take any horseshit about my personal life from you! Okay, so I didn't call for back-up, but nobody got hurt but me; the pistol was my personal property, and I'll be happy to reimburse the department for the radio. And if you suspend or reassign me, or even put a reprimand in my jacket, *I'll* ask for a review board and defend my conduct and my record there."

To Larsen's astonishment, Herrera backed down.

"All right, all right, keep your shirt on," the chief said, and both men sat down again. "I want you to see a doctor immediately, and I want to see his report."

"Yessir," Larsen said.

"And don't you fuck around with this Admirer guy again unless you've got backup. Now get out of here."

"Thank you, chief," Larsen said, and he got out of there.

The young resident looked at the CAT scan and then at Larsen. "This is clear, but you're lucky you don't have a skull fracture. You were out for several hours, and it takes one hell of a wallop to do that. If you'd come into the ER last night, I'd certainly have admitted you for observation. There's no doubt you were concussed, but if you've gone this long without keeling over, you're probably not going to die."

"I'm glad to hear it," Larsen said.

The resident scribbled rapidly on Larsen's chart, then wrote a prescription. "I want you to go home and stay in bed for twenty-four hours." He ripped the prescription form off the pad. "Take one of these every four hours; they'll relax you and help with the pain. And if you experience any nausea I want you back in the ER pronto."

"Yes, Doctor."

At home, Larsen took one of the pills and sat down on the bed. He picked up the phone and dialed Chris's number.

"Hello?"

"It's Jon."

"What about the fingerprint? Did you identify him?"

"No, there was no match in anybody's fingerprint files—ours or the FBI's. That means he's never been arrested, never been in the armed services."

"Oh," she said.

"But when we pick him up, the fingerprint can put him in that guest house, so we can add a battery charge to the list."

"That's good. How are you feeling?"

"Tired. I saw a doctor, and he gave me a prescription. I'm to stay in bed for twenty-four hours."

"You do that. Want me to come and make chicken soup?"

"That's a nice offer; I'll take you up on it when I'm in a condition to appreciate it more. Have you heard from him today?"

"Of course. Just the roses, though. Melanie takes them to a children's hospital out in the Valley every day. I never thought I'd be sick of the scent of roses."

"Don't you be alone for a minute," Larsen said. "He's never attempted anything except when you were alone."

"Don't worry, Danny and Melanie have me covered. You get some rest, and call me tomorrow, you hear?"

"You can count on it." He hung up and fell back onto the bed, exhausted.

He slept from two in the afternoon straight through until dawn the next morning, and when he woke up, he felt human again, if a little fuzzy from the drug. He got into some jeans and a sweatshirt and went out for a walk while the air was fresh and cool. He had gone only half a block when he saw the van.

It was parked across the street. A Ford, gray in color, no windows in the rear. Larsen crossed the street and walked around it and tried to see inside. There was nothing that would offer a clue to the identity of the owner. He made a note of the license number and looked for any other distinguishing mark—a dent, a repainted door, anything. There was nothing. He wondered how many vans like this were in the Los Angeles area; hundreds, probably, but he didn't like the coincidence of finding one on his block. Was Admirer hunting him now? That didn't make any sense. The man could quite easily have killed him, if that was what he had wanted.

Larsen ran back to his house. He hadn't even locked the door, and now he went from room to room, looking for something disturbed, out of place. He found nothing.

When he was sure he was alone in the house, he called the station.

"Officer Martinez," the duty cop said.

"It's Larsen; I want you to run a plate for me." He read off the license plate number of the van.

"Just a sec," the cop said, and the sound of computer keys tapping came over the phone. "Got it. Belongs to an '89 Toyota Corolla at a West Hollywood address."

"Hang on," Larsen said. He ran out his front door and looked down the block; the van was gone. He went back into the house and picked up the phone. "Report the plate as stolen; it's currently on a late-model Ford van, gray, last seen in Santa Monica fifteen minutes ago. Arresting officer should hold the driver on the stolen tag and on a charge of battery; I'll make the case. Call it an APB."

There were more keystrokes. "It's in the computer," Martinez said.

"Add a note to page me immediately on arrest."

"Done."

Larsen hung up and went back to bed, annoyed and depressed. This jerk had run rings around him, humiliated him, and he was tired of it. But he was also just tired, and he needed rest. He fell asleep again, desperate for some notion of what to do next.

CHAPTER

27

On Saturday morning, after a couple of days'
rest, Larsen rose early, took a walk, and, seeing no sign of the gray van, returned to the
house and made himself some breakfast. The phone
rang.

"Hello?"

"It's Chris. How do you feel about the beach?"

"Pretty good. You have a particular beach in mind?"

"Malibu."

"Sounds good."

"Pick me up at ten, and bring a swimsuit. I'm
buying lunch."

"You've got a deal."

Larsen hadn't had time to replace his windshield, so
they drove out to Malibu with the windshield frame

down and the wind in their faces. She gave him an address.

"Whose place is this?" he asked.

"It's the house I'm building," she replied. "I haven't been out there since the accident, and I want to see how the place is coming. I use 'see' in the figurative sense. You'll have to do my seeing for me."

"Glad to."

"I talk with the construction foreman a couple of times a week and send money when I'm asked to, but I'd like an objective eye cast on what's been done, and I want to see how I feel about the place."

"How you feel about it?"

"Since the fall the thought of going out there scares me a little. I want to see if I can get rid of that feeling."

They arrived at Big Rock, and Larsen found the address. She gave him the combination of the lock on the construction fence, and then they were in the house.

"First impression?" she asked.

"Wow."

"What do you mean, 'wow'?"

"I mean, wow, what a neat place!"

"Tell me what you see."

"Well, they've got the roof on, and the cedar shingle siding. It's the color of new wood right now, but it'll turn gray when it's weathered. The windows are in, and most of the interior walls have been drywalled. I'd say you're only a few weeks from completion."

She took his hand. "Okay, we're in the entrance hall now, so we'll turn right and start with the kitchen." She took him that way, then through the living room.

"Great view of the ocean," he said. "I like the big windows. Hey, the deck looks finished."

"Let's go out there."

"I haven't seen the rest yet."

"I'll show it to you later."

They moved out onto the deck. The sun was warm and there was a nice breeze from the Pacific.

"There's a drop-down staircase to the beach," he said. "Want to go down there?"

"Let me just stand here for a moment first," she said. "Is there a railing?"

"Don't worry, you can't fall again." He put her hand on the railing.

"Then you go and get our stuff, and I'll just commune with nature for a minute."

"Sure." He went to the car and unloaded it, bringing back their beach clothes and their lunch, then dumped them all on the deck.

She reached for her beach bag. "Bring your suit and come along; I'll show you the rest of the house."

They looked into her study and the guest room, then ended up in the master suite.

"This is going to be a wonderful room," he said. "Great space, and that marvelous view, too."

"I'm going to change," she said. "You use the guest room."

"Okay." He went into the half-finished guest room, hung his clothes on a sawhorse, and got into his swimsuit. "You decent?" he called from the hallway.

"Just a second . . . now."

He went into the master suite and saw her in the bikini. Her jeans and underwear were in a pile on the floor.

"Wow again," he said.

"Thanks," she laughed. "I needed that." She held out her hand. "Now let's go back to the deck and down to the beach."

He led her to the rear of the house and found the release for the stairs. After he had taken their things down to the sand, he led her down the steps.

"Last time I made this trip it didn't take nearly as long," she said. "There are some rocks here, aren't there?"

"Yes, several good-sized boulders." He placed her hand on one.

"That's the sort of thing my head landed on, they tell me."

"How do you feel about being out here again?"

"I feel great, just angry that I can't see it yet."

"That day will come."

"I'm already seeing light better, and people are definite shapes instead of just blobs. You, for instance, are a very handsome shape."

"You're not so bad yourself," he said. He spread a blanket out and they settled onto it.

"How about a sandwich?" she said. "I'm hungry."

"Me too." He opened the cooler and spread the food on the blanket, then opened a bottle of white wine. "What a spread!"

"Thank Danny; he's great with food, as long as he doesn't have to cook it."

"Thank you, Danny," he said, biting into a smoked-salmon sandwich.

"Tell me about where you live," she said.

"I live in the house my folks built before I was born," Larsen said. "In an old Santa Monica neighborhood."

"I thought you told me you lived in an apartment."

"Well, I do, in a manner of speaking. I divided the

house and made two apartments upstairs, and I live in the downstairs. I guess that's an apartment instead of a house."

"Is it nice?"

"It's a little old-fashioned, but it's my principal asset, so I've hung on to it."

"Your parents are dead?"

"Eight years ago, within a week of each other," he said. "Mother died of cancer, and Dad had a stroke a few days later; never regained consciousness. I've always thought he just couldn't go on living without her."

"That's very romantic."

"I suppose it is," he said. "What about your folks?"

"Both still living, back in my hometown."

"Where's that?"

"A little place called Delano, Georgia."

"Your accent isn't southern."

"Ah kin do it if ah feel lak it," she replied. "They beat it out of me in acting school, in New York."

"Do you get home much?"

"I was there last year for a few days. People make such a fuss it embarrasses me. They just can't believe that a Delano girl made it into the movies. My folks come out here at least once a year, though. I haven't told them about my accident; they'd be out here like a shot."

"I'm glad you still have your folks," he said. "I miss mine; they were good people."

"Is Larsen Swedish?"

"Norwegian. My grandfather came to L.A. in 1911 and worked as a carpenter; did well enough to get my father through law school. He did most of the work on my folks' house after they were married, as sort of a wedding present. He died when I was twelve, so I remember him well."

"I would like to have known you when you were twelve," she said.

"No, you wouldn't have; I was hopeless with girls."

She reached out for his face. "You're doing okay now," she said, kissing him.

This was the second time she'd done that, Larsen thought, and he'd better give the girl some help. He kissed her, and they lay back on the blanket. Larsen was getting excited now, and so was the young woman in his arms. She wrapped a leg around his and pulled his thigh between her legs.

There was a loud noise, and Larsen looked up to see a substantial piece of Sheetrock bouncing off the boulder next to them. He looked up in time to see the stairs from the deck being pulled up. "Stay right here," he said, "I'll be back."

"What was that noise?" she asked. "Where are you going?"

"I promise I'll be right back."

By the time he found a way around to the front of the house, there was no one there. He looked into each room, and when he came to the master suite he saw that Chris's clothing had been scattered around the room. When he gathered it up, he saw that her underwear was gone.

Larsen gathered up her other things, got his own clothes from the guest room, then went back to the deck and lowered the stairs.

She heard him coming. "It was him, wasn't it?"

"Could be."

"Let's get out of here."

He handed her her jeans and T-shirt, and she

quickly put them on over her bikini. He got into his clothes and handed her her shoes. "I'm afraid he took your underwear," he said.

Chris gave an involuntary shudder. "Ugh," she said. "I'm sorry to end such a nice day, but . . . "

"I understand," he said. "We'll go somewhere for lunch."

"Forgive me, Jon, but I'd rather be alone for the rest of the day."

"Alone?"

"I'm sorry, I meant at home. We'll have our sandwiches there."

"All right."

He led her back up the stairs and through the house, looking around at the nearly completed dwelling. The workmanship looked very good, he thought. Everywhere wires stuck out of the walls where electrical outlets and switches would be. Next to the front door was a plastic box with a light-emitting diode panel at the top. He felt around it, and the front panel opened to reveal a keypad. The alarm system looked nearly installed.

Back in the car and headed toward Bel Air they were quiet for a while, thinking their own thoughts.

Larsen was the first to speak. "Your builder's name is Moscowitz?" He had seen the sign.

"Yes, Mike Moscowitz."

"How did you find him?"

"He did some work on the Bel Air house when Brad and I first moved into it. At that time he was doing mostly remodeling, but by the time I started thinking about building, he was doing new houses. I liked what he had done at the other house, and my architect liked his bid, so I gave him the job."

"Are you happy so far?"

"Very. He's been very good about my not being out here to look at things."

"Do you like him personally?"

"Yes. He seems like a very nice man. I've never had a conversation with him, though, that wasn't about building."

"I'd like to talk with him. Do you mind?"

"Mike doesn't know anything about this Admirer thing, and I'd prefer to keep it that way. The more people that know about it, the more likely it is to end up in the tabloids, and God knows I don't want that."

"Sure, I understand." He didn't mention it again.

CHAPTER

28

Chris sat on a cushion, sipping a strange orien-
tal tea and listening to Graham Hong talking
about not much of anything. He seemed to
sense that she was nervous, and he was trying to
put her at ease.

"Well," he said finally. "In all my years in this
town I've had students with all sorts of motives. I've
had ninety-seven-pound weaklings who wanted to
prove themselves to some girl; I've had studio exec-
utives who wanted to intimidate their competitors;
and, of course, I've had movie stars who wanted to
look lethal in their next film." He sighed. "But you,
my dear, are the first student I've ever had who
came to me because he actually wanted to kill somebody. Are you absolutely certain about this?"

"I draw the line when somebody starts stealing
my underwear," Chris replied.

"This is a serious matter, Chris, and you should
take it seriously."

"Graham, I've told you about this man and what he's been doing to me. I've done everything I can to stop him; I've called the police in, and they've done everything they can. Nothing has worked. I'm convinced—and you can say I said this if you have to testify in court—that he's eventually going to kill me if he can, and I'm determined not to just sit around and wait for that to happen. I have a good life, my vision is improving, and I'm not going to let this bastard take it away from me."

"I understand how you feel," Hong said. He helped her to her feet and escorted her into the large studio room. "Now," he said. "There are a number of ways to kill someone quickly with your hands, but because you cannot see your assailant, most of them are not available to you." He stopped.

"Go on," she said.

"Come to think of it, perhaps none of them are available to you. All these techniques rely on a quick strike to a vulnerable area, and most of them rely on having the room to achieve some velocity with your hand."

Chris felt his fingers at her throat.

"For instance, if you aim an edge-of-hand blow at a man's Adam's apple, if you take a full backswing, step into the blow, and swing *through* the neck you will crush his trachea, and unless someone immediately performs a tracheotomy, he will die. But consider the problem; in order to perform this attack you must step away from your opponent and strike a very small spot, and you cannot do that. Nobody can. Oh, there may be some Zen monk somewhere who could do it, but I couldn't, and neither could you."

Chris felt he was speaking as much to himself as to her, and she remained quiet.

Hong sighed again. "On reflection, I think it is not possible for you to kill a strong male opponent with your hands. You might be able to strangle another woman or a child, but not a man."

"So what can I do?" Chris asked.

"You can hurt him so badly that he will break off his attack. Most people don't understand the role of pain and shock in a fight. They go to the movies, and they see the leading man hit a dozen times by three bad guys, and then, suddenly, he gets mad and wipes the floor with them. That's not the way it works. Pain is immediately debilitating; it makes you want to curl up into a ball and lick your wounds. Professional fighters are trained to go on fighting in spite of the pain, but even they will eventually succumb to it. So what you must do is inflict as much pain as possible as early in your struggle as possible."

"And how do I do that?"

"First, you must wait for your opponent to make the first move; you must wait for him to close the distance between you, because you can only operate close, when you can *feel* him."

Chris gave an involuntary shudder.

"Exactly," Hong said. "The idea of having him close to you is repugnant, but you must overcome that, because it is your only chance. Remember the black widow spider, who lures the male into her presence so she can kill him. She must be your model."

He stepped close to her. "Now, reach out and put your hands on my shoulders."

Chris found his shoulders quickly.

"Now you know where I am, so you can hurt me." He reached down and pulled her knee into his crotch. "If you hit me here, hard, while placing a hand at the back of my neck and pulling down, you can disable me for anywhere from half a minute to ten minutes, depending on how determined I am. But the crotch is a difficult target, because it can be defended so easily by turning or blocking a blow. Your best bets are the head and neck." He took her left arm and placed it around his neck. "If you can achieve this position you can inflict great damage on your opponent."

"I've never had any trouble achieving this position," Chris said wryly.

Hong laughed. "Yes, but I hope not with such murderous intent." He became serious again. "With your arm around my neck you can find my throat, my nose, and my eyes. Make a fist."

Chris made a fist.

Hong placed her fist at his throat. "A hard punch here will be very discouraging to your opponent. And I mean *hard*. As hard as you possibly can." He took her left hand and placed it on his face. "Now you can feel where my nose and eyes are. A hard punch to the nose will break it, and sometimes . . . " he opened her fist and placed the heel of her hand against his nose ". . . a hard drive upward can drive shards of bone into the brain. A broken nose will bleed a lot, and the sight of his own blood can often frighten an opponent quite badly."

Chris felt for Hong's eyes.

"Yes," he said. "That is his most vulnerable point. Every human being is terrified of damage to the eyes. If you can hold his head with your arm and drive your thumb—hard enough to break it—into his eye, you will blind him in that eye, or, at the very least, make him *believe* that you have blinded him, and that, in itself, may make it possible for you to overcome him."

Hong put his arms around Chris and pulled her close to him. "This may be your best position of all. He is holding you; both your hands are free to inflict pain, and you *know* where he is."

He put her arms around his waist. "So," he said, "I have two hands free." He cupped his hands and placed them over her ears. "Strike here with both hands cupped, and you will momentarily increase the air pressure in his ear canals so much that the eardrums will burst, and that is excruciatingly painful. He will let you go, I promise you, and he will not be able to do much for a minute or two after that except hold his head while you do other cruel things to him."

"What cruel things?"

Hong demonstrated. "Grab his hair and bring his face down to meet your rising knee; bring your knee up into his crotch; break his nose with your fist; put your thumb into his eye. Don't be content to hurt him once—*keep on* hurting him. Something else, even if he pins your hands to your sides, you are not helpless." He placed his palm above her forehead at the hairline. "This is the hardest place on your body; if you pull your head back and strike him hard in the nose, his nose will break, but your head will not. That should make him let go of you."

For an hour Hong made her practice hitting him, then he gave her a sand-filled dummy of a man's upper torso. "Take this home and practice hitting it as hard as you can; it's important that you know how hard you can hit. This will give you confidence."

Chris hit the dummy. It hurt.

"Remember," Hong summarized, "lure him in close; grab him or let him grab you; then go for the eyes, nose, or throat. And always hit hard."

CHAPTER

29

L arsen sat at his desk and waited for paper. There was a time when he would have had to do a lot of legwork to get this information, but today all he had had to do was make a few phone calls and wait. He heard the distinctive ring of the fax machine.

Larsen got up from his desk and walked down the hall to where the big machine sat on its cart. He stood and waited while it whirred and ground out a sheet of paper. A cover sheet; he threw it away and forced himself to wait until the machine had finished. More than twenty sheets of paper waited for him in the bin. He picked them up and went back to his office.

The California Department of Motor Vehicles had sent him a computer printout of every Ford van registered in Los Angeles County and its neighboring counties during the past two years, sorted by model name. A quick glance through the stack of sheets told him there were several hundred, and color was not mentioned in the record.

Most of the vehicles were owned by companies, and he skimmed through the list, placing a check mark next to those registered to individuals. A little more than halfway down the list, he stopped. A van had been registered in August of the previous year to the Moscowitz Construction Company, Inc., of Los Angeles. He made an effort to keep his pulse down as he continued through the list.

When he had finished he had, in addition to the Moscowitz van, vehicles registered to four individuals whose first or last name was James. It was a start, and he wasn't about to waste time trolling through all the company-owned vans. He looked up a number and dialed.

"Moscowitz Construction, this is Jenny."

"'Morning, can I speak to Mike Moscowitz, please?"

"He's over at the Santa Monica site; I'll give you the number there." She gave him the number.

"I'm on my way to Santa Monica right now," Larsen said. "Can you give me the address?" He scribbled her answer. It was no more than four blocks from his house. "Thanks very much."

"Can I say who called, in case you miss him?"

Larsen hung up and grabbed his coat, then hesitated. He had gotten into trouble last time for not requesting backup. That had been in his jurisdiction, which would have been easy, but this was Santa Monica, and asking for backup would be more complicated. The hell with it, he decided.

Moscowitz's project was an old two-story house not unlike Larsen's own, and it seemed to be undergoing a thorough renovation. Larsen cruised past the place slowly; the gray Ford van was parked outside, and, checking the license plate against the printout, he saw that the right plate was attached. There was no sign of anybody, but hammering and sawing could be heard from inside the house.

Larsen parked the car and walked slowly back toward the house. He was at a disadvantage, he knew, because if Moscowitz was Admirer, he would know Larsen on sight. As he climbed the front steps, Larsen unbuttoned his jacket to make his weapon more accessible.

As he entered the open front door Larsen saw a man of medium height and weight standing at the bottom of the stairs speaking to a worker on the landing. The man was holding a black plastic briefcase in his left hand and wearing a baseball cap. Larsen waited until the man stopped speaking.

"Mike Moscowitz?" Larsen said, tensing.

The man turned and looked at him.

Larsen waited, ready for anything.

The man smiled. "That's me," he said.

No apparent recognition. "I wonder if I could have a few minutes of your time," Larsen said.

Moscowitz didn't budge from his spot. "That depends on what it's about," he said.

"It's about renovating a house," Larsen said.

Moscowitz smiled more broadly and walked toward Larsen, his hand out. "In that case I've got all the time in the world."

Larsen shook the man's hand. "My name is Jon Larsen; I own a house something like this one a few blocks from here, and I'm thinking of having some work done. I've noticed the work going on and I wondered if I could take a look at what you're doing here."

"Sure, glad to show you around." He waved a hand. "This place was built right after World War II, just as soon as materials became available. It was built right, and that sure helps when you start to renovate. What about your place?"

"Early fifties; it was built right, too. In fact, my grandfather did all the carpentry and a lot more."

Moscowitz looked at him. "Larsen? Was your grandfather by any chance named Lars?"

"That's right."

"My grandfather was named Lenny Moscowitz. He used to play chess with your grandfather all the time. Grandpapa would take me over to Lars's house with him. I think Grandpapa did some work on your house, too, although that was before my time."

"Well, that's something," Larsen said, laughing. "So you're, what, the third generation of Moscowitzes in the building trade?"

"Fourth. My great-grandfather was a carpenter in Russia, and that young fellow up there on the landing is my oldest boy, Lenny, so he's the fifth."

This guy can work on my house anytime, Larsen thought. "A family operation."

"Well, that's putting it a little strongly when one of the family is a teenager," Moscowitz said. "I catch him gazing into the middle distance two or three times a day."

"Sounds like a girl in the picture," Larsen said.

"You bet there is, and he won't bring her home to meet us. What kind of a girl would that be?"

"I wouldn't worry too much about it," Larsen said. "He'll either get over it, or he'll bring her home."

•

"I live for the day," Moscowitz said. "Did you call the office to find me?"

"Yes."

"Jenny answered the phone. That's my wife; she runs the business end, raises hell if my bids come in too low."

Larsen felt very much on the wrong track. This guy didn't square with the alienated types who became stalkers. "Mike, what sort of day do you work?"

"Me? I'm at work by seven, and Jenny and me, we don't get home until seven, so it's a twelve-hour day most days, and all too often on Saturdays. Once in a while, when we get a little gap between jobs and we're a little flush, we take a couple of weeks off, but it doesn't happen all that often. Lenny there gets a few years under his belt, maybe I can relax a little."

This guy didn't have time to be a stalker. "Mike, can we sit down somewhere and talk for a minute?"

"Don't you want to see the house?"

"Maybe later; this isn't about work." Larsen showed him the badge.

Moscowitz waved a hand at the stairs in front of them. "Step into my office." He took a seat on a step.

Larsen sat down beside him. "This is in confidence, okay?"

"Okay."

"One of your clients, Chris Callaway, is being annoyed by somebody."

"How annoyed?"

"Seriously annoyed. I can't go into detail, but there's some reason to be concerned about her safety."

"She hasn't been out to the house in Malibu for weeks. Something to do with this annoyance?"

•

"Sort of."

Moscowitz nodded. "Most clients aren't willing to build a house on the phone. I knew it must be something. Who's annoying her?"

"We don't know; that's why I'm talking to you."

"Why me?"

"How many subcontractors are you using on Chris's house?"

"The usual—framer, plumber, electrician, alarm guy, roofer, drywall guy, whatever it takes."

"Can you give me a list of them, please?"

"Sure, I guess so." Moscowitz took a battered address book from his briefcase and read out a dozen names and addresses while Larsen took notes.

"How many of these have had any contact with Chris?" Larsen asked.

"All of them, I guess, except the roofer and the drywall man. She hasn't been out there since they started work."

"Any of them drive one of those?" Larsen asked, pointing through the open door at the van.

"Probably," Moscowitz replied. "It's a pretty popular vehicle in the trade."

"Anybody you can remember?"

Moscowitz shrugged. "Tell you the truth, I don't notice cars much. Just about everybody who works for me drives a van or a pickup. Guys have got tools and stuff to carry, you know?"

"Has anybody who's worked for you on the Callaway house asked a lot of questions about Chris?"

"Sure, most of them; they all know she's a movie star. I mean, they don't go around drooling after her; they're pretty cool, but they like it that they're working on a movie star's house. They go home and tell their wives and friends, you know? But these guys have worked on movie stars' houses before. They're not knocked out."

Larsen nodded. He opened his notebook to his list of vans. "Any of these guys work for you? Michael James O'Hara; James B. Corbett; James M. Rivera; Marvin B. James?"

"None of them rings a bell," Moscowitz said. "Who are they?"

"Guys who own Ford vans like yours and have James in their names. Anybody work for you named James? Either first or last name?"

"Jimmy Lopez, my plumber. He's on your list, there, as Lopez Plumbing Contractors."

"What's he look like?"

"Six two, big, maybe two-twenty, pot belly, black hair and mustache, about fifty."

"That's not my man."

"I'm glad to hear it."

"This guy is medium height and weight, medium brown hair."

"Like me?"

"Like you, but younger."

"Isn't everybody?"

Larsen laughed. "This is beginning to sound like a dry hole."

"Sorry, wish I could help."

"You can. If anybody shows up at the Callaway house who fits the medium description and who drives either a gray Ford van, like yours, or a red motorcycle, I'd really appreciate a call." He gave the builder a card.

"Okay," Moscowitz said, handing over his own card, "and if you get serious about your house, call me."

"I'll do it. Anybody whose grandfather worked with my grandfather can't be all bad. And it may be sooner than you think." Larsen shook hands with the builder and left.

Lenny Moscowitz came down the stairs and stood next to his father. "Was that about work?" he asked.

Moscowitz shook his head. "Nah. That was a cop."

The boy didn't speak for a moment. "What'd he want?" he asked finally.

"Checking up on who works for me. Cops are always checking up."

"Did you tell him what he wanted to know?"

"Nope." Moscowitz tore Larsen's card in half and dropped it over the banister into a cardboard box full of rubbish.

"Pop, what is it with you and cops?"

"Kiddo," Moscowitz said, punching his son playfully in the gut, "if you had grown up in the sixties, you wouldn't have to ask."

CHAPTER

30

Danny Devere left the CBS Television Studios in Burbank at three-thirty, exhausted. He had been doing hair since six A.M.—a three-part miniseries with lots of women—and all he wanted now was to get to Chris's and stretch out on a sofa. When he stopped at the gate to wait for traffic, his brakes felt a little spongy, and he made a mental note to add this symptom to the list of items to check when he next had the car serviced. He headed toward Beverly Hills.

Danny was forty, and the first thirty years of his life had not been easy. Born in a hardscrabble industrial town in western Pennsylvania, he had known he was different from most other boys from the age of five, but he had been smart enough to keep it to himself. Finally, at the age of fifteen, driven almost mad by the necessity of maintaining a heterosexual facade and keeping his sexuality a secret, he had lied about his age, joined the navy, and for the first time found other young men who felt the same way he did, and who didn't bother to keep it a secret, at least when they were off duty. But he had also found that, no less than in Pennsylvania, he would have to be tough enough to defend himself against those men who, although they loved a blow job aboard ship, loved just as much to do a little queer-bashing when on liberty. He had lost a good friend in a men's room in Manila, when four of his shipmates had entertained themselves by kicking the boy to death. From that time on, Danny didn't wait for others to start fights; instead, he started them himself, and at the slightest provocation. After a few of these, his shipmates trod lightly around him.

For this reason, and because of his native courage, Danny had never feared Admirer, as he had learned not to fear any bully. He abhorred guns, but since the day he had bought one for Chris, he had carried a very sharp folding knife secured to his ankle with two stout rubber bands. He knew from his experience in liberty ports how to use it, and although he had never killed anybody, he knew exactly how to do it. He had already decided that, given the opportunity, he would kill Admirer, and with the greatest of pleasure. He entertained fantasies of showing the man various of his severed appendages.

He had been driving uphill for some minutes now, and as he crested the mountain ridge that separated the San Fernando Valley from Beverly Hills, another sports car overtook him and cut in front of him too quickly, forcing him to brake hard. The brakes held for a moment, then let go completely. He found himself headed down a steep and winding

Beverly Glen with his braking foot to the floor, quickly gaining speed.

Danny was an experienced, even expert driver, and although he was alarmed, he did not panic. He shifted the automatic transmission down a notch, then into the lowest gear, which slowed his acceleration, and looked for a driveway, a hedge—something that would stop the little car without killing him. Then there was a metallic *snap* and the car gained speed again. He whipped the gear lever back and forth, trying to find park or reverse or any gear that would slow him down, but the transmission was now useless, and Danny knew the only thing that would stop the car was a solid object.

The most inviting solid object available, because it was moving in the same direction, was the sports car that had recently passed him, and Danny did something wholly unnatural: he aimed at the car's rear bumper, hoping a same-direction collision would at least slow him down.

The driver of the sports car, however, interpreted the situation differently. Glancing into his rearview mirror and seeing Danny's convertible closing on him from behind, he inferred an angry motorist who had been cut off and who now wanted to catch up. The sports-car driver sped up, relishing the race.

"What are you doing, you idiot?" Danny said aloud as he saw the little car accelerate. It was a good time to remember that, as usual, he had not fastened his seat belt. He struggled with it and gratefully heard it snap home.

Traffic was light at this time of day—at least, as light as it got—and the two cars had the upper part of Beverly Glen momentarily to themselves. Danny had driven this road hundreds of times over the years, and he knew every bend; but he was unused to the bends coming at him so quickly. He tried to think ahead, and he realized that at the bottom of this hill was Sunset Boulevard, if he managed to get that far. After that there was a dogleg left, then UCLA and hundreds of students on foot. His heart sank. If he couldn't find a way to stop the car before Sunset he was going to have to do something noble.

The sports-car driver now figured he had a maniac on his hands. He was doing better than seventy down this mountain, and the guy was still right on his bumper. He took his hands off the wheel for a moment and raised them in surrender, then started to brake. For his trouble, he got a firm clout from behind. Terrified now, the driver grabbed the wheel and tried to get out of the maniac's way. He cut too sharply to the left, and his car went into a flat spin.

Danny passed the sports car, which was momentarily pointed in the opposite direction, and glimpsed the car briefly in his rearview mirror as it completed a turn of approximately seven hundred and twenty degrees, then stopped. "Lucky bastard," he said aloud. "If I had that kind of suspension I'd try that, too." The good news was that his collision with the little car had taken a good fifteen miles an hour off his speed, but that was now building again. Suddenly

Danny knew what he was going to do. There was traffic coming up the mountain now, but no car in front of him for another mile. At the end of that mile, he remembered, was a driveway that left Beverly Glen at a slight angle, and at the bottom of the driveway was something that might possibly save his life.

He tried not to look to his right, because the drop-off was precipitous, and at the bottom were dozens of houses, tightly packed. If he went off the road to his right, he would have a short flight and end up in somebody's living room, hamburger. On his left was a steep bank going up and many utility poles. Danny rounded a curve to his right doing eighty or so, and left it in a four-wheel drift that took him to the opposite side of the road before he could correct. Coming up the hill was a Mack truck, towing God knew what, and he managed to miss it by a hair. Where the hell was that driveway?

He knew the people who lived there, and it was tough enough not to miss it at normal speeds; at his present velocity he had a millisecond to make the entrance, and he felt relief when he saw the striped mailbox that marked it. He braced himself for the swerve, and to his surprise, made it; he was off Beverly Glen now, and hurtling down two hundred yards of gravel driveway that was about to turn sharply to the right, a turn he had no intention of trying to make. Dead ahead, he saw his salvation; then, in a heart-stopping moment, he saw a flash of blue water. He had forgotten that between him and his objective lay a lap pool.

•　　•　　•

Danny now had no choice; he was committed. Out of a crazed curiosity, Danny looked at the speedometer: eighty-five miles an hour. He pointed the car straight ahead and, at the bend in the driveway, he and the convertible left the ground. The driveway's edge fell away to an embankment, at the bottom of which lay the pool. The car flew straight over the pool, and Danny caught a glimpse of an astonished woman lying on a chaise to his left, talking on a cordless phone. "Afternoon, Agnes," he murmured. Amazingly, the car maintained its directional stability, and when it struck the ground it did so on all four wheels. Danny saw a glorious sight rushing at him.

The car struck the tennis court fence and carried it down the court, making a horrible noise. Next it hit the net; the steel wire supporting it snapped like a thread, and car, fence, and steel poles met the fence at the opposite end of the court. The thoroughly mangled car was netted like a trout.

Danny didn't see anything after the first fence, because the airbag was in his face. When the thing collapsed, he struggled to take a breath and then fainted. His last conscious thought was to wonder why the airbag hadn't worked when he struck the sports car, and to thank heaven it hadn't.

CHAPTER

31

When Larsen got back to his office, another piece of paper he had requested was on his desk. He took off his coat and bought a cup of bad coffee from the machine in the hall before he sat down and picked up the document—the arrest record of one Myron Aaron Moscowitz. He had requested it that morning, and after his interview with the builder, he was surprised there was such a record.

In October 1968, Moscowitz had been charged with possession of less than one ounce of marijuana and resisting arrest. Disposition: a $1,000 fine and thirty days on the county farm. They were tough on potheads in the sixties, he reflected. "Resisting arrest" probably meant he had given the cop some lip and had gotten his ear cuffed for it. He wondered what the experience had done to Moscowitz's opinion of policemen, and if that opinion might have colored the information he had given to Larsen that day.

Larsen thought about it. The builder had been polite, affable, but had he detected something else? Come to think of it, apart from the list of subcontractors, which Larsen had insisted on, Moscowitz had given him zip. Couldn't remember what kinds of cars people drove. He thought of half a dozen people he knew, and he could remember exactly what each of them drove. Why couldn't Moscowitz?

He looked at the arrest record; a full set of fingerprints was attached. He picked up the phone. "Hi, it's Larsen; could you bring me that print you picked up at the Millman guest house? I'd like you to compare it to a set I've got here."

He stared at the whorls of Mike Moscowitz's fingerprints and thought about his peculiarly unsatisfying conversation with the man.

The fingerprint man showed up a minute later. "Whatcha got?"

Larsen handed him Moscowitz's record. "Check your print against this set," he said.

The fingerprint man held up a card with a single print on it and looked back and forth from card to card. "You got a loupe?"

"Will a magnifying glass do?"

"Sure."

"No sleuth should be without a magnifying glass," Larsen said, rummaging in a desk drawer. "Here." He handed it over.

The fingerprint man placed the two cards on Larsen's desk, moved the desk lamp over them, and scrutinized first one, then the other through the magnifying glass.

"Close, but no cigar."

"What?"

"At first glance I thought they might match, but not under the glass. These are from two different guys."

Larsen was half relieved—he'd liked the man—and half disappointed. "Thanks," he said, and the fingerprint man left.

After his conversation with Moscowitz, he probably wouldn't have looked closely at the subcontractors, but the fact was he had nowhere else to go in his investigation. He spread the computer printout of van owners on his desk, got out his notebook, and started to compare the two.

Lopez Plumbing Contractors

Jimmy Lopez was the only James, but no van.

Bud Carson Framers

No van.

Gianelli Electrical

No van.

Keyhole Security

Bingo. He ran quickly through the rest of the list: no more Ford van owners among the subs. Moscowitz had said it was a popular van in the building trade, but there were only two Ford vans in a dozen outfits, if you included Moscowitz's.

Keyhole Security's address was a P.O. box number, and he wasn't about to start dealing with the post office to get an address. He tried the phone book; there in the Yellow Pages was Keyhole, in Santa Monica. Everybody was in Santa Monica today.

He found a government directory and the right phone number. "Afternoon, this is Detective Larsen, Beverly Hills PD. I need a copy of the business license of Keyhole Security." He gave the address.

"Let me check my index," the woman said, and he heard her keyboard clicking. "Right. I'll print it out and mail it to you today."

"Can you fax it, please?" He gave her the number. "And as soon as possible?"

"Sure, baby," she said, and hung up.

To his surprise, the fax machine rang two minutes later. He was waiting for the license as it came out of the machine, and he began reading it on the way back to his office.

OWNER & OPERATOR: MELVIN JAMES PARKER.

He sat down at his desk and took a couple of deep breaths, tried to slow down. First application two years ago; passed the police check through the Santa Monica department—he couldn't get a license for a security business if he had a criminal record. Four employees (that was then, maybe more by now). Description of business: installation and maintenance of alarm systems, audio and video electronics and telephone equipment; supply of security personnel, armed and unarmed; supply and maintenance of security vehicles. Not licensed for private investigations, but into absolutely everything else. M. James Parker fit Admirer like a glove.

Then a little negative worm squirmed into Larsen's mind. If Parker had gone through a police check then he would have been fingerprinted and his prints would have gone into the central registry. Why, then, when they ran the print from the Millman guest house, didn't it turn up Parker? Two reasons occurred to him: one, the Santa Monica police didn't print him as they should have, or they didn't file the prints; two, the guest-house print belonged to somebody else, maybe a maid.

Larsen picked up the phone and called a detective he knew on the Santa Monica force.

"Gene, it's Jon Larsen. Your people did a check on a guy a couple of years ago for a security company business license, name of Melvin James Parker. He was supposed to be printed, but it looks like for some reason the prints never made it into the system. Can you get hold of the original record and transmit the prints to me?"

"Hi, Jon; nice to hear from you. How you been? How's tricks? Are you enjoying being a policeman?" The voice dripped with sarcasm.

"I'm sorry, I just haven't got time for small talk. Can you get me the original record?"

"From two years ago? Everything goes to Central Records after a year, pal. You can go down to the warehouse and rake through that stuff as good as I can, if you got a week to spare."

"Thanks, Gene."

"Delightful chatting with you, asshole." He hung up.

Larsen sighed. He had plenty on Admirer, but without the fingerprints he couldn't make Parker as Admirer. And he couldn't just drag Parker in and fingerprint him, either, or strip him and search for a tattoo, not without probable cause, and owning one of several hundred Ford vans in greater L.A. didn't constitute probable cause.

He got on the computer to see if a motorcycle was registered either to Keyhole or to Mel Parker, and the answer was negative. Maybe he registered the machine some other way.

He rested his forehead on the glass of his desktop and tried to think of something. Well, he might as well go and get a look at Parker, but he'd better not let Parker get a look at him, because Parker knew him, and he'd be on his guard. Larsen did not want Parker on his guard. He got up and struggled into his coat.

The phone rang.

He picked it up. "Larsen."

"Jon, it's Chris."

"Hi, how are you?"

"Terrible. I'm in the emergency room at Cedars-Sinai. Danny has had a horrible car crash, and he's demanding to see you. They're having an awful time with him; can you get down here right away?"

"I'm on my way." Larsen ran for his car.

CHAPTER

32

The emergency room at Cedars-Sinai was not as busy at this time of day as at midnight, when the gunshot victims started to come in, but business was not bad. Mothers with sick children were lined up with dogbite victims and the odd drug addict, and there was a hum of activity about the place.

Larsen found Chris sitting on a bench with Melanie.

"Oh, God, I'm glad you're here. Danny's half nuts, and they won't let me be with him," Chris said.

"Where is he?"

Melanie pointed at a curtain at the end of the hall. "Down there."

"You two stay here, and try and be calm. I'll see what's happening." He walked down the hall and parted the curtain. Danny Devere was lying on a treatment table, and a doctor was stitching a long wound in his lower left leg. An IV was running into his arm. Danny was mumbling in a nonstop stream, and only an occasional epithet was understandable.

A nurse holding a tray of instruments turned and glanced at Larsen. "You. Take a seat outside."

Larsen produced his badge. "I have to talk with your patient."

The young doctor glanced up from his work, saw the badge, and continued sewing. ER people weren't impressed with badges; they saw too many of them.

"Take a hike," the nurse said.

"Hang on," the doctor said wearily. "You can talk to him while I'm working." He continued suturing. "Come around to the head of the table and ask your questions. Don't be too long, he could still go into shock."

Larsen eased between the nurse and the wall, grabbed a steel stool, and sat down, so he would be close to Danny. "Danny, it's Jon Larsen. Looks like you're doing pretty good. You wanted to talk to me?"

Danny turned his head toward Larsen, but that seemed to hurt, and he closed his eyes. "Thank God," he said. "The other cops seem to think I'm a drunk driver or something. At four o'clock in the goddamned afternoon!"

"Talk to me, Danny, and I'll talk to them."

"Fucking Admirer did it," he said.

"He ran you off the road, like Melanie?"

"No, he did something to the car. I couldn't stop it."

"How do you know Admirer did it?"

"I'm fucking psychic, Jon; now will you talk to those goddamned cops and do something about this? My leg hurts like hell, and I'm tired of being treated like a criminal. They wanted me to take a blood test."

Larsen looked up and saw a uniformed Beverly Hills officer standing at the opening in the curtain. "Go ahead and let them give you the blood test, Danny; I'll talk to them. Now what happened?"

"I was coming back from the Valley, and my brakes went at the top of the ridge. I tried to stop by hitting another car, but it didn't work, and then I remembered these friends' house with a tennis court, so I just aimed the car at the court, and the fence stopped me."

"Smart move," Larsen said. "You just take it easy and get some rest, okay? I'll come and see you tomorrow."

"Thanks, Jon. Is Chris here?"

"She's outside with Melanie."

"Will you take care of her tonight? Melanie has to go home to her kids."

"Sure; don't worry about Chris." He stepped around the table. The doctor seemed ready to bandage Danny's leg, and Larsen motioned him over. "How is he?"

"He's got a bad gash in his left leg, which you just watched me close; he's got a lot of bruising here and there, but otherwise he seems to be okay. There's no internal injury that I can find, but we're going to hang on to him for a day or so and see if anything develops."

"Thank you, Doctor. He seems to be in considerable pain."

"I'm aware of that; we'll give him some morphine and put him to bed."

Larsen gave the doctor his card. "I'd appreciate it

if you'd notate his records to the effect that I should be contacted if there's any change in his condition for the worse."

"Sure."

Larsen stepped through the curtain and took the uniformed cop's arm. "I'm Larsen, Detective Division; bring me up to date."

"That guy in there is some kind of maniac, or he's very drunk. He drove down Beverly Glen at eighty or ninety, rammed another car, and scared the shit out of a lady before he dumped his car into her tennis court. Wiped it out."

"He'll agree to the blood test now; I think you'll find he's sober."

"You know this guy?"

"Yes; he's a potential witness in a case, and he thinks the perp doctored his car. Tell me, was his driving consistent with having no brakes?"

"Yeah, could be."

"Go ahead and make your report; write it up as referred to the detective division, and put my name on it." He gave the cop a card. "Also, I want the wreck impounded, so our man can go over it."

"Okay," the cop said, "that shortens my day." He handed Larsen a clipboard. "You want to sign right there and put down your badge number?"

Larsen signed, and the cop left. Larsen walked back to where Chris and Melanie were waiting. "Danny's going to be fine," he said. "He's got a cut leg and some bruising and they're going to keep him overnight for observation, but tomorrow he'll be his old self."

"Thank God," Chris said. "Why was he so anxious to talk to you?"

"Melanie, why don't you go on home? I'll take care of Chris."

"Chris," the secretary said, "I'll be glad to stay if you need me."

"It's all right, Melanie. Go home to your kids."

Melanie took her leave, and Larsen led Chris to his car. When they were inside, Chris spoke up again.

"You didn't answer my question," she said.

"I'm sorry; I didn't want to upset Melanie. Danny thinks that Admirer screwed up the brakes on his car, and the investigating officer says that's consistent with what happened."

"Exactly what did happen?"

"Danny was coming down Beverly Glen when his brakes stopped working. He had the presence of mind to drive into a tennis-court fence; I'm sure that saved his life."

"Do you think Admirer did it?"

"I've had his car impounded, and we're going to find out. In the meantime, you're going to stay with me tonight."

"I'd better go by the house and get some things."

"Do you mind if I lend you something to sleep in? I'd just as soon not go back to your place right now."

"You think Admirer is still watching it?"

"I don't know, but let's proceed on the basis that he is."

"You certainly have sneaky ways to get a girl to stay over."

"I couldn't pass up an opportunity like this."

"I'm glad," she said.

Larsen reached over and took her hand. "I'm going to tell you something, but I don't want you to ask any questions, all right?"

"All right."

•

"I've got a solid lead on who Admirer may be. I have a feeling we may be nearing the end of all this."

"Who is he?"

"You promised not to ask any questions."

"That wasn't fair; you tricked me."

"Look, I may be wrong about this, and I don't want to go into it with you until I'm sure. I just want you to know that there's some hope that this won't last forever."

"Well, okay," she sighed. "I guess I can wait. I've waited this long."

Four cars back in the traffic behind them, a red motorcycle kept pace with them all the way to Santa Monica.

CHAPTER

33

Larsen led Chris into his house and switched on the lights in the living room. Outside the sun was sinking into the Pacific. "Here we are," he said.

"It's nice to know when the lights are on," Chris said. "It's still bad in low light, but pretty soon I won't be bumping into the furniture anymore."

"Let's keep that from Admirer," Larsen said. "I'd just as soon have him think you're blind as a bat." He hung his jacket and pistol in the hall closet, then led her to the counter that separated the living room from the kitchen and helped her onto a barstool. "Can I get you a drink?"

"God, I could use one. Got any bourbon?"

"Sure."

"Rocks only, please."

He poured them both a drink and touched her glass with his. " 'Better times than these,' " he said.

"Hear, hear," she said, and sipped her drink. "Where have I heard that line?"

"It's from 'Garryowen,' the riding song of Custer's Seventh Cavalry. The Seventh still uses it, I think. It was also used as the title of a Vietnam war novel by somebody named Winston Groom."

"That's where I've heard it; I read the book a long time ago and liked it."

"So did I."

"Speaking of novels, there was one on your sister's tapes that interested me called *Light of Day*, by Karen Copeland."

"I don't know it."

"It's about the problems of a young woman who's blinded in an accident. Her blindness is difficult, of course, but an even bigger problem for her is getting her family and friends to accept that she can live alone and lead a fairly normal life."

"Sounds good."

"It's better than that; there's some very powerful stuff in it, and it's funny, too. I believe it would make a terrific film, and I think I could bring a lot to the part."

"I'm sure you could."

"I've already asked my manager to pursue the film rights. If I can option it at a reasonable price, I want to adapt it myself and see if I can get it made."

"Have you ever written anything?"

"Not since college, when I wrote a play. I was torn between writing and acting in those days, and I'm not entirely sure I made the right choice."

"I don't see why you can't do both."

"I've been too busy up until recently, but these days I don't have a damned thing to do, so I've already started dictating some scenes, and Melanie is typing them up."

"That's great." He took some steaks from the freezer and put them in the microwave to thaw. "How do you like your beef?"

"Medium rare."

"I'm glad you're not a vegetarian; we'd have to order in a pizza."

"A steak sounds good." She took another sip of her drink. "So, what kind of a house am I sitting in?"

"Oh, I guess it's vaguely mission in style. I think I told you my folks built it before I was born."

"Yes. What have you done to it?"

"Well, I divided the upstairs into two apartments, and I opened it up a little downstairs. There used to be a wall between where you and I are right now, so I took that down and put in the bar. It makes everything seem bigger and lighter. I need to rip out the kitchen and bathrooms and replace them; I might call your friend Moscowitz about that before long."

"I recommend him highly."

"What about your subcontractors? Any of those you particularly like?"

"I've met most of them, I guess, but my instructions have always gone through Mike to them, so I haven't dealt directly with any of them."

"I see."

"Except the burglar alarm guy."

"Oh?"

"Yeah, his name is Mel something-or-other; I met him out at the house and went through the whole place to decide what I needed in the way of window and screen sensors and smoke alarms and panic buttons and all that stuff. He was very good about explaining it all, and I'm satisfied that I'm getting the right system."

"This was before your accident?"

"Yes, just a few days."

"What does he look like?"

"Oh, about my height, I guess—five eight or nine, well-built, sandy hair . . ." She stopped and her mouth dropped open. "Oh my God."

"What?"

"He's Admirer, isn't he?"

"Jesus, you're too sharp for me. I didn't mean for you to know I suspected him."

"When are you going to arrest him?"

"Hang on, I'm not in the least certain that he's our man, not yet. I've got to get his fingerprints to compare to the one we found in the Millman house."

"Why don't you just drag him in and fingerprint him, then sweat the whole story out of him?"

"You've been seeing too many old movies. These days we have to have something called probable cause before we can arrest somebody. If I pull him in I have to have his permission to fingerprint him, and he's not likely to agree to that. If I printed him anyway, his lawyer would get the case thrown out of court, and we don't want that."

"But you know all this stuff he's done, don't you?"

"Sure, but I can't prove he's the same guy who did it."

"The bastard," she said vehemently.

"Tell me, did he do the system for the Bel Air house, too?"

"No, that was already installed when Brad and I bought it. It's never worked properly, either, and after all that's happened, I was thinking of calling Mel in to fix it." She laughed. "How about that?"

"That's not a bad idea," Larsen mused.

"What? Invite him to the house?"

"Let me think about it; we might be able to turn such a visit to our advantage."

The microwave beeped, and Larsen took out the steaks. "These are ready for the grill, I think. You hungry?"

"Always."

Larsen began seasoning the meat.

Chris cocked her head to one side. "Your doorbell is about to ring."

"What? You going psychic on me?"

"Wait," she said.

They waited, but nothing happened.

"That's funny," she said.

"What's funny?"

"You know, since I haven't been able to see I've had to rely a lot more on my hearing, and I think it's become more acute."

"What did you hear?"

"I heard someone on your front porch," she said.

"You wait here for a minute, and I'll check," Larsen said.

"Don't be long."

"I'll hurry." He went to the front-hall closet and took his pistol from the holster; he opened the front door. Nobody there.

Larsen stepped out onto the front porch and looked around. Nobody. He leaned back inside the front door and called out to Chris. "I'm going to walk around the house once. You okay?"

"Go ahead," she called back.

He saw her reach into her jeans pocket and remove the little Italian pistol he had taught her to shoot. Not a bad idea, he thought.

Larsen retrieved a flashlight from the coat closet, then turned to his left and walked to the corner of the house. He stuck his head around the corner for an instant, then pulled back. He hadn't seen anyone. He stepped off the front porch and began walking toward the back of the house, the darkened flashlight in his left hand, the pistol in his right. There was enough light left in the sky to see fairly well, and he saved the light for when he might see something move.

No one was out back or on the other side of the house. Outside his bedroom window he stepped over a small pile of flagstones that had been left over from building the patio. After his tour he let himself back in the front door. "It's me," he called to Chris. "Don't shoot."

There was no response.

He stepped into the living room and looked around. She was gone. The pistol held ready, he ran through the house to the back door, kicked open the screen, and stepped outside, the flashlight ready to point, the weapon ready to fire. Nobody. He ran quickly to both sides of the house for a look, then returned to the back door, looking at the fence at the end of his backyard and wondering if anyone could get over that. Now he was frightened.

From inside the house he heard a door open, then another noise. He opened the back screen quietly and stepped into the hall. As he did, Chris came out of the bathroom to his right, holding her pistol. Suddenly, she turned toward him and raised the weapon.

"It's me! Don't shoot!"

"What are you doing there?" she asked, lowering the gun. "I thought you were out front."

"I came back in and you were gone," he said. "Scared the shit out of me."

"I'm sorry," she said apologetically. "I had to use the bathroom."

"How the hell did you know where the bathroom was?" he asked.

"I could hear the water running in the toilet. It's a distinctive sound."

"I keep meaning to fix that."

"Don't—not for a while, anyway; it's useful."

He laughed. "Come on, let's get those steaks on the fire."

They returned to the kitchen, but he kept the pistol in his hip pocket.

CHAPTER

34

They ate their steaks hungrily, with a salad and a bottle of California cabernet, avoiding the subjects of Admirer, Danny's accident, or anything that might ruin their dinner. Larsen dug some ice cream out of the freezer and they had dessert, then he cleared the table. Chris insisted on helping with the dishes, and although he had a serviceable dishwasher, he didn't discourage her. He liked having her standing next to him doing something domestic, even if it seemed a strange setting for a movie star.

"Does the movie actress thing make you at all uncomfortable?" she asked suddenly, as if reading his mind.

"It did a little, at first," he admitted. "Less so now."

"Good; it's an artificial barrier and I don't want barriers between us."

"You have to admit we live in different worlds," he said, handing her a plate.

"We live across town from each other, that's all."

"Bel Air is a lot farther than across town. It's a thousand miles, at least. So is Malibu."

"I was afraid that might bother you," she said, wiping a cup. "I wish it didn't."

"I had to deal with something like that once before," he said. "When I was at UCLA."

"Tell me about it."

"There was this very beautiful girl, and I was nuts about her, and we were pinned for a while."

"What happened?"

"She took me home to San Diego—La Jolla, actually—for a weekend. La Jolla is a very ritzy place, and her parents had one of the more noticeable houses there, overlooking the Pacific. Her father was a lawyer, like mine. No, not like mine; he was the managing partner of a very major firm in San Diego, and when at dinner the first night I described my father's practice, not without some pride, he burst out laughing. I don't think he meant to, but he was an insufferable snob, and I told him to shut up. He recovered from that and apologized, but Sherry, my girl, was incensed that I would speak to her father that way, no matter what he had said about *my* father. Make a long story short, I took the bus back to L.A. that night. We were hardly rich, but my father earned a respectable income, and we were solidly middle class. I didn't think we had to kowtow to anybody."

"Quite right," Chris said. "What happened with the girl?"

"I waited for her to apologize for her conduct—I was quite stiff-necked in those days—but instead she mailed my fraternity pin back to me. We didn't speak to each other again, until last year."

"Last year?"

"I ran into her on Rodeo Drive. She had gained a lot of weight, and she had two horrible children in tow. We had a minute's polite conversation—she's married to a La Jolla dentist—and we went on our ways."

"I hope you're not quite so stiff-necked these days."

"I hope not, too."

"My father is a pharmacist in Delano, Georgia."

"Then you're not far above me?"

"Well, he does own the drugstore."

"Only one?"

"Just the one."

"I can live with that, I guess."

"But Bel Air and Malibu are harder to live with?"

"I'm afraid so."

"Let me tell you about my fabulous wealth and position. About the time I started getting work out here I married an actor—Brad Donner. We were both just getting started."

"I've seen him in several things," Larsen said. "He's good."

"Yes, and he's done very well—better than I, in fact. It's easier for men out here. Brad is not the world's brightest man, but he made one very good career decision. Remember a movie called *Man in Blue*?"

"Sure; a very good cop flick, I thought."

"So did the whole world, and Brad was smart enough to take a minimum salary and profit participation. That paid for the Bel Air house and made us fairly secure. When we were divorced, the community-property law gave me half the marital assets, including half the house, plus about half a million in cash. I had saved some money, and with smart handling by my business manager, Jack Berman, it grew to about three hundred thousand. So when the Malibu house is finished and the Bel Air place sold, I should end up with a paid-for house and about half a million dollars. Do you think that's too rich to be comfortable with?"

"Well, due to my father's diligence in making insurance payments, I've got a paid-for house in Santa Monica and about three hundred thousand in investments, and I don't owe anybody anything, so maybe we're not so far apart after all."

"I'm glad you see it that way," she said.

"Of course, if we're both reasonably successful at our careers, I'll end up with a pension in eight more years, and you'll make millions."

"Let's cross that bridge when we come to it," she said.

"I guess if you're going to cross a bridge, that's the time to do it," he agreed.

"There's another bridge we have to cross," she said, slipping an arm around his waist, "and I think it's time we did it."

"We seem to keep getting interrupted," he said.

"Not tonight," she murmured, kissing him.

They stood at the kitchen sink with their arms around each other, becoming more and more aroused.

"I can't find my way to the bedroom," she whispered. "You'll have to lead the way."

He swept her into his arms and carried her across the house to the bedroom, then set her on the bed while he got out of his clothes. She was already taking off her heavy T-shirt, and the dim light from the window revealed the lines of her breasts and waist. Larsen sat on the bed and buried his face in her breasts, kissing the nipples; he was already naked, and he helped her with her jeans.

Then they were stretched out on the bed, whispering to each other, kissing, caressing. She reached across his body and pulled him on top of her, then guided him inside her.

Larsen took a deep breath, and before he could let it out, the window next to the bed caved inward with a roar, and, accompanied by thousands of shards of glass, an eighteen-inch-wide slab of flagstone crashed onto the bed next to them.

Chris screamed, and Larsen rolled off the bed, taking her with him, landing on his back, with her weight crushing the broken glass into him. Larsen turned and shoved her under the bed. "Stay there and don't come out until I tell you to," he whispered.

He got to his feet, scooping up his trousers as he ran across the glass shards. He got quickly into his pants and yanked the heavy automatic pistol out as he tore toward the front door, ignoring the pain in his back and feet. From outside he heard a motorcycle engine leap to life and the gears engage.

He fumbled for his car keys as he burst through the front door, in time to catch a fleeting glimpse of the motorcyclist tearing down the street. This time he had a shot at the guy, he thought, and if he could catch him he wouldn't need to worry about his fingerprints.

His unmarked patrol car was at curbside, and Larsen dived into it, key at the ready. It started instantly, and he was off down the street after the disappearing motorcycle.

•

Then he felt a series of hard bumps and heard the sound of metal grating on concrete. The car was hardly moving. Swearing, he got out and walked around the car. All four tires had been slashed to ribbons. "SHIT!" he screamed into the night. He heard neighborhood doors and windows opening. Humiliated, he pulled the crippled car to the curb, then ran back into the house.

"Chris?" he shouted as he came through the front door.

"I'm here," she called back. "I'm all right."

He ran to the bedroom, then became more careful as he made his way through the broken glass. He picked up the naked girl and made his way to the guest room. "Shhhh," he whispered over her sobbing. "It's all right; we're both all right."

Her arm was over his shoulder. "Your back isn't all right," she said. "You're bleeding horribly."

"I'll get into a shower in a minute," he said, turning down the bed and tucking her into it. "Then you can put something on it for me." He brushed her hair out of her eyes and kissed her tears away. "I'll be right back," he said. He placed his pistol in her hand. "This will take care of you."

A few minutes later, still standing under the stinging water, he became the third person to resolve to kill Admirer at the first opportunity.

35

Larsen greeted Mike Moscowitz and walked him to the bedroom. Outside, a police mechanic had jacked up the patrol car and was changing the wheels. "I hadn't expected to call you this soon," Larsen said, pointing at the window. The large flagstone still lay on the floor.

Moscowitz whistled. "That really made a hole, didn't it?"

"It did."

"Burglar? Vandal?"

"Neither."

"This have something to do with what you came to see me about?" Moscowitz asked.

"Yeah."

"You said somebody was bothering Chris Callaway?"

"She was here last night."

Moscowitz looked at the floor. "Look, I didn't realize this was so serious. I'm afraid I wasn't very cooperative when we talked."

"Are you feeling more cooperative now?"

"I've been thinking; there's a couple of my subs who've got a van like mine. One of them strikes me as, well, a little odd."

"Which one?"

"Name's Mel Parker; he's doing the security system for the house."

"What's odd about him?"

"Well, I don't know, he's a pleasant enough guy, fairly nice-looking, but . . . "

"But what?"

"He just makes me a little uneasy. He came highly recommended to me from a friend who's in the business, and God knows, he's done a first-rate job with his installation. He's just a little creepy."

"How do you mean?"

"It's not the scar . . . "

"Scar?"

"His upper lip. Looks like one of those, uh . . . "

"A harelip?"

"Not anymore. It must have been fixed when he was a kid, and it's not a bad scar, it just makes his mouth sort of grin all the time, even when he's not grinning."

"The teeth are exposed, you mean?"

"Yeah, even when his mouth is closed."

"Chris didn't mention that."

"Well, he smiles a lot, and that keeps you from noticing; it's when he doesn't know you're looking at him that it's noticeable."

"What else about him?"

"He's got dead eyes."

Larsen paused. "How do you mean?"

"Well, you remember that guy who shot Reagan a few years back?"

"Yeah."

"And the guy who shot John Lennon? They both had dead eyes."

"Describe them."

"Well, it's like no matter what expression is on their faces, their eyes always look the same—expressionless, dead."

Larsen knew what the builder meant; he had seen them often enough in mug shots. "What else about him bothers you?"

"Once he told me about this experience he had on a job. He was installing an alarm in a big house in Pacific Palisades, and he was working outside the master bedroom window, and the lady of the house was lying on the bed, naked, you know, doing herself. And he said he just stood there and watched her, didn't care if she saw him or not."

"Did she see him?"

"He sort of implied that she did, but she didn't care. I thought that was weird; I couldn't have stood there and watched that; I'd have been embarrassed. It bothered me that he wasn't embarrassed."

Larsen nodded. "Thanks, I'm glad you told me."

Moscowitz looked at the shattered window. "I wish I'd told you sooner. I hope I haven't said something about an innocent man."

"Don't worry, nobody's going to bother him until we're sure he's our man."

"About the window, Jon, I'll pick one up this afternoon and have it in by tonight. I'll charge you for the window—my wholesale price—but the labor's on me."

"That's not necessary, Mike."

"I know it isn't, but I'd feel better if you'd let me do it."

"All right, thanks."

The two men shook hands, then left the house.

Larsen stood and marveled at Danny Devere's car. "How the hell could anybody survive that?" he asked Bernie, the chief police mechanic.

"The car did what it was supposed to: collapsed in sections, pretty much preserved the integrity of the passenger compartment. He had his seat belt on and, maybe most important, he had an airbag," Bernie said.

"What did you find?"

"Well, when a car's this torn up, there's some guessing involved."

"What do you guess?"

"There was a hole, like a pinhole, in the hydraulic line to the brakes. It could have been made in the crash, of course, but it looks to me like the hole was so small that not much fluid would leak until the brakes were used. So every time he used the brakes, he'd squirt out some more fluid, until there wasn't enough left to be effective."

Larsen nodded. "Anything else?"

"The transmission shift cable was gone, and I would say, though I couldn't swear in court, that somebody had cut all but a strand or two of the cable, and when the driver is up there at the top of Beverly Glen and his brakes don't work, he gets a little panicky, maybe, maybe a lot panicky, and he yanks the gear lever around, trying to slow the car down, and the last of the cable snaps."

"You're saying we're not going to get anybody for doing this?"

"You may get him; you're not going to prove it. The car's just too much of a mess. But if I was you, I wouldn't give the driver a ticket, either. The guy ought to get a medal for driving it into that tennis court. Can you imagine what could have happened if he had just ridden the thing all the way down to Sunset and hit that traffic? That was one cool customer."

Larsen grinned. "Would you believe he's a very gay little hairdresser?"

"You're shittin' me!"

"I shit you not."

Bernie burst out laughing.

Larsen sat at his desk and pondered how to proceed. He thought of staking out Keyhole Security and waiting to get a good look at Mel Parker, but the idea of tiptoeing around the bastard galled him.

Finally, he picked up the phone and dialed.

"Keyhole Security," a woman's voice answered.

"Mel Parker, please."

"May I say who is calling?"

"A prospective customer. Tell him Mike Moscowitz referred me to him."

"Just a moment."

Parker came on the line. "Hello?"

"'Morning, I'm looking for a burglar alarm, and Mike Moscowitz recommended you."

"That's nice of Mike," Parker said, "Mr. . . . ?"

"Larsen. Jon Larsen."

There was a long pause on the other end. "Right, Mr. Larsen," Parker said finally, his voice steady. "What sort of system did you have in mind?"

"Something pretty comprehensive."

"Home or business?"

"Home."

"Why don't I come and take a look at your situation?"

"Perfect." Larsen gave him the address.

"I've got some service calls to make this afternoon, but I could stop by on my way in. Are you available around six?"

"Absolutely perfect."

"I know the street," Parker said. "I'll see you at six."

"I'll look forward to it," Larsen said. When he put down the phone, his hand was trembling.

36

Melvin James Parker stood on the opposite side of the screen door and looked at Larsen. "Hi," he said. "I'm Mel Parker.

His gaze was as Moscowitz had described it: flat and dead. Larsen pushed open the screen and let him into the house. Neither man offered to shake hands.

"Nice place," Parker said, looking around.

"Thanks."

"So, what do we need here?"

"Why don't you tell me?"

Parker handed him a pair of brochures. "These are two systems we offer; one is pretty basic, the other can expand to be as elaborate as you like. Why don't you take a look at those while I have a look around?"

"Sure," Larsen said. He didn't glance at the brochures. Instead, he followed Parker at a discreet distance while the man wandered around the house, inside and out, and made notes on a clipboard.

Parker was not a large man, but he was well-built, with the look of someone who'd gotten his physique from hard work, not lifting weights in a gym. In spite of his repaired lip and defective gaze, he was not an unattractive person. He was cool, too, Larsen had to concede. To walk right in here and pretend he didn't know who he was talking to took a tightly controlled psyche.

Larsen had the pistol in a shoulder holster and his jacket on, and he was unable to prevent the fantasy of shooting Parker in the back of the head from flitting through his mind.

When they were back where they started, Parker sat at the bar and worked up his estimate. Larsen stood in the kitchen, watching him with real fascination. When Parker had finished, he tore off a carbon copy and pushed it across the counter. Larsen picked it up and glanced at it. "How about a beer?" he asked.

"Why not? It's the end of my day."

It's closer to the end than you know, Larsen thought. He took two Carta Blancas from the fridge and grabbed two glasses.

"No glass for me," Parker said, but it was too late; Larsen had already started to pour.

Larsen shoved the glass across the bar and waited for Parker to pick it up. Parker didn't hesitate.

"Take a look at what I've done," he said, nodding at the paper. "I've used a combination of window and screen sensors, depending on what was already there. Every door is covered, there's a motion detector in here . . . " He paused. " . . . and a panic button next to the bed in the master bedroom." He met Larsen's gaze straight on.

"I guess that's a useful place to have a panic button," Larsen said.

"Everybody's prone to panic—under the right circumstances," Parker said.

"What happens if the alarm goes off?" Larsen asked, though he didn't much care.

"A signal is transmitted to our central office, and we telephone you. If there's no answer, we call the cops; if you answer, we expect to hear a code word from you, and if we don't hear it we call the cops. If the panic button goes off, we call the cops immediately." He took a pen from his shirt pocket and made ready to write. "What would you use for a code word?" he asked.

"How about Admirer?" Larsen asked.

Parker's strange eyes showed no reaction. He wrote down the word on the form. "Oh," he said, "there are two smoke alarms included, too. That's important."

"Yeah," Larsen said, glancing at the form.

"I think you'll have a hard time beating the price," Parker said. "Twenty-seven hundred even, tax included. What business are you in?"

"I'm in the cop business," Larsen replied.

"It's good you realize that even a cop needs security," Parker said. He stopped smiling, but the teeth were still there. "Even a piece under your arm isn't always enough to protect you."

"A cop has a lot more going for him than a piece," Larsen said. "Street scum have a way of forgetting that."

"Oh, yeah," Parker said, smiling again, "you've got all that scientific backup these days, haven't you? Computers and stuff."

Larsen smiled back. "Mostly we have other cops.

Cops don't take it lightly when somebody screws with one of their own."

Parker laughed aloud. "One for all and all for one, huh?" He laughed again.

There was a large kitchen knife near Larsen's right hand, and it was all he could do to keep from grabbing it and plunging it into Parker's throat. "We always laugh last," Larsen said. "Always."

"Whatever you say," Parker said, glancing at his watch in a manner that was bored and dismissive. "Well, thanks for the beer," he said, standing up and strolling toward the door.

Larsen followed him to the door. "It was the least I could do for the chance to meet you."

"Be sure and let me hear from you," Parker said, walking out the door.

"Oh, you'll hear from me, when you least expect it," Larsen called after him.

Parker didn't turn, but raised a hand and gave a limp wave. He got into his gray Ford van and drove away.

Larsen crossed the room quickly. With one finger he tipped Parker's beer glass, then got another finger under the bottom. Using just the two fingers, he held the glass up to the light.

"YES!!!" he shouted.

37

Larsen went in to work feeling better than he had in weeks, with Parker's beer glass in a Ziploc bag beside him on the front seat. He parked the car in the garage under the building and, unwilling to wait for the elevator, ran up the stairs to his office, clutching the plastic bag tightly.

He went straight to the fingerprint team, but he was greeted by two empty desks in their office. A secretary walked past in the hall.

"They're on a job," she said.

"When will they be back?"

"My best guess is after lunch."

Larsen emitted a grunt of frustration. He went to Elgin's desk, set the glass on it, and wrote a note requesting an immediate comparison with the Millman guest house print. ASAP! he added.

He went back to his office, hung up his coat, and dug in his bottom drawer for a warrant form.

Chief of Detectives Herrera stuck his head in the door. "What's happening with the Callaway case?" he demanded.

"I expect to ID the perp this afternoon; I'm typing up the warrant now."

"About fucking time," Herrera said. "Send me your report the minute you get in from making the arrest."

"Yessir," Larsen said, and rolled the warrant form into his typewriter. This was going to be a very favorable bust for him, and the papers were going to eat it up. Larsen didn't care much about the papers, but he knew that Herrera did, and it would gall the chief to see a subordinate getting the space. He knew a reporter at the *Times* who would give it big play. He'd arrange for the woman to "accidentally" be at the station when he brought in Parker, then Herrera couldn't accuse him of seeking out the reporter.

Larsen typed the warrant with a light heart.

Chris and Melanie picked up Danny from Cedars-Sinai at mid-afternoon in Melanie's station wagon. Danny gave both of them a big hug and kiss, then hobbled out to the car on crutches that were a little too long.

"Danny, there have been developments," Chris said as she settled him into the backseat.

"Tell me."

"Jon has identified Admirer."

"Who is the sonofabitch?"

"It's a man named Mel Parker—the same Mel from Keyhole Security in Santa Monica who installed the alarm system at the new house. He's the guy in the gray Ford van. Jon got his finger-prints last night, and he's going to make the arrest this afternoon."

"Not if I can help it," Danny muttered under his breath.

"Sorry," Chris said, "I didn't get that."

"I need to make a stop, Chris, and I'm all out of wheels. Do you and Melanie mind?

"Not at all," Chris said.

"Glad to," Melanie echoed.

"Oh, Danny, I brought your checkbook, as you asked." She handed him the folder.

"Thanks, Chris. I want to go to the BMW dealer on Santa Monica Boulevard."

"Are you going to buy a new car?"

"I don't think I'll be driving the old one soon, and I've always wanted a BMW, so what the hell?"

"Go for it," Melanie said.

When they reached the dealership, Danny struggled out of the car.

"We'll wait for you," Chris said.

"No need; I'm planning to drive the new car home."

"Danny, isn't it a little soon? You're supposed to be taking it easy."

"I'll take it easier when I have this off my mind," he said. "I'll see you back at the house; I should be home in a couple of hours. Do you mind waiting if I'm late, Melanie?"

"It's okay," Chris said. "Jon's coming over after work, and we'll hear everything."

"Great, see you later." Danny hobbled into the dealership. There was a black sedan of the Five series on the floor. Danny opened the door and got behind the wheel. Beautiful.

A salesman approached. "Yes, sir, a beauty, isn't it?"

"What's your lowest cash price?" Danny asked.

"Let me do some figuring," the salesman said.

Danny looked at the man. "I don't want to dance; I want to buy a car."

"I can probably manage a six-percent discount," the man said.

Danny had been reading up on the car, and he knew what the markup was. "Make it eight percent, and you've made a sale."

"I'd have to talk with my manager," the man said.

"Remind him that the Mercedes dealer is just down the street," Danny said.

The man scurried away and came back with the manager, who took a deep breath.

Danny held up a hand. "Don't start. I know what this car cost you, and I want eight percent off. I'll pay sales tax and documentation, but don't talk to me about paint sealants and floor mats. I'll give you a check; you can call the bank. Is it a deal or not?"

"Nothing to trade? No financing?" the manager asked.

"Straight cash."

The manager shook his head. "That's a little close to the bone for me," he said.

Danny got out of the car, shoved the door shut with a crutch, and aimed himself at the door.

"All right, all right," the man called after him. "Deal."

Forty-five minutes later, Danny drove his new car out of the dealership and up Santa Monica toward

La Cienega. A couple of blocks up the street, he saw the sign—he'd looked up the address while he was waiting for the car. He smiled tightly and gave the sign a wave as he drove past.

On La Cienega he pulled up in front of the shop where he'd bought Chris's gun, got out of the car, and swung into the building, wrestling with the swinging glass door.

"Mr. Devere, isn't it?" the man behind the counter said.

"Right. I'm in the market for some more firepower."

"Something specific in mind?"

"The only handgun I've ever fired was a Colt .45 automatic, and that was nearly twenty years ago, in the navy."

"I've got a nice used one," the man said, opening a showcase.

"No, no, that's too heavy for me. I used to have to fire the goddamned thing with both hands. I want something lighter, but I want plenty of stopping power."

"Long range or close?"

"Close," Danny said. "I'm no marksman."

"New or used?"

"It's only going to be fired once, so used should do it."

"Let's keep it simple, then," the man said, removing a snub-nosed revolver from the case. "Smith & Wesson .38 Special, the old detective's favorite. Use a soft-nosed load and it'll stop a water buffalo in his tracks. It's two-fifty—no, you're becoming a good customer; we'll say two hundred."

"Sold. And give me a box of soft-nosed cartridges for the pistol."

"Holster?" the salesman asked. "Got a nice clip-on for your belt."

"Throw that in, too."

While the salesman wrapped his purchases, Danny wrote a check. He clipped the holster onto his belt, shoved the pistol into it, picked up the ammunition, and left the shop.

Back in his car, Danny loaded the pistol and holstered it. He drove back to Santa Monica Boulevard, found Keyhole Security, and parked the car so that he could see the little parking area in front of the building. The gray Ford van was parked there. All he had to do now was wait.

38

It was after three before Larsen got a call from the secretary in fingerprinting.

"They're back," she said, and hung up.

Larsen tried to keep from hurrying but failed. When he arrived at the office Elgin was hunched over a lightbox with a loupe. "Just a second," he said to Larsen.

While Larsen was waiting, Chief of Detectives Herrera strolled up. "Got your perp ID'ed?" he asked.

Larsen nodded toward Elgin.

Elgin stood up straight. "Congratulations, Jon," he said. "You got three real pretty prints there—first, second, and third fingers."

Larsen heaved a sigh of relief and produced his warrant. "I'm going to go get this signed," he said to Herrera. "I'll want backup for the arrest."

"Hang on," Elgin said. "These are beautiful

prints, but they don't match the one from the Millman guest house."

"What?" Larsen said weakly.

"The prints from the glass are not from the same guy as the print from the guest house. Maybe it was the cleaning lady's print or Millman's. Who knows?"

Larsen tried not to sag in front of his boss; he knew he had turned red.

"So where are you now?" Herrera asked.

"Well, I'm better off than I was last week," Larsen replied. "At least I know who the guy is."

Herrera shook his head. "Jesus Christ."

"Chief, I want to surveil him."

Herrera looked at him in disgust. "You know I haven't got the manpower for a proper surveillance. You've let this case suck up all your time, and now you want to suck up everybody else's. You want to surveil him, do it yourself."

"I can't do it properly alone," Larsen said.

"Then do it half-assed, the way you do everything else," Herrera said, and stalked off before Larsen could reply.

Elgin shrugged. "Sorry, Jon; I thought you had your man for a minute there."

Danny had almost dozed off when he saw the gray van move. It backed out of its place, left the parking lot, and turned west on Santa Monica Boulevard.

Danny got his car started and, after waiting for a lot of cars to pass, executed a quick and illegal U-turn. The van was almost to the beach before Danny caught up with it.

He slapped his forehead. If he was going to follow the guy, he certainly couldn't do it like he was hooked to his bumper. He dropped back and let a car get between them.

At the beach, the van turned left and headed south toward Venice. Danny followed, making certain to stay well back. The van headed into Venice, the neighborhood of canals and small houses near the beach. It made a couple of turns, then moved into a street a little shabbier than the others, and finally stopped before a freshly painted bungalow surrounded by a high chain-link fence. As Danny got closer to the van an electric gate opened, and the van drove into the garage. The gate closed behind it.

Danny stopped and waited for Parker to come out of the garage. He looked up and down the street; no one in sight. Danny wasn't very mobile, so he would call the man to the fence and shoot from the car, a distance of no more than eight feet. As he waited he looked up and saw strands of razor wire entwined in the spires of the iron fence. A sign at the front gate read GUARD DOG ON DUTY. The man was certainly security-conscious.

Parker never came out; he must have entered the house directly from the garage. Next door, two small boys came outside and began to play with a dog. Cursing, Danny drove away.

Chris sat with her tape recorder and worked on dictating her screenplay while Melanie typed up the pages. The novel was short and ideally structured for a film, so the work had gone quickly. The phone rang.

"Hello?"

"Hi, it's Jack. I've tracked down the agent who represents Karen Copeland, and he's willing to option the book for a year for ten thousand dollars against a purchase price of a hundred thousand, second year's option five thousand, not to apply to the purchase price. I think it's reasonable; want me to go ahead?"

"Oh, yes, please, Jack! Oh, thank God! If I'd done all this work and not been able to get the rights I'd shoot myself!"

"Don't do that, sweetie."

"Jack, I'm almost done with a first draft, and I'd like for you and Ron to read it."

"Sure, send it over."

"We'll have it typed up soon, and I will. I'm anxious for your opinion. I'll send you a check for the ten thousand, too."

"Fine. How's it going otherwise?"

"Very well; my vision is improving, and I want to go back to work before long."

"Good news. I gotta run. 'Bye."

"'Bye."

Chris hung up as Melanie came into the room. "We've got the rights!" she crowed.

"That's wonderful, Chris!"

"As soon as you can get it typed up, send a copy to Jack and one to Ron, and we'll get this show on the road." She heard a car pull up outside. "See who that is, will you?" Involuntarily, she felt for the pistol in the pocket of her jeans.

"It's Danny," Melanie called from the front door, "and he's driving a really terrific BMW. And here comes Jon, too."

"Great, I can tell everybody the news." Chris heard Danny struggle through the door with his crutches and Jon's low voice behind him.

Both men came into the room, and when Danny

had been settled on the sofa, Jon sank into the wing chair opposite Chris.

"Why is everybody so cheerful?" Chris asked. Something was clearly wrong.

"You first, Danny," Jon said.

"I don't want to talk about it," Danny replied.

"Jon, what's wrong?" Chris asked.

Jon sighed. "Palmer's prints didn't match the one in the Millman guest house."

"But they had to match!" Chris said, stunned.

"Not necessarily. We never knew for sure that the one print we found was Admirer's. It could have been anybody's—maid's, real-estate agent's, anybody's."

"What does this mean?"

"It means that I can't prove that Parker is Admirer. Not yet, anyway."

"Then you can't arrest him?"

"No. Not until I have probable cause to do so."

"Oh, no, no; it's not over."

"Not yet, I'm afraid."

"What are we going to do now?"

"We're going to have to wait until Parker makes a mistake, that's all."

"What kind of mistake?"

"Something that will connect him to Admirer directly."

"How long will that take?"

"There's no way of knowing," Jon said. "In the meantime, we just have to be very, very careful. I'm going to start following Parker wherever he goes. If I can find out where he lives, that might help us."

Danny spoke up. "I know where he lives."

"How would you know that?" Jon asked.

"He lives at 1825 Little Canal Road in Venice. I followed him there this afternoon."

"Danny," Chris said, "you shouldn't have done that."

"Danny, I hope you weren't thinking of doing something stupid," Larsen said.

"I was thinking of doing *something*," Danny said vehemently. "I don't like it when people try to kill me. I learned a long time ago not to sit around waiting for people to hurt me."

"Danny," Jon said, "if you were entirely healthy, I'd put you up against just about anybody, but I don't think you're in any kind of shape to go picking fights with Parker."

"I wasn't going to pick a fight," Danny said. "I was going to kill the sonofabitch."

"Don't tell me you've got a gun, too," Larsen said.

"I certainly have," Danny replied.

"Great, now *everybody's* got a gun."

Chris broke in. "Danny, will you let Jon handle this?"

"Like he's handled it so far?" Danny asked.

"That's not fair," she said. "Jon has to operate within the law."

"Well, I don't," Danny said.

"Danny, listen to me," Jon said. "This situation is bad already, and if you go taking potshots at Parker, you could make it a lot worse. You have a nice life; don't go screwing it up by getting yourself put in jail."

"Are you going to put me in jail, Jon?"

"I could, and right now. Threatening to kill someone is against the law, and you could get two to five years for it. Now, I know you're frustrated—God knows, I am, too. But you're not going to be of any help to Chris if you start behaving stupidly."

"He's right, Danny," Chris said. "Please promise me you won't try anything like that."

"Oh, all right," Danny said. "I was just mad, I guess. I won't hunt him down and kill him. But I promise you, if he tries anything else, I'll defend myself."

"That's reasonable," Jon said. "Just be sure the threat is real before you act on it."

"Okay, but what are we going to do next? We can't just sit around and wait for the guy to hurt Chris."

"Well, he isn't making any mistakes, so we're just going to have to force an error."

"And how do we do that?" Chris asked.

"Leave that to me," Jon replied.

39

L arsen found the street easily enough. It was
just after 7:00 A.M., and the neighborhood had
only begun to stir. A couple of doors from
where he was parked, a woman came out on her
front porch to collect the morning newspaper.

Larsen had already cruised the street twice to get
a good look at the house. It was like a fortress.
Venice, although efforts were being made to gentrify
it, was still a high-crime neighborhood, with burglary being at the top of the list. Still, though he had
seen a few security company signs in the neighborhood, nobody had gone to quite the same lengths as
Parker to protect his property. Larsen couldn't recall
having seen any house, outside of south-central L.A.
or Watts, that appeared so fortified.

Larsen sipped his coffee and resisted the tempta-
tion to read his newspaper. An all-news channel
was on the radio, and that made up for the lack of

something to do while he waited. He had always been an impatient surveillant, had hated the waiting game, and his years on the force had not mellowed him. He had to wait until almost eight-thirty before Parker's gates suddenly swung open and the van backed into the street.

Larsen waited until Parker turned the corner before following. Anybody paranoid enough to have barbed wire around his house might keep an eye on his rearview mirror. He caught up on the stretch along the beach and checked his own mirror to see if the other member of his team was in place. He picked up the handheld CB radio and said, "Okay, change places." Then he moved into the right-hand lane.

Danny passed him slowly in the shiny new BMW and took his place two cars behind Parker's van. Larsen was driving his half-restored 1965 Mustang convertible with the top up. He reckoned he still had two hundred hours of work to do before the Mustang could take its place proudly beside the MG in his garage.

The rush-hour traffic made it easy to keep pace, because nobody could move very quickly. Larsen reckoned Parker would stop by his office before he went on his day's rounds, and he was right.

When the gray van was in the Keyhole Security lot and Parker had gone inside, Larsen spoke into the radio again. "Okay, partner, back to the house. Follow me."

"Gotcha," Danny's voice came back.

Larsen drove back to Venice slowly; he wanted the denizens of Little Canal Road to go to work before he did. He pulled over to the curb in the street behind Parker's house and waved Danny alongside.

"Reporting for duty," Danny said, saluting smartly.

"The front of the house doesn't look too inviting," Larsen said. "I'm going to see if I can work my way through here to the back. You go around the block and park three or four doors down from the house and watch the front. If you hear an alarm go off from the house, drive away. If a police car shows up on the block, somebody may have called the cops or I may have tripped a silent alarm, so say clearly, three times, 'Security, security, security,' and drive slowly away. If, on the other hand, Parker himself shows up, say 'Mayday, mayday, mayday,' and get the hell out of there. Got that?"

"Right."

"Okay, go park your car."

Danny drove away, and Larsen got out of the Mustang and locked it. You couldn't be too careful in this neighborhood. Two houses down the street, more or less behind Parker's house, was a boarded-up derelict bungalow, and he headed for that. The houses were spaced widely enough for him to walk between the derelict and the house next door, which didn't look much better, and he was soon in the backyard. A narrow alley separated the rows of houses.

It was obvious which house was Parker's, even from the rear. A chain-link fence enclosed the backyard, and the familiar razor wire snaked along the top of it. Larsen walked down the alley, stopped at Parker's fence, and looked around. He could hear a television from somewhere, but he didn't see anybody at the windows of the neighboring houses. He seemed to have the morning to himself. He grabbed an empty garbage can from a row in the alley and trotted along the narrow opening between the chain-link fence and the six-foot picket fence enclosing the yard next door. He put down the garbage can and, using the chain-link to steady himself, climbed on top of the can at a point where the fence met the house.

He was wearing an army field jacket left over from his days in the National Guard, and from one of its commodious pockets he took a zippered tool kit and removed a pair of wire cutters. He snipped the razor wire at the end closest to the house and very carefully folded back a three-foot length of it, then donned gloves and hoisted himself to the top of the fence. As he did, he glanced at the roof of the house and noticed two skylights. Those might give him a point of entry, he thought, or at least let him have a look inside.

He climbed onto the roof and walked toward the nearest skylight, glad that he had worn sneakers, and examined the edges of the clear plastic. Inside, fixed to the wooden frame, he saw a narrow plastic box with a wire leading away from it. Parker seemed to take his own advice where burglar alarms were concerned.

Very few houses were impregnable, Larsen knew from four years on the burglary squad. There were two ways to deal with a house that was thoroughly wired: if you knew enough about alarms you might disable the equipment and operate at your leisure; or, if you were electronically illiterate, you could smash your way in and loot quickly, hoping to depart before the police arrived. Larsen well knew that his colleagues often did not arrive within the advertised two-minute time frame.

Larsen was not entirely unfamiliar with electronics, but he did not feel confident attacking an alarm system installed by an expert in his own house. Nor did he long for a few nerve-wracking minutes of search time while he wondered how close the local law was, and he certainly did not wish to have to explain to the LAPD why a Beverly Hills officer was present in the home of one of its taxpayers in his absence.

Given the circumstances, it seemed that his best hope was simply to get a look at the inside of the house from the outside, and the two skylights should be helpful. He cupped his hands around his eyes to cut the glare of the sun and peered down into the residence.

He found himself gazing into the uplifted eyes, some twelve feet below him, of the largest Rottweiler he had ever seen. The animal resembled more a small bull than a dog, and it was emitting a low rumble of a growl that he could feel in his fingertips against the skylight. Thanking heaven that he had not broken into the house, Larsen quickly surveyed the room, found it to be a sparsely equipped kitchen, then moved on to the next skylight.

The Rottweiler moved with him, following his footsteps across the roof. The dog was now in the living room, which contained a new-looking sofa and a very large television set, and little more. This was consistent with someone who had recently moved out of a furnished guest house.

By laying his cheek against the skylight, Larsen could see a corner of the bedroom, and against the wall was a Samsonite suitcase like the one he had seen on the bed of the Millman guest house.

Larsen was not sure what he had been hoping for—perhaps the Navajo rug or a wallful of photographs of Chris—but whatever it was, he hadn't found it. While everything he saw was consistent with his matching of Admirer and Parker, he could see nothing that would establish the fact sufficiently to justify an arrest warrant. It was going to be necessary to look into the windows from the ground, particularly the garage, which he hoped would contain a red motorcycle. Taking care to first wipe any fingerprints off the skylights, he padded across the roof to the back of the house. He looked for a place where the gutter seemed strongly attached to the house, found it near the back door, and let himself dangle from the gutter for a moment before dropping the final six feet to the ground.

As he rose from a squat to his full height, he found himself facing the back door and, to the right of that, a good-sized picture window. He happened to be looking directly at the window as it exploded, sending glass everywhere, and, simultaneously, a piercing, whooping alarm went off and the Rottweiler sailed through the air into the backyard.

Larsen did not hesitate. He ran at the patch of fence from which he had removed the razor wire. The Rottweiler had landed off balance and rolled, giving Larsen just enough time to plant one foot against the fence and leap to the top. At that moment, the Rottweiler came for him.

He had one leg over the fence and was struggling to get the rest of his body over it when the dog left the ground, snapped its jaws loudly shut, and fell back, brought up short by the jean leg to which he held fast.

Larsen had both hands on the top pipe of the fence and one leg over it, but hanging from his leg was at least a hundred and seventy-five pounds of squirming, thrashing beast, which was not about to let go. Larsen felt himself slipping back into the yard.

He had no doubt that if he allowed the dog's feet to touch the ground, the animal would use the opportunity to connect with Larsen's leg instead of his trousers, and would then eat his way upward.

With one enormous effort, Larsen managed to get an arm over the fence and grip it from the other side. This gave him a moment's purchase that allowed him to begin swinging his leg. In a weird kind of rhythm with the whooping alarm, he got the tenacious dog swinging through an arc, and, straining to increase the animal's velocity, he managed to strike the side of the house with the dog's body.

The dog grunted and let go. Larsen, with his remaining strength, got his body over the fence and dropped. He struck a patch of weeds on his back, knocking the breath out of him, and then the Rottweiler flung himself at the fence, his teeth inches from Larsen's face. Larsen was very grateful that the fence was more resilient than the picture window.

He struggled to his feet, using the garbage can for support, and shuffled as quickly as he could toward his car. The dog followed him along the fence, making awful beast noises, while Larsen struggled to get breath into his body. As he crossed the alley, he heard a distant, crackling voice from his breast saying, "Security, security, security," then, "Mayday, mayday, mayday."

Larsen reached his car with his keys in his hand, but he did not need them to open the door. The driverside window had been smashed, and the radio was gone. He immediately regretted that he had not yet found the time to install an alarm in the car.

He started the Mustang and, sucking in deep breaths, drove as slowly away as the adrenaline pumping through his veins would let him.

CHAPTER

40

Larsen was driving back along the beach when his radio crackled again. "Buy you a cup of coffee, boss?"

"I could use it," Larsen said into the radio.

"I'm at the Beach Diner; I'll order you a cup."

Larsen looked up and saw the diner, with Danny's black car parked outside. He pulled into the parking lot and found Danny sitting in a booth with two cups of coffee.

"Sounded like all hell broke loose," Danny said. "I expected to be bailing you out by now."

"All hell is a fair description," Larsen said, exhibiting his mangled jeans.

"You shouldn't wear such good jeans," Danny said. "A cheaper pair would have torn away."

"I'll consider that the next time I do some second-story work," Larsen said. "By the way, did I hear you broadcast *both* warning signals?"

"You sure did. When the alarm went off I started driving, and as I came around the corner the cops passed me going the other way, and a second later, the gray van went by, too. I can see how the cops might have been in the neighborhood, but how did Parker get there so fast?"

"His alarm system warned his office, and he probably has a car phone. He must have been nearby."

"He'll know someone has broken in now, and he'll suspect you."

"Maybe not; that neighborhood has more than its share of burglars. By the time I got back to my car the radio was gone."

"This has not been a profitable day," Danny said.

"I wouldn't say that." Larsen told him what he had seen in the house. "Everything there reinforces Parker as Admirer, even if it isn't enough for a bust."

"Is it always so tedious, being a cop? Isn't it ever easy to arrest somebody?"

"Very often it is. Mostly we deal with repeat offenders, and they can be easy to trace. Also, we get a lot of convictions on information from informants. Parker is the toughest kind of perp—no record, which means nothing is known about him, and very bright. And, if he fits the usual stalker profile, he has the advantage of believing that what he is doing is perfectly all right. He has nothing to feel guilty about."

"You mean he's crazy?"

"Not in the sense you mean. Look at Parker—he's a functioning, even successful member of society, has his own business. Not only that, he's a *trusted* member of society. He's in and out of people's homes all the time. It would be tough to get a jury to convict him on anything but the most damning evidence. Certainly he's warped in some way. I wouldn't want to live his personal life."

"Such as it is. You think he does anything in his off time except bug Chris?"

"Probably not, and he does it even while he's working. Remember, a lot of what's happened to Chris has occurred during business hours. His work takes him all over, and he can come and go as he pleases. He also has skills that help him: he can bug a telephone, wire a house, disable a car, scan police radio frequencies. So far, he's anticipated me every step of the way, except maybe this morning. And I have a feeling that anybody who's as paranoid as he is isn't going to think that an ordinary burglar set off his alarm this morning."

"In that case, shouldn't you be worried?" Danny asked.

"Oh, I don't think he'll come after me."

"Why not? He doesn't seem to give a damn what the police think of him, and you've invited him to look over your house—that was a smart move—you've made it easy for him."

Larsen felt himself blushing. "I guess it wasn't the smartest move to let him in my house, but I wanted his prints badly, and I got them."

"A lot of good it did you."

Larsen blushed again. "You're sounding more and more like the chief of detectives."

"I don't mean to be critical, Jon, I'm just trying to figure out what we can do about this guy, short of taking him somewhere and putting a bullet in his head."

"Put that thought out of your mind," Larsen said.

"Look, I know we're not going to do that, but I still like thinking about it."

Larsen laughed. "If Parker had any idea what kind of a guy you are he'd be on his way to another state."

Danny's face changed.

"What are you thinking?"

"He doesn't know what kind of a guy I am, does he? He thinks I'm your regular faggot hairdresser, and that I'll fold like a lily if he blows on me."

"Probably."

"You know, when I was in the navy—this was in my extreme youth—and some musclehead from the ship started hassling one of my gay mates, I'd put myself in the way. He'd think I was another wilting pansy, so I'd sucker him in and beat the shit out of him with a pipe, or sometimes whittle on him a little bit."

"Jesus, Danny, now *I'm* scared of you."

"My point is, he's already had one shot at me, and he figures I got lucky. Why don't we persuade him to take another shot?"

"That could be very dangerous, Danny."

"I don't mind being bait, not if it gives me first dibs on this guy."

"Danny . . ."

"I'll bet he's a homophobe; bet it would drive him completely nuts if somebody put his hand on his knee."

"Danny . . ."

"I'm liking this more and more."

"Danny, you've got a hurt leg."

"Oh, yeah, I forgot."

They were both quiet for a while, sipping their coffee. Frustration was thick in the air.

"Maybe there is a way to smoke him out," Larsen said.

Danny shrugged. "As Ross Perot likes to say, I'm all ears."

41

Mel Parker got to work late the following morning; he'd had to wait for the guy to come and install the new window—this time with divided windowpanes and a steel frame. He'd had to spend some extra time with Buster, too. The dog was high-strung, and his experience the day before had unsettled the huge animal badly. Still, his security system had worked, and nobody had gotten inside. He wondered how the hell anybody could get away from the dog alive. He wondered, too, if the intruder might have been more than a burglar.

Parker started his day by checking the alarm calls from the night before. Only three, a good night. He called each of the customers and ascertained whether there had been a break-in or a false alarm: all three had been false alarms. He counseled them on how to prevent this circumstance in the future, and told them that he was always available if they needed more schooling on how to operate their security systems.

He then checked the call-in responses from his ads in the *Los Angeles Times* and *Los Angeles* magazine. Only a couple today; sometimes there were as many as a dozen. Business was very nearly booming. He called them back and made appointments for the afternoon, since he didn't have to do an installation today.

He looked at his schedule for the past week and saw that there was one sales call he hadn't followed up on—the cop. That had been an awkward encounter, and he hadn't liked it; he had no intention of calling him back. He'd let the cop make the next move, if any.

His morning went well, until the mail came. He separated the bills and put them in the bookkeeper's out box, then picked out the checks and set them aside for deposit later that day. Then he came to a plain, square envelope with no return address. He turned it over; it was postmarked L.A., and it was addressed to him in childlike block capitals.

He opened it and read the message inside, which seemed to have been written in crayon or lipstick. It read, in its entirety:

I KNOW ABOUT YOU.

Sweat broke out on his forehead and under his arms. He turned the page over and looked at the back. Nothing. He examined the envelope again. Cheap dime-store paper. What the hell?

He had been very, very careful. He had never been so careful in all his life, and now this? Somebody knew? Who knew? Who could possibly know? He had been too careful for *anybody* to know.

In his mind he went over every step he had taken, every move he had made, and it was seamless, absolutely seamless. He had fooled them all, and he had made it stick.

And now this. Somebody knew.

He got up from his desk and walked to the plate-glass window that let him look down into his operations room. Below him sat four operators, looking at their computer screens and drinking coffee. An alarm came in, and one of them took it. Parker reached back to his desk and pushed a button on his phone so he could hear it.

A phone was ringing; a woman answered.

"Hello, this is Keyhole Security," an operator was saying.

"Oh, hello; I'm afraid I did something to the alarm," the woman said nervously.

"May I have your code, madam?" the operator asked.

"Oh, the code, damn it, what is it?"

"I'll have to have the code or call the police, madam."

"It's . . . oh, shit, Harry has told me half a dozen times—please don't call the police, he'll give me hell."

"I'm sorry, madam, for your own protection I'll have to have the code or call the police."

"Rover! No, Bowser, that's it, Bowser!"

"That's correct, madam. Your alarm will reset itself now. Please call us if you have any problems."

Parker switched off the phone's speaker and looked at the operators. Could one of them have found out something? Or somebody on one of the other two shifts? These people saw him more often than anyone else.

A buzzer signaled someone at the front door. An operator looked through the peephole, then answered it, received some sort of package, and signed for it. He was coming upstairs.

There was a knock on his office door.

"Come in."

"Package for you, Mel," the man said.

"Thanks." Parker waited until the man had gone, then set the box on his desk and opened it. A dozen roses. He found the little envelope with the card.

I KNOW WHAT YOU DID.

Parker sat down, grabbed a Kleenex from the box on his desk, and wiped his perspiring face. His hands were trembling.

He could lose the business. All that work, and it could go right down the tube. He got up and began pacing back and forth, back and forth, like some caged animal, trying to think how this could have happened, trying to find his error.

But he could not find it. It was all seamless, it really was, it was perfect, perfect.

But why this? Why now? Who could possibly know? He sat asking himself this question over and over. He rested his head on a cradle of his arms, as he had done in school so many years ago.

"Sweet and low, sweet and low, wind of the western sea," the teacher had sung while they napped and rested. It was soothing remembering that, back when he was another person, before all the trouble started.

He raised his head and looked at the card again.

DEAD EYES

I KNOW WHAT YOU DID.

Could it be the cop? How could the cop possibly know? It couldn't be the cop, but he would find out who it was, and he would make him sorry.

CHAPTER

42

Danny sat cross-legged on the floor of Chris's study, using one of her lipsticks to write notes to Parker. "How about 'I'M GOING TO EXPOSE YOU'?"

"I like it," Chris said. "Do another one."

"How about, 'YOU'RE GOING TO EXPOSE YOURSELF'?"

The two of them roared with laughter.

"Oh, God," Chris said, wiping away a tear. "I don't remember the last time I laughed like this."

"It's about time we had the laugh on him," Danny said.

The phone rang, and Chris picked it up. "Hello?"

"Hi, it's Jon. Any reaction?"

"None. Oh, we haven't received any roses today—not yet, anyway."

"That's something, at least. What we need now is some sort of excuse to get you and Parker in the same place in public."

"That's easy," Chris said. "The Malibu house is near-ly finished, and next week I'm going to throw a party for all the people who've worked on the construction."

"Perfect! He won't suspect a thing."

"What do you plan to do?" Chris asked.

"I'm still working on that," Larsen said. "Just make sure you invite Parker."

"Mike Moscowitz is doing the inviting; I'm buying the beer."

"I'll talk to Mike; he knows I suspect Parker, and I don't want him excluding the guy."

"I'll leave it to you, then."

"Dinner tonight?"

"Love to."

"I'll come get you after work; see you then."

Larsen hung up and began going through the material in his in box. There was a phone message from somebody called Helen Mendelssohn; the name was familiar. He called the number and got an answering machine.

"Hello, this is Helen; please leave a number, and I'll call you back."

"This is Jon Larsen, returning your call." He left his number and hung up. Who the hell was Helen Mendelssohn? He couldn't remember.

He opened an interoffice envelope and pulled out a plastic sheet with three fingerprints on it. At the top was Parker's name. He looked idly at the prints and thought about them. When he had run the print from the Millman guest house, he hadn't turned up anything, because the owner didn't have a record, so he had thought Parker didn't have a record. He'd have had to be printed by the Santa Monica police when he applied for a license to operate a security business. There was a gap here he hadn't closed.

He took a sheet of stationery and wrote on it:

Elgin—I'd appreciate it if you'd run these prints as anonymous and see what we turn up.

Larsen

He put the prints back into the envelope, walked it over to the fingerprint department, and left it on Elgin's desk.

When he got back to his desk, the phone was ringing. "Hello?"

"Jon, it's Danny; I think you'd better come over here."

"What is it?" He could hear Chris crying in the background. "What's happened to Chris?"

"She's all right, but I'd rather not explain on the phone."

"I'll be there as soon as possible."

Larsen did something he rarely had occasion to do: he put the flashing light on top of the car and drove very fast down Sunset to Stone Canyon. He took the light off a block before Chris's house, but he didn't slow down.

He ran up the front steps and walked into the house without ringing the bell. A cardboard gift box was on the floor beside the door, and Larsen stopped. This must have been what upset Chris. He tucked a finger under the lid and lifted. A pair of eyes stared at him from the box.

It was the severed head of a dog, a small mutt of some kind, he thought. He closed the box and went into the study. Chris had stopped crying and was sitting in her usual chair looking drained.

"Hi," Larsen said.

Danny got up. "Come with me."

"I've seen it." He went and knelt beside Chris's chair. "It was for shock value, that's all; it doesn't mean anything."

She seemed to relax. "Thank God. I didn't know what to think. The idea that he would *kill* some living thing in order to shock me. It's really disgusting."

"I'll get rid of it," Larsen said. With his head, he motioned Danny to follow him. Larsen put the box in the trunk of his car, then turned to Danny.

"It's a death threat," Larsen said.

"That's what I thought," Danny replied. "Did we push him too hard?"

"Maybe. Can you take a few days off from work?"

"I don't have a job for another ten days; I'll turn down anything new."

"Thanks. I think one of us should be with her at all times, and armed."

Danny patted his trousers pocket. "It's loaded."

"I think you should ask Melanie to stay at home, too."

"How long?"

"Let's say until after the party for the house-builders."

"You think this is coming to a head?"

"If it isn't, we'll try to bring it to one at the time of the party."

Danny handed an envelope to Larsen. "Will you drop this in a mailbox for me?"

Larsen looked at it. "Sure. What does it say?"

Danny told him.

"That's appropriate."

"I've arranged to have some more roses delivered, too."

"Can't hurt."

"I hope it does."

CHAPTER

43

P arker was opening the mail, and when he got to the plain, square envelope he began to shake. He ripped it open and read the message.

YOU ARE DISGUSTING.

Parker cringed as a thought struck. There was a knock on his office door.

"Package for you, Mel," a voice said.

He went to the door and took the box. He already knew what it contained, but he had to open it; he couldn't help himself. The roses were there; another note, too.

FILTH LIKE YOU DOESN'T DESERVE TO LIVE.

Parker winced. He opened his office door and threw the flowers down the stairs.

Downstairs, four operators raised their heads from their computers and looked at the window of Parker's office.

He went back inside and closed the venetian blinds, then sat down at his desk. He began to weep. What did these people want from him? He'd never hurt anybody, not really. Why were they doing this to him?

Larsen was at his desk when Elgin walked in with the results of his fingerprint search. He tossed an envelope onto the desk. "Go figure," he said, and walked out.

Larsen opened the envelope and removed the report. The fingerprints belonged to one James Melvin Potter. Who the hell was Potter? Go figure, indeed.

He turned to his computer, called up the records program, and entered the name.

Searching . . .

The computer stopped searching. On the screen appeared the face of a much younger Mel Parker.

James Melvin Potter had been convicted of child molestation and aggravated assault and sentenced to five to fifteen years. He had served his whole sentence without parole at an institution for the mentally ill in northern California and had been released three years ago, against the recommendation of the director of the institution. His present whereabouts were unknown, but he was believed to have left the state.

Admirer was Parker, Parker was Potter. And now Larsen had something on him, though not much. He had falsified his application for a business license, a misdemeanor. Larsen could turn him in to the Santa Monica police; his business license would be revoked, and he'd be fined; he'd lose his business, but he would still be on the street. Larsen badly wanted him to lose more than his business.

He found the number of the institution and asked for the director, whose name was Michaels.

"This is Dr. Michaels."

"Dr. Michaels, my name is Jon Larsen; I'm a detective with the Beverly Hills Police Department."

"How can I help you, Detective?"

"I'm calling about a former patient of yours, one James Melvin Potter."

"Ah, Jimmy, yes."

"His criminal record says that he served his sentence without parole and that you recommended against his release."

"That's quite true. I felt he wasn't ready to be returned to life in the community, but his sentence had been served, and he wouldn't consent to voluntary commitment."

"Why did you feel he wasn't ready to be returned to society?"

Michaels sighed. "He was in for molesting a small boy, and I felt that in his time here we helped him deal with that problem, that he wasn't likely to relapse."

"Then why didn't you want him to leave?"

"The young man was intensely paranoid, fearful of just about everything. We helped him a lot with that, too, but I felt we needed at least another year of treatment before he'd be fully functional."

"Suppose I told you that he was living alone in a large city and had started a successful business."

"What kind of business?"

"Security—burglar alarms, that sort of thing."

"I think he'd be ideally suited to such work," the doctor said. "He was always brilliant with technical things; our maintenance staff hated to see him go. And what more could one ask for when paranoid about the security of one's home than a true paranoid, someone who'd do the worrying?"

"You have a point, I guess. Do you think that Potter might be dangerous?"

"Not to children, I'd say. I can't think of him as being dangerous to anyone but himself, unless he felt himself seriously threatened."

"What kind of threat?"

"Almost any kind—physical, of course; he'd certainly fight back. But he could have all sorts of difficulties with anyone he thought meant him ill."

"Could he become violent in such a circumstance?"

"Certainly. Mind you, he might go along apparently normally for years before such an explosion occurred."

"Would his mental condition improve, back on the street?"

"Unlikely, without extensive therapy, and although I recommended a man to him, he would have none of it. You have to understand that such a personality could function quite well when he did not feel threatened. It doesn't surprise me that Jimmy could operate a business; he was very bright."

"I believe he may be involved in the obsessive harassment of a young woman," Larsen said.

"Really? That's very surprising," Michaels said. "Jimmy's sexual orientation was ambiguous, but certainly the tendency was toward homosexuality. People like Jimmy rarely form attachments of any kind, let alone obsessive ones. Society would tend to see him as a neuter."

Larsen didn't know what to say.

Michaels stepped in. "Of course, untreated, his illness could exhibit new permutations," he said.

"Thank you, Doctor," Larsen said, and hung up. He didn't know what to think.

CHAPTER

44

Jack Berman was on the phone, and he was brimming with good news. "Chris, it was an inspiration to send it to Jason Quinn and Brent Williams; they both love it."

"I'm so glad," she said. "Will they take the meeting?"

"Three this afternoon, at your house."

"Great."

"Tell me, why did you want to send it to these two guys, after they way they dumped you from the western?"

"Because they're both right for it. Jason will be good as the doctor, and Brent's best work has always been on a smaller scale."

"Not many people in this town can let bygones be bygones for the sake of a project. You're a real pro, kid."

"Thanks, Jack. I hope you'll be here, too. I want you to produce."

"I'd love to; it's been a long time."

"It's like roller-skating; you never forget how."

"I hope you're right. See you at three."

Chris began to work on not being too excited; it wasn't a good idea to get too excited before a meeting like this one.

Larsen sat in the Mustang across the street from Keyhole Security and waited. He had been waiting for most of the morning, and by the time Parker finally left the building and got into his van, Larsen had nearly dozed off.

He fell in a couple of cars behind the van as it drove west on Santa Monica Boulevard, then made a left and a right and continued on Wilshire. He followed the van into Brentwood and drove past the house where Parker stopped. He turned a corner, got out of the car, and, from behind a palm, watched Parker ring the bell and enter the house.

Parker was there for nearly an hour, probably a sales call, Larsen reckoned. When he left, he drove to a house in Beverly Hills, and this time he took his tool kit with him. Half an hour later, he pulled into a delicatessen on Melrose and had lunch. Larsen ate in his car and waited.

There were two more apparent service calls, one at a house, the other at a doctor's office, then the van pulled into a parking garage under an office tower on Wilshire. Larsen gave him two minutes to park and get out of the van, then drove into the garage. He went down two levels, looking for the van, and suddenly came up against a dead end. Turning quickly around, Larsen drove back through the garage, checking every parking space. The van had disappeared.

• • •

Chris greeted Brent Williams, the director, and Jason Quinn, the actor, in her study and introduced them to Danny. Both men already knew Jack Berman.

She was using this meeting as a rehearsal for looking directly at people, a habit she had lost since the damage to her sight. She could see their shapes well enough, and she concentrated on gazing at the point where she knew their eyes to be. She settled her guests and Danny took orders for coffee and soft drinks, then Jack called the meeting to order.

"Chris and I are delighted that you both like the script," he said. "Chris has asked me to produce her film, and this afternoon I thought we'd just talk informally about casting and where we might take the project."

Jason Quinn spoke up immediately. "I have what I think is a terrific idea," he said, "and I want to get the reaction of all of you."

"Go ahead, Jason," Jack said.

"Well, it's clear to me that the two leads are both potentially Academy nomination material, with the right people in the parts. Chris, I'm flattered that you thought of me, and I'm certainly very interested. But I think that the casting of the girl is critical; we need someone who's established, and yet who has a reputation for versatility and good dramatic work."

Chris warmed to this description of her abilities.

Jason continued, "I think we ought to send the script to Annette Bening."

There was a shocked silence in the room, which Quinn didn't seem to notice.

"I know she hasn't worked since the baby, and I think this project is just the sort of thing to bring her back. I think she'll love it." He looked around the room for a reaction.

Jack Berman broke the silence. "Jason, I think there's been some miscommunication here."

"What?" Quinn asked. "What do you mean?"

"Well, Chris has developed this project from scratch; she found the material, she optioned it, and she has adapted it."

"I'm aware of that," Quinn said.

"And I thought you were aware that she plans to play the role herself."

Quinn looked shocked, then embarrassed. "Oh," he said.

"I trust you have no objection to that," Jack said.

Quinn looked uncomfortable. "Well, I'm afraid I see the project in a different light." He turned toward Chris. "Chris, I hope you don't think this is a criticism of your work as an actress, but for strategic reasons, my agent and I don't feel I can be associated with this project unless the role of the girl is played by a major star, like Annette."

Chris started to speak, but he continued.

"I think that to play a blind person calls for something special in an actress, and I think Annette has that."

Chris could not help herself; she began to laugh.

Quinn bristled. "I did not intend that to be funny," he said. "I feel very strongly about this."

"I'm sorry, Jason," Chris said, "but there's an irony at work here that you're not aware of."

"I don't know what you mean," he replied.

"It's just that right now, I'm giving a performance; I'm playing the part of a woman who can see."

"Chris, I don't have the slightest idea what you're talking about."

"I mean that I'm acting. I can't see. I've been blind since my fall some time back, and although my vision has improved and I expect to recover fully, at this moment I can't see the expression on your face, although I can guess what it is—equal parts of surprise, irritation, and consternation, I would hazard."

Quinn made a sort of grunting noise.

Chris worked hard to keep the anger out of her voice. "Jason, I own this project, and although I have asked Jack to produce, I intend to exercise a considerable degree of control over the way it is developed, particularly over casting. The part of the girl has already been cast; she is to be played by me. But I understand your strategic concern for your career, and since you feel you need a major star to play opposite, then I don't think we need to take any more of your time."

Quinn grunted again, and she watched him get to his feet and start for the door.

"Oh, and Jason, would you please leave your copy of the script?"

She heard it hit the floor.

When he had gone Brent Williams was the first to speak. "Chris, I want to thank you," he said. "I've just spent ten weeks working with that arrogant, insensitive sonofabitch, and it delights me to hear somebody speak to him that way."

"Thank you, Brent."

Williams continued. "I want to say that I never saw anybody but you in the role, and the fact that your sight has been impaired reinforces my opinion."

Jack spoke up. "How do you think this project should be developed, Brent?"

"Well, if Jason had been involved I'd have wanted to go to Centurion with it, because they love him in the western. But since he's not, I think we should package it as a quality, low-budget film with a ready-made script and cast. In order to do that, of course, all the principals are going to have to defer compensation, but if the picture is a hit, and I think it will be, then we'll all do a hell of a lot better with profit participation than with big salaries."

"I agree," Chris said. "What do you think about the script?"

"I think it's basically right. I think it's a little too enclosed at the moment—it reads like a stage play made into a film. But I don't see any problem with opening it up visually and making it look good. I . . ."

Danny came into the room. "Excuse me, all, but you're going to have to get the hell out of here. The house is on fire."

Larsen sat at the parking-lot exit and looked up and down Wilshire. Parker had at least a five-minute start, and that meant he had no chance to find him in this city. Then he slapped his forehead. Of course. He slammed the Mustang into gear and roared out of the garage toward Bel Air.

When he arrived at Chris's house a fire truck was parked out front, and a column of black smoke was rising from a back corner of the house. He saw Chris standing on the lawn with Danny, safe. He reversed into a driveway and tore off down Stone Canyon; he drove up every side street looking for the van, but to no avail. The bastard had outsmarted him again.

CHAPTER

45

The three of them sat at Larsen's dining table and ate takeout Chinese food.

"... and I managed to throw some clothes out the window, and Brent got the cars out of the garage," Danny was saying. "That's all we saved."

"It was an old house," Larsen said. "It went up like tinder. I'm sorry you lost so many things, Chris."

"I feel stripped bare," Chris said. "Absolutely naked. Oh, hell, there wasn't a lot in that house that I would have moved to the new place, but what there was was stuff I've had for a long time—furniture, photographs, bound copies of scripts. Some of it I can never replace. Maybe I'm overreacting, but I feel as though everything has been taken from me."

Larsen reached for her hand, but the phone rang; he went to answer it and talked quietly for a few minutes, then came back to the table.

"That was the arson investigator from the fire

department; he found the remains of some sort of timing device and a detonator attached to a five-gallon can of gasoline."

"A timer?" Danny said.

"I don't think he meant for it to go off immediately; something must have gone wrong."

Chris put down her fork. "You mean he intended it to go off later, like while we were asleep?"

"Maybe," Larsen said.

"Oh, come on, Jon," she said. "He was trying to kill us."

"Possibly," Larsen said.

Danny spoke up. "I think it's time she knew."

"Knew what?" Chris demanded.

"Jon and I thought the dog's head was a death threat; we didn't want to frighten you."

"Well, I'm frightened now," she said, and she meant it.

"I think we have to treat it as attempted murder," Larsen said. "That's what my report is going to say."

"Christ, I hope this doesn't get into the papers," Chris said. "I don't need the industry aware of this while I'm trying to get a film financed. They'd never be able to insure the production, and you can't get anything made without completion insurance."

"I asked the arson man to keep the report under lock and key," Jon said, "and it won't get out of my office. If it gets reported at all it'll be as just a house fire."

"What about Parker?"

"I still can't touch him," Larsen said.

Danny leaned back. "Well, I can touch him."

"Danny, we've been through this already," Larsen said. "Going after Parker is not going to help."

"It would help me," Danny said.

"It wouldn't help either you or Chris."

"He's right, Danny," Chris said.

"Oh, all right," Danny said. "I won't blow the bastard away. Not yet, anyway."

The doorbell rang, and everybody jumped. Larsen stood up.

"Stay here," he said. He walked toward the front door, yanking the pistol from its holster as he went. He held the weapon at his side, switched on the front porch light, and opened the door a crack. "Yes?"

A uniformed man stood at the door, and another waited at the edge of the porch. "You Larsen?" he asked.

"That's right; who are you?"

"My name's Greer; a Mr,. Jack Berman arranged for some security here."

"Let's see some ID," Larsen said.

Both men produced a plastic card.

Larsen compared the photographs to the faces on his front porch; they matched. He opened the door and stepped outside.

"Jon?" Chris called from the living room.

"It's okay," he called back. "I'm going to be out-side for a minute. There's no problem." He turned to the security man. "You're not from Keyhole Security, are you?"

"No, sir; we're from Knight Guardian, in Beverly Hills."

Larsen knew the firm. "Okay, let's do it this way: one of you on the front porch in the light, so you can be seen; the other in the backyard."

"All right," Greer said. "Max, you go around back." He glanced at his watch. "We'll have some relief at about four A.M."

"You fellows want some coffee?" Larsen asked.

"We've got some in the car," Greer replied. "Don't worry about us."

Larsen went back inside and left them to their own devices.

"Who was it?" Chris asked.

"Jack Berman has sent a couple of private cops to keep an eye on us tonight, and I must say, I think it's a good idea."

"What about after tonight?" Danny asked.

"I'm working on that," Larsen said. "One of my upstairs tenants is out of town for a week or so. I'm going to put you two upstairs for tonight, and in the same room."

"I'd rather sleep with you," Chris said.

Danny laughed. "So would I."

"The last time we slept here we got a big rock through the window, remember? If he tries anything tonight, it'll be downstairs, and he'll have me and the two guards to contend with. Tomorrow we'll find you some more secure quarters, until the Malibu house is finished."

"By the way," Danny said, "remember who installed the security system at Malibu?"

"I remember. The day after the party, we'll get a new security company on the job and disconnect Keyhole. A few new wrinkles in the system might be in order, too."

"Will that keep him out?"

"I hope we won't have to worry about him, but if we do, we can change the codes in the system and install additional equipment. That will effectively shut him out, I think."

"Do you have a security system here, Jon?" Danny asked.

"No. But we have the two guards, at least for tonight. Let's all get some rest; tomorrow we'll make some moves."

CHAPTER

46

Larsen hung up the phone and looked at the expectant faces of his houseguests. "Okay, I think we're in business."

"So where am I living?" Chris asked.

"You know the old Del Mar Beach Club on the beach in Santa Monica?"

"No," Chris said.

"I know the place," Danny said. "It was built back in the twenties, and it was a big hangout for the stars, especially the ones with beach houses—Douglas Fairbanks, Chaplin, that bunch."

"Right, Danny," Larsen said. "A few years ago it was taken over by the Pritikin Institute, which is a diet-and-exercise outfit. Anyway, a friend of mine is an assistant manager there, and he's arranged for the two of you to move into a suite on the top floor as Mr. and Mrs. Richard Hedger. It's very comfortable, and you'll have a view of the beach."

"How long do we have to stay there?" Chris asked.

"I think you should stay there until we've removed Parker from the scene, and I think we can do that at the construction party next week."

"Do we have to stay inside all the time?" Danny asked.

"I think you should, because Parker's business isn't all that far away, and he takes the road along the beach to work and back home every day."

"How are we going to get Chris over there without Parker seeing us?"

"I've got an idea about that," Larsen replied. "In a few minutes, you get into your car, Danny, and I'll take Chris to the Mustang through the kitchen entrance to the garage and tuck her down in the backseat. Then we'll leave, and he can't follow both cars. Chris, you give Danny a list of the things you need; Danny, you go shopping; I don't care where. Drive all over town, if you like."

"What are you and Chris going to be doing?" Danny asked.

"I'm going to drive around for a while, and when I'm certain nobody is on our tail, I'm going to take Chris to the hotel, through a service entrance at the side of the building. When you've finished your shopping, and you're sure you're not being followed, deliver your goods to the service entrance, then drive around some more and park your car in a lot just up the hill. You can see it from the hotel. Take a walk on the beach, make sure you're alone, then beat it back. The suite number is 1200; it's on the top floor on the beach side. We'll talk some more then."

"Okay," Danny said. "Chris, what do you want me to bring you?"

"Oh, get some jeans and sweaters, I guess, and a suitcase to put them in. You know what kind of makeup I use, and I think we ought to have something to read. Oh, and some pajamas and underwear. Neiman's has the stuff I like."

"And I was going to Frederick's of Hollywood," Danny said, shaking his head.

Larsen got Chris settled in the backseat of the Mustang, then put the top up.

"How long do I have to stay like this?" Chris asked, her voice muffled by the blanket he had put over her.

"A long time, so stop bitching; I gave you a pillow, didn't I?"

"But it's hot!"

"It won't be when we get rolling."

"Oh, all right."

Larsen pressed the remote control that opened the garage door, then started the car. He backed out into the street, past Danny, who was waiting with his motor running. Danny turned east, and Larsen went west. He drove down the beach, through Venice, then headed for Marina Del Rey, making a conscious effort not to look in the rearview mirror.

"You okay back there?"

"Better," she said.

"Hang on." He drove into the marina complex and found a drugstore. "I'll be right back," he said.

"You're leaving me here?"

"Not for long, and I'll always have the car in sight." He went into the drugstore and bought a couple of things for himself, then returned to the car. "I'm going to put the top down," he said quietly. "That way, if he's following us, he'll get the idea that I'm alone." He unlatched the top, stowed it, and snapped on the cover. "Beautiful day for a drive," he said, trying hard not to look around for a van or a motorcycle.

"Thanks, I needed that," she whimpered.

Larsen got back into the car and drove to Long Beach, stopped for gas, and bought some magazines.

"I have to go to the bathroom," she said from under the blanket.

"You should have done that before we left."

"I did, but I have to go again."

"You'll just have to hold it." He left Long Beach and drove into Orange County, using a random series of streets, and gradually worked his way back north, glancing only occasionally in the rearview mirror. He hadn't seen anything following them since they left Santa Monica.

Finally he got on the freeway and took the turnoff for Santa Monica. He drove down Santa Monica Boulevard and checked the parking lot at Keyhole Security as they passed. The van was parked in its usual spot. He made a few more random turns, drove in one side of a parking lot and out the other, then stopped and looked back. Nothing followed him out of the parking lot. He drove straight to the old Del Mar Beach Club, turned into the covered service entrance, then whipped the blanket off Chris. "We're home, kiddo," he said, laughing, as he helped her out of the car and onto the receiving platform. He walked her through the kitchen and took the service elevator to the twelfth floor. The key was in the door of the suite, as arranged.

"Well, it's sunny," Chris said, looking around at the shapes of the furniture.

"Walk around a little, and get the lay of the land,"

Larsen suggested. "The bedroom is to your left; twin beds, and the bath is to your left again."

Chris moved around the suite, feeling for furniture and locating the light switches. "Now that I can see more of the light I like a lot of it," she said.

There was a knock on the door. Larsen left Chris in the bedroom and closed the door, then drew his pistol and went to the door.

"It's me," Danny's voice said from outside.

Larsen let him into the room and helped him with his packages.

"Christ, I spent a fortune," Danny said. "You never realize what stuff costs until you have to buy a lot of it at once. Where's Chris?"

Chris came out of the bedroom and hugged Danny. "You didn't really go to Frederick's of Hollywood, did you?"

"No, but I got the sexiest stuff Neiman's had." He reached into a shopping bag and pulled out a dark wig. "And I got you a disguise," he said. "Got one for me, too; we can take walks on the beach."

"Oh, no, you don't," Larsen said.

"Listen, I can make her look like Ava Gardner; nobody will ever know."

"Well, all right," Larsen said reluctantly, "but do a good job, and go armed, both of you."

"Fear not," Danny said.

"Any problems, call me," Larsen said.

Danny held up a cellular telephone. "You can reach me on this."

Larsen wrote down a number on the back of his card and gave it to Danny. "This is my cellular number." He took Chris's hand. "You going to be all right?"

"Sure."

"Don't give this number to too many people," he said.

"Just Jack and Melanie."

"Good. By the way, you can eat in the dining room, but it's all no-fat, low-calorie stuff.

"Swell," Danny said, patting his flat belly. "I guess I'm a little overweight at a hundred and thirty-five."

"I'll bring back dinner tonight," Larsen said, "and you can do some shopping tomorrow. There's a little kitchenette through those doors."

"I think I'll send out for a pizza," Danny said.

"For God's sake, don't!" Larsen groaned. "The smell will drive the dieters nuts!"

He kissed Chris good-bye, took the service elevator down, and drove his car out of the loading bay, looking both ways. He didn't see anybody.

CHAPTER

47

He pulled up in front of an auto-painting shop and stopped. "$129.95 ANY CAR—DIAMOND FINISH," the sign said. He had seen the place advertised on TV. He didn't feel comfortable in it anymore. He thought about paint, and as he did, he glanced up the street and saw the Ford dealer's sign. Wouldn't hurt to look, he thought.

He drove up the street and turned into the lot; a salesman was at the van's door before he could get out.

"Afternoon," the man said. "Can I show you something?"

"Maybe," he said. "I've got this real nice Ford here, it's what, not quite a year old, got, let's see, thirteen thousand miles on the clock, and it's nice, you know? But I've been thinking, maybe it's a little grim for me, thinking I might paint it, put some windows in the back, fix it up a little."

"That's a lot of grief to go through when I've got two dozen beauties right over there," the salesman said, making an expansive gesture. "Why don't we see if there's something that catches your fancy?"

"Well, I'll take a look, but I don't want to get into a lot of money, you know?"

"Don't worry, I'll go easy on you."

The salesman hopped into the passenger seat and they drove half a block to a row of gleaming vans parked along the street.

"Something customized?" the salesman asked, pointing at a vehicle. "Fully equipped camper?"

"Nah."

"Something more austere?" the salesman asked, slapping another van on a fender.

"Something in between," he replied.

"Got three of a very nicely equipped number right over here," the salesman said, leading the way.

"That's more like it," he said, peering through the window of a dark blue van.

"Got four captain's chairs in leather, very nice."

"Do the rear chairs come out easily?"

"Yes, indeed, just pull a couple of pins, you can use 'em in your living room."

He opened the rear door and felt the carpeting. "Not bad." He walked around the van once, then read the list of equipment on the window sticker. "I wouldn't mind a decent sound system," he said.

"That one's got the top of the line, AM/FM stereo and tape, six speakers. I can do you a CD player for a little more."

"That wouldn't be cheap," he said.

"I'll make you a real good deal."

"Why don't you take a look at my van," he said, handing over the keys.

The salesman walked around the van, checked the mileage, then drove it around the block. After a few minutes of haggling, they made their deal.

"I'll give you cash, now."

"You got a loan on your van?"

"Nope."

"You got the title with you?"

"Yep."

"Then we'll have you out of here in fifteen minutes," the salesman said.

They went into the showroom, and he produced his title.

"Want it registered this way?" the salesman asked.

"Right. It's my business name."

"There's only a P.O. box. Want to give me a street address?"

"The box number is all you need."

He signed the documents, reached into a hip pocket of his jeans, extracted a folded stack of bills, and started counting.

"Exactly right," the salesman said, counting the money. "You always carry that amount of cash around with you? That's dangerous."

"I never met anybody who could take it away from me."

He got into the new dark blue van and drove away.

The salesman drove the gray van around back to the service department and got out.

"What's up?" the service manager asked.

"Just took one in trade. It's in good shape, but it needs cleaning up. Can you put somebody on it?"

"How's the interior?" the service manager asked, walking around to the rear of the van.

"Pretty good. It's only got, what, thirteen thousand miles on it."

The service manager opened the rear doors. "Shit, Harry, did you see this before?"

The salesman walked around to the back of the van and looked inside. "Goddammit!"

"Looks like he's been killing hogs back here. It's been shampooed, I guess, but shampooing wouldn't handle this."

"You think it was blood?" the salesman asked. "Should we call the cops?"

"Nah, if it's blood, it's from an animal, and I'm not about to get involved with the cops." He popped the snaps holding the carpet in place and yanked the whole thing out the back of the van. "You better go around to parts and order a new carpet for this thing before the Man sees it." He rolled up the soiled carpet and stuffed it into a large trash can.

"Shit," the salesman said, "that'll have to come out of my pocket, too."

"You should have done your job right," the service manager said. "I got no sympathy for you. I hope for your sake the rest of this thing's as advertised."

"I hope so, too," said the abashed salesman. He wondered what the hell that guy had been doing in the back of his van.

CHAPTER

48

Larsen arrived at his post late and looked for the gray van. It was not in the parking lot. This made him nervous until he reflected that there was no way Parker could know where he had Chris stashed.

He waited outside Keyhole Security until nearly lunchtime, then took out his pocket cellular phone and dialed the company's number. After all, he still had security business to discuss with Parker.

"Good morning, Keyhole Security."

" 'Morning, may I speak with Mel Parker, please?"

"Mr. Parker isn't in; may I take a message?"

"When do you expect to hear from him?"

"I'm not sure; he won't be in for a few days."

Larsen began to feel uneasy. "Out of town?"

"I don't really know; he called in this morning and just said that he wouldn't be in for a few days. Is there something I can help you with?"

"No, that's all right; I'll call back later." Larsen hung up the phone and immediately dialed Pritikin and asked for Suite 1200.

"Hello?"

"Chris, it's Jon. Everything okay?"

"Just fine; Danny's gone out for some groceries."

"Have you been out of the room at all?"

"Nope. Just been working on my screenplay."

"Good. I'll stop by a little later today." He hung up and thought for a minute, then he started the car and drove toward Venice.

He cruised down Parker's block twice and saw no sign of life at the house. This was as close as he could get; he wasn't about to go over the back fence again.

Suddenly there was nothing to do. He drove slowly back to Beverly Hills and went up to his office. There were a dozen phone messages on his desk, and he began returning the calls. Between calls he went to the coffee machine and noticed a hum of activity in Homicide. Another detective joined him at the machine.

"What's up?" Larsen said, nodding at the busy group of desks.

"A lady out for her morning run found a head up in one of the canyons," the man said.

"Just a head?"

"Yeah, a woman, apparently in her twenties."

"Got an ID?"

"You ever tried to ID a corpse from just the head?"

"I have to admit I haven't."

"Hope you never have to."

"What about dental records?"

"Well, the FBI doesn't keep a file on dental

records. There's an artist over at the morgue doing a drawing of the head now. We'll advertise that, and when somebody recognizes her, then we can run a check on the dental work."

"Well," Larsen said, "I don't guess you can run a picture of a head in the papers."

Chief of Detectives Herrera walked up. "How nice to see you in the office," he said to Larsen.

"I've been on surveillance," Larsen said.

"You haven't ID'ed that perp yet?"

"Soon."

"Swell," Herrera said. "When are you going to wrap this one?"

"Soon, I think."

"How long you been saying that?"

Larsen sipped his coffee and didn't reply.

Herrera walked away.

"He been on your back?" the other detective asked.

"Sort of."

"Watch him; he's a mean one."

"I'll do that," Larsen said. He tossed his empty cup into the trash can and went back to his office. The phone rang.

"Detective Larsen."

"Mr. Larsen, this is Herbert Mendelssohn."

There was that name again; Larsen struggled to place it.

"My daughter was having a problem with a stalker early this year."

Now he had it; Helen Mendelssohn had been one of his cases. "Of course, Mr. Mendelssohn; how is Helen?"

"Well, she hasn't heard from the guy in a while, or she would have called you."

Larsen remembered everything now. An anonymous admirer had sent her some small gifts and written some notes over a period of about a month, then the contacts had stopped. It was one of Larsen's inactive cases.

"I'm glad to hear that," Larsen said. "Is there something I can do for you or Helen?"

"Well, I'm not sure if I'm doing the right thing," Mendelssohn said. "I guess I'm supposed to call another department, but since we know you, I thought I'd just ask your advice."

"Of course."

"Helen's boss called me this morning and said she didn't show up for work. That's unlike her, so I went over to her apartment. I have a key, so I let myself in and had a look around. She wasn't there."

"Had anything been disturbed?" Larsen asked.

"No, the place was neat as a pin."

"Nothing unusual at all?"

"Well, there were some flowers there that had been delivered; still in the box, but no card. Normally, Helen would have put flowers in water right away. It's not like her to leave a dozen roses in a box and let them die."

Larsen felt a trickle of apprehension run down his bowels. "Well, I'll be glad to look into this for you, Mr. Mendelssohn."

"Thank you, I'd appreciate that. I've heard that the police don't take missing persons very seriously."

"Usually missing persons turn up without an investigation," Larsen said, "so we normally wait twenty-four hours before launching an investigation. But since I know Helen, and I agree, she isn't the type to just disappear, I'll be glad to check on it. Tell me, Mr. Mendelssohn, do you have a recent photograph of Helen?"

"Yes. We took some nice pictures at a barbecue last month. I think I can find them."

"Is your address still the same?" Larsen asked, looking in his drawer for the file on Helen Mendelssohn.

"Yes."

"I'm going to be out that way in a few minutes; I'll stop by and pick it up."

"Thank you, Mr. Larsen; I appreciate your attention to this. We're worried sick."

"I understand," Larsen said. "I'll be there in half an hour or so." He hung up the phone. "Long shot," he said aloud to himself, "but worth checking on." He had nothing else to do anyway.

CHAPTER

49

Larsen pulled into the Mendelssohn driveway and got out of his car. It was a beautiful house, warm and inviting. He recalled that Mendelssohn had retired a couple of years ago from his job as chief financial officer for one of the big studios.

Mendelssohn met him at the door with the photograph. "Will this do?" he asked. It was a good head shot.

"Fine," Larsen replied. "You said you had a key to Helen's apartment?"

"Yes. She left one with us for emergencies."

"Would you mind if I had a look at her place?"

"Sure, I'll come with you."

"That won't be necessary," Larsen said. "If you could just let me have the key."

Mendelssohn went back inside for a moment, then reappeared with the key. "Here's the key; you'll call me if you find out something?"

STUART WOODS

•

"Of course. And I'll get the key and the photo-graph back to you just as soon as I can."

The apartment was in a small upmarket condominium development up in one of the canyons. Larsen put the key into the lock and opened the door without touching the knob.

It was as Mendelssohn had said—very neat. It looked more like the show apartment for the development than a place where somebody lived. He guessed that the girl's parents had bought it for her. Helen Mendelssohn was, as he recalled, an apprentice in costume design, not the sort of work that paid for a place like this.

The roses were on the living-room coffee table; he lifted off the lid with his pen and looked for a card, but there was none.

Nothing else in the living room caught his attention; he entered the kitchen and walked around opening cupboards and examining their contents.

In the woman's bedroom the clothes were put away perfectly, and the bathroom was spotless. He was thirsty, and he went back to the kitchen for a drink of water; he found a glass and went to the refrigerator for some ice cubes. There was little in the fridge in the way of food, and on the bottom shelf was a familiar-looking box. Larsen slid the shelf out with his pen and flipped up the lid.

It was a cat's head this time, and suddenly Larsen felt sick about Helen Mendelssohn. He put the box back in the fridge and went back to his car, leaving the key under the doormat.

• • •

•
280

The trip was superfluous, really, but it had to be made. At the city morgue he showed his badge to an attendant. "I want to see the head picked up in Beverly Hills this morning," he said.

"Sure," the attendant replied. "Been a regular parade of folks in here this morning wanting to see it. You'd think nobody'd ever seen a head before. I turned down a hundred bucks from one of those supermarket tabloids that wanted to photograph it."

The Los Angeles morgue had not wasted an entire body slab on this case. The head was in a stainless-steel drawer in a cold room, wrapped in a sheet. The attendant unwrapped it almost tenderly, Larsen thought, and when the head was exposed he knew he didn't need the photograph; he remembered the face well.

"Can I use your phone?" he asked the attendant.

"Sure. You through with the head?"

"Yes. You can put a new tag on it; the name is Helen Mendelssohn." He spelled it for the man. "That's an official ID," he said. "I knew the girl, and there's no point in putting her parents through an identification."

"If you say so," the attendant said. "There's the phone."

Larsen called Beverly Hills Homicide and got the right detective on the phone. "This is Jon Larsen; I've got an ID on the head that turned up this morning."

"How the hell did you do that?" the detective asked.

"She was an inactive case of mine. I knew her, and I have a photograph from her parents. I've ID'ed her myself, so don't call them. I'll handle that part of it. And do me a favor, will you? Stop the artist's drawing from being released to the newspapers."

"Sure."

He gave the detective the address of Helen's apartment. "The key's under the doormat, so you won't have to break in. There's a cat's head in a box in the refrigerator, too; make sure you go over the box for prints."

"What's a catshead?"

"The head of a dead cat."

"Yuck. You know who did this, Larsen?"

"No, but it could be the same guy that's involved in another stalker case I'm working on." He hung up and walked slowly back to his car.

The Mendelssohns were glad to see him at first. He sat them down in the living room.

"Have you finished with the key yet, Mr. Larsen?"

"Not yet." He hesitated, then took a deep breath and plunged in. "I wish there were an easier way to tell you this, Mr. and Mrs. Mendelssohn; I'm sorry to have to tell you that Helen is dead."

There was an audible gasp from the girl's father, and the mother burst into tears.

Larsen waited for him to quiet her, then continued. "Her . . . remains were found up a canyon this morning, and the case is already being intensively investigated."

"Was it that stalker fellow?" Mendelssohn asked.

"I have reason to believe it was, but it may be a while before we know for sure."

"Do you know who he is?"

"Not for certain; we have some leads, though. I think he may be stalking another young woman."

"I hope you get the bastard," Mendelssohn said.

"We will, I promise you. Mr. Mendelssohn,

there's something else I have to tell you, however unpleasant it may be."

"What could be more unpleasant than what you've already told us?" Mendelssohn asked.

Larsen tried to look the man in the eye. "I'm afraid that only Helen's head has been found. They're still searching the canyon for the rest of her body."

Mendelssohn stood up and paced the room while his wife wept again. "These crazy people," he said. "You've got to get them off the streets."

"I know; we're trying. It won't be necessary for you to identify the remains; I've already done that. The coroner's office will contact you when Helen's body is ready for an undertaker."

Mendelssohn sat down next to his wife again and tried to comfort her.

Larsen stood to go. "There's going to be a lot in the papers and on television about this. I would suggest that you not talk to anybody but the police about what's happened. Your phone will be ringing a lot, so you might ask a friend or a relative to answer it for you. Also, there's a team going through Helen's apartment for evidence; it might be best if you didn't go there for a few days. Someone will return the key to you when they're finished."

Mendelssohn stood up and offered Larsen his hand. "Thank you for coming here personally to tell us," he said. "I'm grateful for that, at least."

"I'm very sorry for what's happened," Larsen said. "I hope we have a quick resolution."

Larsen sat in his car for a few minutes, trying not to cry. He hated to cry.

CHAPTER

50

Larsen drove absently toward Santa Monica, his thoughts on the head of Helen Mendelssohn and the pain of her parents. He felt glad that he had been able to tell them of her death before they read of it in the newspapers or, worse, saw it on television. He wondered: if he had done something differently in the case, would it have turned out differently? He thought not. He couldn't have stayed on a case when the stalker had ended contact. Or apparently so. Had Helen Mendelssohn continued to hear from him?

Certainly, she had received the roses and the cat's head. A cat's head in a box would frighten anyone; and what the hell was it doing in the refrigerator? Was she so obsessively neat?

Had Parker done this? If so, how did it connect with Chris's case? And why hadn't he told Homicide about Parker? He knew the answer to that one; they'd bust him in a hurry, and then they wouldn't be able to hang it on him. Parker would walk. And he didn't want Parker to walk.

He was nearly to the hotel, and he passed the parking lot. Danny's car wasn't there, and that meant that Chris was alone. He accelerated. Convinced that he hadn't been followed, he parked at a meter in front of the hotel, next to a dark blue van.

He ran up the steps and across the lobby to the elevator. He pressed the button and waited impatiently; he didn't like the idea of Chris being alone. Others, plump dieters dressed in sweat clothes, crowded into the elevator car with him, and stops were made on nearly every floor. Finally, on the twelfth, he hurried down the hall. As he approached the end he saw that the door stood ajar.

Alarmed now, he drew his pistol and held it near his right ear. Flipping off the safety, he edged along the wall toward the door, fearful of crossing the threshold. He stopped and listened for a moment, but all he could hear was a fluttering noise from inside the room. Taking a deep breath, he pushed open the door with a foot and stepped into the room, the pistol before him.

A window was open, and the curtains fluttered in the breeze. He moved into the bedroom, the pistol still ready, but no one was there. He checked the bathroom and the kitchenette; nobody.

Alarmed now, he ran down the hall. Unwilling to wait for the elevator, he took the fire stairs, descending as rapidly as he could without breaking a leg. At the bottom he shoved open the emergency door to the street, then, realizing the weapon was still in his hand, he holstered it.

He ran to the corner and looked both ways, toward the service entrance, then back toward the parking lot. No sign of her. He ran back up the street, noticing Danny's car parked at a meter near his, then around the corner of the building. A concrete walkway led to the beach, and he sprinted down it until he came to sand, then stopped and looked desperately around. A couple were on a blanket thirty yards away, basking in the late-afternoon sun and talking; the next cluster of people was a couple of hundred yards to his left, and he turned in that direction, trotting with difficulty through the loose sand. He stopped; someone had called out.

"Jon!"

He turned and the couple on the blanket were waving to him; he ran toward them, puzzled.

"Hello!" the woman called out.

He realized that they were Chris and Danny. "What the hell . . . ?" He sank to his knees on the sand, out of breath.

"What's wrong?" Chris asked. Her hair was black, and she was wearing huge sunglasses.

"I thought . . . " He couldn't find the breath to speak.

"You thought something had happened to us?" Danny asked.

Larsen nodded. "The door was open; you were gone."

"The maid needed to clean the room," Chris said, "so Danny disguised us and we went for a swim. We're perfectly all right."

"The maid must have left the door open," Danny said.

Larsen sank onto the blanket and lay on his back.

"I'm so glad you're all right," he said. "I was so worried."

"We're okay here," Danny said. "There's no way he can know."

"What's new?" Chris asked. "Any progress on Parker?"

Hardly, he thought. "No. He seems to have gone away; his office said he was out for a few days, and there doesn't seem to be anybody at the house. I'll check again tonight. I don't suppose he's getting your notes, Danny. Maybe that's why he's vanished."

"Oh, the hell with him," Chris said. "Let's go out to dinner tonight."

"Out?"

"Why not? You think Parker frequents good restaurants?" Danny asked.

"Maybe not," Larsen admitted.

"Let's go to Market Street." Chris asked. "The place that Tony Bill and Dudley Moore own. Dudley sometimes plays piano."

"Where is it?"

"In Venice."

"Oh, no; we're not going anywhere near Venice."

"Well, we're sure not eating at the Pritikin Hotel," Danny said. "I had a look at the food, and if I start eating there I'll waste away to nothing."

"I'll decide," Chris said firmly. "Let's go and get cleaned up, and I'll make a reservation somewhere. Trust me."

"I'll trust you," Larsen said. "God knows, we need a night out."

CHAPTER

51

Chris chose the Maple Drive Cafe, and Larsen liked it. They were given a booth at the rear, still in earshot of the piano, but nicely private.

They dined well and were into a second bottle of wine before Larsen began to relax and realize that he was having a good time. It seemed a very long while since he had had some pleasant experience that had not been interrupted by Admirer, and he devoted himself to enjoying it.

He was especially enjoying Danny, who was at once bitchy and funny. Danny knew everybody in town; he had done the hair of most of the important actresses, and he was greatly in demand by both the studios and the independents.

Larsen had known many homosexuals, some of them cops, but he had never had a friend who was gay, and he was enjoying his new one. Danny was affectionate, hilarious, and brave, and he was no threat to Larsen's relationship with Chris. Danny, in fact, seemed to take the role of a benevolent brother who wanted to see his sister happy, even if it was with a policeman.

Danny was telling a story about one of the old-time movie queens he'd known in her later years.

"I'd been working as an assistant to Robert Koenig, who was very big at the time, and Bobby was shacked up with some chorus boy and didn't make it to work, so there I was, trembling, wondering what the hell I was going to do with her hair, which was awful, take my word for it. I was about to suggest a wig when she looked at me in the mirror and saw that I was less than confident.

"She got up from her chair and turned around to face me—she was a head taller than me, of course. She reached down and took me by the lapels and just about hoisted me off my feet; then she gazed at me like a rattlesnake at a rabbit, and she said, 'Listen to me, you little faggot. Today we're shooting my only decent scene in this movie, and if you fuck up my hair I'll beat the shit out of you.' Then she sat down."

"What did you do?" Larsen asked.

"I didn't fuck up her hair," Danny said. "That little chat had a curiously calming effect on my nerves, and I made her look great. She would never let anybody else do her hair after that, and I used her patronage to leave Bobby and go out on my own. I don't care what anybody else says about her, she was a great lady."

Danny raised a hand for a waiter. "I'm buying; no arguments." He paid the check, and the three of them walked out of the restaurant arm in arm.

• • •

Back at Pritikin, Danny let them out of his car. "I'm going home," he said. "It ain't much, but my clothes are there, and besides, I haven't spent this much time in a bedroom with a woman since I left my mother. It's unnatural."

"You watch yourself," Larsen said quietly, so that Chris wouldn't hear him. "This isn't over yet."

"Don't worry, I'm still carrying," Danny said, slapping his pocket. "You kids enjoy."

The lobby was deserted, with not even a desk clerk in sight, and as Larsen rang for the elevator, he was so caught up with the thought of spending a night alone with Chris that he didn't notice the delivery box of flowers laying on the front desk.

Larsen put the chain on the door, and they began undressing in the living room, abandoning their clothes there as they worked their way toward the bed. Two people in one twin bed made it small, but they didn't let it bother them; Larsen was grateful to finally be alone in bed with Chris, secure from interruption. They made love sweetly, passionately, with tender regard and with abandon, and for the first time in his life Larsen understood the meaning of two people becoming one flesh; he could not tell where his body ended and hers began. They found release together, and Larsen was sure their cries could be heard a couple of floors down.

Chris wiped the sweat from his forehead and kissed it.

"Lower," he said.

She worked her way down his body and took him in her mouth. "Is this low enough?" she asked, pausing for a moment.

"Oh, yes," he said as she began again. He wouldn't have believed he could have two erections so close together, but there it was. He held her head in his hands, ran his fingers through her hair. He tried to pull her on top of him, but she wouldn't let go until he had come again.

She put her head on his shoulder. "How are you?"

"I can't make a fist," he replied.

"That's okay," she laughed. "You won't need to now."

"That's one I owe you," he said.

"And I'll collect, too," she said.

They fell asleep pressed against each other, oblivious to all else.

He didn't know what time it was when he woke, and at first he didn't know what had awakened him. Then he knew; it was the sound of a door latch operating. Opening or closing? He couldn't tell.

Slowly, so as not to awaken Chris, he slipped out of bed, tiptoed naked to the closed bedroom door, and pressed his ear against it. There was a sound, but he couldn't place it. Then he realized that his gun was in the living room with his clothes, and so was Chris's little automatic.

He heard the latch noise again, and he was almost certain he heard the outside door of the suite close. Very, very slowly he turned the bedroom doorknob and opened the door half an inch. He put his ear to the opening and listened hard. He could hear nothing but the wind off the Pacific rattling the windowpanes.

He opened the door a foot and looked into the living room, now lit by part of a moon. The room seemed empty. He stepped through the door, looking around him, ready to defend himself. His coat was on the coffee table, and the pistol was inside it, still in its holster. He freed the weapon and flipped off the safety, turning slowly around in the room, watching for any motion. He seemed to be alone.

He reached for a lamp on a small table and switched it on. The light illuminated the room sufficiently for him to notice the only thing that had changed. Near the door was a small chest of drawers with a mirror hanging above it. A tube of Chris's lipstick rested on the chest, and there was writing on the mirror in bright red.

YOU'LL NEVER GET AWAY FROM ME.
A.

Then he looked at the front door and saw that the chain was off the latch.

CHAPTER

52

Larsen sat and watched Chris sleep in the morning sunlight. When she showed signs of waking, he put the pistol back into its shoulder holster. She opened her eyes and felt for him.

"Jon?" she said sleepily.

"I'm over here," he said. "I woke up earlier than you, so I got dressed."

"Why didn't you wake me?"

"It was too early. Besides, I like watching you sleep; you're like a little girl."

She smiled. "I'm hungry."

"So am I. Come on, get dressed, and I'll buy you a good breakfast."

"We've got some cereal here," she said.

"I'm hungrier than that. Anyway, it's time we got out of this place."

"Where will we go?"

"Back to my house."

"He'll find us there, won't he?"

"I've begun to think that he'll find us anywhere, so what the hell? I'm going to stay with you from now on, so if he finds us, it's okay with me." It was, too. All he wanted was one clean shot at the bastard.

"Where are my clothes?" she asked, sitting up.

"On the other bed." He loved looking at her naked.

"Are you looking at me?" she asked.

"Yes."

"I think I like it."

"I know I do."

"Why don't you come back to bed for a while?"

"That's a wonderful idea, but I've got you all packed and ready to go. Let's make love where we belong, not in this place."

"Sounds good to me," she said, feeling for her clothes.

"I laid out some fresh things; I hope you'll approve of my choices."

"Let me guess: jeans and a T-shirt."

"You're clairvoyant."

"I'm without anything else to wear."

"We'll fix that; we'll get Danny to take you shopping properly."

"We're getting awfully bold, aren't we?"

"We're going to be bold from now on." The son of a bitch had been there when they were making love, and Larsen was going to find a way to kill him for it. Fuck probable cause.

He stopped for some things at a little grocery store and then drove home. The house seemed as they'd left it; Chris's Mercedes was parked at the curb. He should have put that in the garage, he thought; it was lucky no one had broken into it.

He made scrambled eggs and smoked salmon for them, opened a bottle of champagne, and mixed it with orange juice. They both ate greedily.

Larsen thought about Admirer's uncanny ability to find them wherever they were, and he decided there was nothing uncanny about it. While Chris did the dishes he went into the garage and flipped on the lights. He slid his shop jack under the Mustang, hoisted it a few inches, put steel supports under the axle, then lowered the car until it rested on the supports. He got a work light on a long cord, plugged it in, and stretched out on his back on the creeper that allowed him to work under the car.

He didn't find it at first. A cursory examination of the car's underside turned up nothing; then he did the job more carefully, and he found it stuck magnetically to the body—just a little plastic box with a short antenna. He pushed out from under the Mustang and then performed the same search under the MG, with the same result. He backed the Mustang into the drive, pulled it to one side, then went back into the house.

"Where are your car keys?" he asked. "I think your car ought to be in the garage."

She pulled them from her pocket and tossed them in his direction. "Thank you."

He drove the Mercedes into the garage and made another search. Another black box. No doubt there was one on Danny's new car as well.

He turned off the garage lights and went back into the house.

"Does it still have a radio?"

"Listen, this is a decent neighborhood, not like Bel Air."

"Sure; I'm lucky it still has axles." She looked reflective. "I wonder if I'll ever drive it again."

"Don't even think about it," he said. "You'll be driving in no time."

"This morning I stood at the window at the hotel, and for a moment I thought I could see the horizon."

"Maybe you did see it."

"I thought I had it in focus for just a second, and then I couldn't get it again."

"Relax, and you'll get well sooner." He left her in the living room, went into his little book-lined study, and made a phone call to a man he knew who specialized in exotic electronics.

"Jim, it's Jon Larsen; how are you?"

"I'm okay, Jon. What's up?"

"I found a bug on my car."

"Sound or location?"

"Location. Maybe sound, too; I haven't looked that thoroughly."

"What do you want to do about it?"

"I want to be able to disable it at will, without actually removing it."

"You mean you want it to work sometimes, but not others?"

"That's right."

"It has an antenna?"

"Yes."

"You're fairly handy, as I remember."

"Yep."

"You want to get a second output to the antenna; you follow?"

"What kind of output?"

"Doesn't matter, but the radio will do fine. Here's

what you do: you mount a switch on your panel somewhere, then you run a wire from the switch to a speaker wire and from there to the antenna of your bug. Then, when your radio is on, all you have to do is flip the switch, and you'll get output from the radio into the bug antenna. What that'll do is screw up the signal the guy's receiving; he'll be getting more signal than he wants, and it'll screw him up, whether he's tracking you on a CRT screen or, more likely, if he has some sort of handheld radio direction finder. Got that?"

"I've got it," Larsen said. He hung up, went back to the garage, and found some wire and some switches in his tool chest, then went to work. The Mustang no longer had a radio, of course, so he concentrated on the MG and Chris's Mercedes.

CHAPTER

53

D anny picked up Larsen and Chris later in the morning, and they went shopping. Chris and Danny combed Rodeo Drive, plus Saks and Neiman's, while Larsen hung back a few yards and watched their backs.

They had lunch at the Bistro Garden, then Chris wanted to buy furniture, so they did Melrose Avenue and the decorators' shops. She needed the most basic things, like beds, so by the time they had finished, the shops were closing. They had an early dinner at Valentino's, then drove back to Santa Monica, walked through the pedestrian district, and found some dessert. It was well after dark when, exhausted, they returned to Larsen's house, where Danny dropped them, then went back to his own home. Larsen didn't tell him about the bug on his car; there was time for that, if it became necessary.

Larsen unlocked the front door and helped Chris in with her packages.

"What's that smell?" she asked.

"What kind of smell?"

"Like a roadkill or something."

"Your sense of smell is better than mine," he said, switching on a light. He started to take the packages to the bedroom, then stopped. There was someone seated at the little writing desk in the living room.

"What's wrong?" Chris asked.

"Nothing's wrong," he said, steering her toward the bedroom.

"Jon, I can tell by the way you stopped and by your voice. What is it?"

"I've just remembered that I have to meet with some other cops here. Come on, you're exhausted; let's get you into bed, and we'll try not to keep you awake."

He settled her in the bedroom and went back to the living room, closing the door behind him. She was sitting at the desk, neatly dressed, her legs crossed, hands folded in her lap, handbag sitting on the floor beside her. He picked up the telephone.

"This is Larsen; get me Martinez in Homicide."

"He's gone for the day," the dispatcher replied.

"Patch me through to him at home," Larsen said. "It's urgent."

Martinez sounded sleepy. "Yeah?"

"Al, it's Jon Larsen; I think you'd better come over to my house. The rest of Helen Mendelssohn has turned up."

Martinez was wide-awake now. "Where?"

"In my living room. You want to get over here with a full team as soon as possible?" He gave the detective his address.

"I'll call everybody, then I'm on my way."

"I guess we'd better call Santa Monica Homicide, too. Will you handle that?"

"It's our call," Martinez said. "Why do we need them?"

"Part of the victim is on their turf. We'd better do it by the book."

"Yeah, okay." Martinez hung up.

Larsen put down the phone and walked around Helen Mendelssohn's body. The long nails were painted a bright red, and two of them were broken; it was wearing jewelry, even; it was dressed in a business suit and seemed ready to go to work, except for the absent head.

He went back into the bedroom to be sure Chris was all right.

She was nearly asleep. "You coming to bed soon?"

"I'll be a while; you go to sleep."

"Mmmm. Okay."

He left her and went back to the living room to wait with Helen Mendelssohn for the cavalry to arrive.

54

They came in force—Beverly Hills Homicide, the medical examiner, a photographer, an ambulance with two attendants, and, finally, Santa Monica Homicide. Larsen kept them as quiet as he could.

"Okay, Jon, we're all here now," said Martinez. "What the hell is this about?"

"I told you I was working a stalker," Larsen said.

"Yeah, now tie it all together for me," Martinez said.

The Santa Monica man spoke up. "Yeah, tie it all together for me, too. You can start by telling me what the fuck you guys are doing working a homicide on my turf."

Martinez turned to the man. "The homicide occurred on *my* turf the night before last, and we've got the head down at the morgue with our tag on it, okay?"

"Well, we've got a lot more than a head," the Santa Monica man said. "We've got legs and arms and a torso, and that's a hell of a lot more than a head."

"It didn't happen here," Larsen explained. "It happened in Beverly Hills, so it's our case. Jurisdiction comes down where the crime is committed."

"Says who?" the Santa Monica man asked.

"Listen," Martinez said, "we called you in as a courtesy, because we're courteous guys. Now if you can't be courteous, get the hell out of here."

"My chief . . ."

"Fuck your chief and the horse he rode in on, pal; we're working this case, and you had better start getting used to the idea. Now, you want to be embarrassed in front of your chief, you bring him over here, and I'll embarrass you."

"Okay, okay," the Santa Monica detective said, holding up his hands. "You work it, I'll watch; you screw it up, and I'll go get my chief."

"Good. Now, Jon, you were going to tie this together for me."

"Right. I'm working a stalker case, anonymous, bothering a young woman for some time now—flowers, notes, then, recently, it got more serious—picture of open-heart surgery and a dog's head in a gift box."

"A real dog's head?"

"Right. And now there's flowers and a cat's head in Helen Mendelssohn's apartment, so I think we've got the same MO going."

"Sounds that way," Martinez agreed. "You've got a lead on the guy, you said."

"A lead, and that's all; it's very tenuous. What it boils down to is we *think* the perp, who styles himself Admirer, drives a gray Ford van and a red motorcycle. My complainant is building a house, and one of the subcontractors has the same van and all the skills necessary to do what Admirer has been doing. I've been surveilling him, and he lost me right before he burned down the lady's house. But I can't prove it was him, and I don't have probable cause to arrest him."

"Why don't we have a talk with him?" Martinez said.

"If you do that, Al, he's going to pull back into his shell, and we'll have nothing but a bad arrest. I want him free to make a mistake, so I can nail him."

"He's also free to do this again," Martinez said, nodding at Helen Mendelssohn's corpse.

"I have a theory about that," Larsen replied. "I think he got frustrated dealing with my complainant, and he killed Helen Mendelssohn to relieve the pressure. I think he'll be okay for long enough for me to make the case."

"That's a dangerous theory," Martinez said. "Can you imagine what the chief is going to say to us if the guy decapitates another woman?"

"Listen, Al, what did you find in Helen Mendelssohn's apartment?"

"Not a fucking thing."

"Right, and you're not going to. This guy is very, very bright, and he hasn't made a mistake yet. You're just not going to get a good bust right now, and that's it."

"So what makes you think he's going to make a mistake sometime soon, if he never makes mistakes?"

"I'm setting something up, and in a few days I think I'll have him."

"You been surveilling this guy alone?"

"That's right."

"Well, the least I can do is pitch in; maybe we can make the surveillance wall-to-wall."

"That would be great, Al, but he's disappeared. He called in to his business and said he'd be out for a few days, and I haven't been able to put him at his house. Last night he was in a hotel where my complainant was staying, so he's around somewhere; he just seems to have gone to ground."

"What's his name?" Martinez asked.

"I'm going to hang on to that for the time being," Larsen said. "I don't want him rousted until I'm ready."

"That's a lot of responsibility to take, Jon. Sure you don't want some help?"

"Do I get to say exactly how much help?"

Martinez sighed. "Okay, you call it."

"And Herrera doesn't hear about it?"

"And Herrera doesn't hear."

"Okay, his name is Melvin James Parker, aka James Melvin Potter. He did time for child molestation and was released three years ago. He changed his name and started a security business, and some way or other he got past the fingerprint check"—he turned to the Santa Monica detective—"which should have been done by the Santa Monica department. I tried to get somebody there to dig out the original application, but no luck; it's in long-term storage."

"I can put a guy on his house and his business," Martinez said. "This is an important case."

Larsen gave him the two addresses. "He moves around a lot, installing and servicing alarm systems, and he's as cunning as a sewer rat. You're going to have to have two cars on him, or he'll make the surveillance."

"I can only spare the two guys, but these two addresses aren't too far apart; when he goes on the move, one can call the other in."

"Fine, and don't mess with his house; he's got the biggest dog you ever laid eyes on—a real monster."

"Okay, no B & E," Martinez said.

The medical examiner approached the group.

"What have you got for me?" Martinez asked.

"From the looks of it, the body was stripped before the decapitation took place and then dressed again; there's not a drop of blood on any of the clothing. The body's been refrigerated, so I can't give you even an approximate time of death. There are a couple of broken nails, so she may have put up a fight; there's nothing under any of the nails, though; she's clean as a whistle."

"Could he have scrubbed her down?" Martinez asked.

"Wouldn't be surprised."

Larsen broke in. "That would line up with the rest of his MO—super careful."

Martinez turned to Larsen. "I don't suppose you've got a motive."

"Yeah, I have; I think he killed her to piss me off."

"*What?*"

"I've been covering the other case very tightly, and I've gotten in his way. Helen was an old target of his, one he'd dropped for some reason, but he figured I had been on the case. That's why he left the body here; he wants to piss me off."

"A very strange motive," Martinez said. "Did it work?"

"It sure did," Larsen said. "I don't know when I've been more pissed off."

The Santa Monica detective spoke up. "Tell you what, you guys work this one. I'm outta here."

55

They were having breakfast at Larsen's house, and Larsen was groggy from lack of sleep. The cops hadn't left until after one o'clock, and he hadn't slept well; he'd kept waking up, thinking there was a headless corpse in his living room, then remembering that it had been taken away.

"I'd like to go out to the house today," Chris said. "The party's tomorrow night, and I move in the following day, so I want to see how Mike is coming along. Will you take me?"

"Sure. I had planned to spend the day with you anyway."

"Not at work?"

"I am at work, and it's nice work if you can get it."

"I'm glad you think so."

Larsen was thinking ahead: the Mustang's bug

hadn't been dealt with, and the MG still had a broken windshield. "Mind if we take your car?" he asked.

"Of course not." She dug into her jeans for the keys. "It needs driving."

They washed the dishes, then went to the garage. Larsen had never driven a Mercedes, let alone a red convertible, and he felt vaguely uncomfortable in the midst of all that leather and luxury. He was accustomed to his still-ratty Mustang and his ancient English sports car. He backed out of the garage and turned toward the east.

"Shouldn't we be going the other way?" Chris asked.

"I'm going to take the long way around," Larsen replied. He drove through the residential streets of Santa Monica, making frequent turns and checking his rearview mirror often. So far, it didn't seem that they were being followed.

As he turned another corner he flipped on the switch that he had installed, then he made for the Pacific Coast Highway. The car was marvelous, he thought as he whipped in and out of traffic and accelerated to overtake other cars. "This isn't bad," he said, "for a new car."

"But you prefer the old cars?"

"Well, I thought I did, but this is something else. If you don't mind my asking, how much did it cost?"

"Eighty-something thousand," she said. "I'm not sure exactly; Jack Berman did the deal, and it was delivered to the house."

"That's more than a year of my salary," he muttered to himself.

"I hope you can find a way not to worry about

things like that," she said. "It's just a car, even if it is expensive."

"I know I should think that," he said, "and I'll try. It just takes some getting used to."

When Larsen pulled up in front of the house, he was surprised to see that a permanent fence had been erected, and an electronically operated gate was being installed. Inside the fence was room for half a dozen cars, and landscapers were laying out flower beds and planting shrubbery.

"This is going to be very nice," he said.

"As long as it's very nice by tomorrow night," Chris replied. "I gave them that deadline."

He helped her out of the car. "It's nice of you to throw a party for the people who worked on the house."

"Nothing nice about it," she said, taking his arm. "I wanted the house finished on time, so I just invited all the workers to come and bring their wives. Mike tells me they've been working harder ever since."

"Good plan," Larsen said. He opened the new front door and they walked into bedlam. Workmen of every kind were running about the house, hammering, sawing, painting. They walked into the living room in time to watch two young men with crowbars start to rip out the picture window. One of them was Moscowitz's son, Lenny.

Mike Moscowitz came to greet them. "Hi, I'm sorry you had to show up just as we're correcting a mistake."

"What's the problem?" Chris asked.

"The window is six inches off center, and I'm embarrassed I didn't know it until now. I've had to get the framers back in to rip it out and reinstall it, and then the drywallers are standing by to redo the walls, and then the painters will be here to get it painted in time for the party. Don't worry, this isn't costing you; it's my fault."

Lenny and the other man looked up at them.

"You remember my boy, Lenny, Jon; and this is Bud Carson," Moscowitz shouted over the din. "Bud's the framing subcontractor, and he's here, himself, covering our mistake."

Jon offered his hand, but Carson just gave a little wave and turned back to the job.

"A little surly, isn't he?" Larsen asked as they walked away.

"He's not in a very good mood this morning," Moscowitz said. "He finished his work weeks ago, and now I've had to pull him off another job to come back and fix this."

Larsen pulled the builder to one side. "Have you heard anything from Mel Parker?"

"Not since I talked to him last week, to invite him to the party," Moscowitz said.

"Did he say he was coming?"

"Yeah, he was pretty enthusiastic about it. He said he was going upstate somewhere to see his mother, but he'd be back in time for the party."

"Thanks," Larsen said. "If you hear that, for any reason, he's not coming, will you let me know?"

"Sure."

Chris tugged at his elbow. "We'll take a look around, Mike, and leave you to get on with it. Come on, Jon, let's see where I'm going to live."

They walked through the house, and it seemed far from finished. "It's always like this near the end of a building job," Larsen said. "You'd never believe they'll be finished in time for you to move in the day after tomorrow, but it looks like they're getting it done. And you'd better expect to have builders in and out of the house for a few weeks, because you'll have a lot of fine-tuning to do."

They entered the master suite and Larsen stopped to admire the rooms. "This is going to be very nice," he said. "I didn't realize on my last visit that you had two bathrooms and dressing rooms."

"I designed it for two," Chris replied, "on the off chance that I wouldn't be spending the rest of my life alone. What would you think about moving in here with me?"

"Is that some sort of proposal?" he asked, surprised.

"It's more of a proposition," she replied. "I'm perfectly serious; I've gotten used to having you around, and I like it. One of these days I might well propose to you, but I think it might be nice if we lived together for a while first."

"It's the best offer I've had all day," Larsen said, "and it certainly is an attractive idea. I'd like to think about it."

"You do that," she said, "and then you make the right decision. Come on, let's go outside."

They walked back into the main hallway, then out onto the deck overlooking the Pacific. They stood with their elbows on the railing, staring out to sea.

"Jon," she said, "I can see the horizon."

He turned to look at her. "You mean those eyes do something besides look beautiful?"

"I mean, I can actually see that ship out there, clear and sharp." She pointed to a tanker creeping along the coast.

"That's wonderful, Chris."

"The only problem is that I still can't see the

beach or you properly. But I'm looking forward to it." She put her hand on his face and kissed him.

Suddenly, from behind them, came an enormous crash, and they both turned.

Lenny Moscowitz was shouting at Bud Carson. "What the hell is the matter with you?"

"Ah, keep your shirt on," Carson shouted back.

"What happened?" Chris asked.

"Looks like they've had a little accident with your living-room window. There's a crowbar sticking through it."

"Jesus Christ!" Lenny yelled. "That was the stupidest move I ever saw!"

"Shut your face, kid," Carson shouted back.

Chris laughed. "Oh, God, let's get out of here; I don't want to hear the explosion when Mike finds out."

On the way back, driving the Mercedes, it suddenly became real to him that he could soon be living with a movie actress on Malibu Beach, and that he could get used to driving this car. The thought scared the hell out of him.

CHAPTER

56

That afternoon, Danny came to stay with Chris, and Larsen went to his office. He found Martinez in Homicide and pulled a chair up to his desk.

"I've heard that Parker has gone upstate to see his mother for a few days," he said. "It's not true, of course, at least for the times we know he's been here, but it's worth checking to see if he does have a mother."

Martinez turned to his computer and summoned up the criminal record of James Melvin Potter. "Here it is; the mother lives in Oakland. I could ask for some surveillance help up there."

"Probably not worth it. Parker told somebody he'd be back in town tomorrow, and I think he'll show."

"Just in time for your get-together?"

"Just in time."

"What, exactly, are you planning?"

"He's coming to a party for the people who built a house; he did the alarm system."

"Is that Chris Callaway's house?"

"You get around, don't you, Al?"

"I do; I think I'd better have some men around that place tomorrow evening."

"No, no, no. He'd smell them a mile away, and I don't want him nervous when he comes to that party."

"Jon, if this goes wrong, Herrera is going to have your badge."

"If this goes wrong, I'll give it to him," Larsen replied.

Back at the house he found Chris taking a nap and Danny stretched out on the living-room sofa reading a magazine. He pulled up a chair.

"We'd better talk while Chris is asleep," Larsen said.

"Okay," Danny replied.

"This is what I want to do tomorrow evening: we'll take two cars to the party, Chris's and my MG. It starts at six, so I'll stay there until the party begins to thin out a little, then I'll say I have to work that evening, and I'll leave the party and drive away.

"I'll go just far enough to be out of sight of the house, then I'll park the car and make my way back up the beach. What I want you to do is, late in the party, go out onto the deck and let down the folding ladder to the beach; then turn off the deck lights and close the sliding doors to discourage anybody from coming out there. Then I want you to leave."

"You mean leave her there all alone?"

"Wait until there's only a couple or two, then go. Make some excuse about having to buy groceries or booze or something. Get into Chris's car and drive toward Malibu. On the left-hand side of the dash and underneath, very near where the hood release is located, there's a little black switch. Switch it to the opposite position."

"What's that for?"

"Parker has placed a bug on Chris's car, my two cars, and probably your car."

"What?"

"It lets him know where we are. The switch will interfere with the bug, and that will keep him from knowing how far you go, if he's watching."

"What if when I go, one of the few people left is Mel Parker?"

"That's the tricky part; you're just going to have to go. Don't go far; do the same thing I'm going to do—come back to the house along the beach, and stay out on the deck with me. There's a little shed out there for storing deck furniture; meet me behind the shed. We won't be seen from the house, even if somebody should come onto the deck."

"What then?"

"I'm going out to the house tonight and plant some small transmitters there. A friend of mine has given me a little receiver that will let us hear what's happening inside the house. Chris will have a code word; when she uses that, we bust in."

Danny listened closely, then sat up and rubbed his eyes. "You mean you're going to use Chris for bait? Is that it?"

"That's it."

"I don't like it, Jon."

"I don't like it either, but I'm at the end of my rope."

"Isn't there some other way?"

"Yes, there is; we can wait for Parker to kill again, and hope to catch him, but . . . "

"What do you mean, 'again'?"

Larsen got up, walked to the bedroom door, and

looked in on Chris; she was curled up tight, fast asleep. He came back and took his chair again. "A couple of nights ago Parker killed a young woman named Helen Mendelssohn. She had been a case of mine a few months ago, but the contacts had petered out. I think Parker became angry that I was interfering with his harassment of Chris, and he wanted to show me that he could rattle my cage."

"I don't get it; how would this murder affect you?"

"The woman's head was found the day before yesterday in Beverly Hills. When you dropped us off after dinner last night, the rest of her body was propped up in that chair over there."

"Without a head?"

"Without a head."

"Jesus Christ! That must have scared Chris."

"Chris doesn't know about it; it's the only time since I've known her that I was glad she's blind. It scared *me* pretty good, though."

"I'm glad I didn't come in for coffee," Danny said. "I would have screamed bloody murder."

"That would have been appropriate," Larsen said.

"I can't believe he bugged our cars," Danny said, shaking his head.

"That's how he knew we were at the Pritikin place."

"He *knew* we were there?"

"After you left Chris and me there the other night, he came into the suite and left a message on the living-room mirror in Chris's lipstick; said she'd never get away from him."

"What did you do?"

"I didn't know he was there until he was gone."

"Why didn't he do something, if he was in the suite?"

"I don't know; probably he didn't realize that my pistol was in the living room, where we'd left our clothes."

"There's something to be said for taking your clothes with you wherever you go."

"You have a point."

"Jon, what if this plan of yours doesn't work tomorrow evening?"

"I don't know, Danny; I honestly don't. Maybe I'll let you kill Parker."

"That would be my pleasure," Danny said.

That evening Larsen met his friend Jim, the electronics expert, at the Malibu house. Jim walked around the house looking at the ceiling. "How many rooms you want to bug?" he asked.

"Living room, dining room, kitchen, master suite, study," Larsen said.

"How many voices you want to listen to? A whole roomful?"

"Not necessary; one or two."

"That makes it simpler and cheaper; I don't have to use very high-tech stuff." He opened his toolbox and went to work.

Two hours later Larsen stood on the beach a hundred yards away, listening to a small handheld receiver.

"One, two, three, four," Jim was saying. "That's the kitchen; now I'm going to the living room."

The test was successfully repeated in each room of the house, then Larsen climbed the stairs to the deck and met Jim.

"Worked like a charm," he said.

"Why do you sound surprised?" Jim asked.

CHAPTER

57

They gathered in Larsen's living room, ready to travel to Malibu. Larsen sat Chris and Danny down on the sofa and drew up a chair; it was time to explain to Chris what she was in for.

He took her hand. "Chris, Danny and I are both going to leave the party toward the end."

"What?"

"We're going to wait until the crowd has started to thin out, and then we're going to drive in opposite directions down the beach, then walk back to the house and go up the steps to the deck."

"Does that mean I'm going to be alone with Parker?"

"Not quite; I want you to hold at least one couple there until we've had time to get into place."

"How will I do that?"

"Offer them another drink; take them on a tour of the house; anything, just to keep them there a little longer. Don't worry, I'll be able to hear everything that goes on in the house over this." He held up the little receiver. "We've got to make Parker believe that you're going to be alone for a few minutes."

"I have to be alone with him?"

"You won't be; he just has to believe it. Danny and I will be on the deck, listening; if you say the words 'You must be crazy,' then we'll be all over you. But we'll wait for that signal."

"You must be crazy," Chris said.

"That's right."

"It certainly is."

"You have your pistol?"

She patted the pocket of her silk slacks. "Right here, and it's probably ruining the line of my pants."

"Just let your jacket drape over it."

"If I'm alone with him, what do I do?"

"Get him to talk, and keep him talking. If you can get him to talk about what he's been doing, Danny and I will hear it, and he will have incriminated himself. We have plenty to charge him with, *if* we can get probable cause. Then we can get search warrants for his home and business, and we'll probably find physical evidence that will connect him with the crimes. When that happens, he's out of your life, I promise you."

"Then it's worth going through this," Chris said resolutely.

Larsen drove the MG and followed the Mercedes out the Pacific Coast Highway toward Malibu. The wind in his face evaporated his nervous sweat, and he took deep breaths to get his pulse down to normal. He took a hand off the steering wheel, and it was trembling.

They arrived at the house as the caterers were unloading food and champagne, and Larsen took the head woman aside. "As soon as you've set everything up, you can leave," he said.

"Don't you want us to serve?" the woman asked.

"No, that won't be necessary. Just set it all up on the tables, and the guests will help themselves."

"Whatever you say," the woman replied, then went about her work.

Larsen walked around the house, checking to see that the bugs were still in place. They were visible, but just barely, since there was no wiring; each transmitter operated on batteries. He walked out onto the deck and checked the reception with his receiver; it was perfect. The sun was sinking slowly toward the horizon, but they had another two hours of daylight. He turned back into the house; it was time to socialize.

The first subcontractor to arrive was Jimmy, the plumber, with his wife and teenage daughter; right after him came Mike Moscowitz and his wife and Bud Carson, the framer, then the electrical man and a flood of laborers, most with their wives or girl-friends. Then Lenny Moscowitz arrived and found himself a beer. They were a good hour into the party before Mel Parker appeared at the door.

Larsen was standing nearby, but he ignored Parker and left it to Mike Moscowitz to greet him.

"Glad you made it back in time," the builder said.

"Me, too," Parker said. "I had to come from Oakland, but the traffic wasn't too bad. You got finished, huh?"

"Well, as finished as you can get before the owner moves in. And there she is; come and say hello."

"Sure."

Chris was talking with a young couple about the intricacies of electrical wiring when she saw two shapes approach and heard Mike's voice.

"Chris, you remember Mel Parker; he did your security system."

"Of course," Chris said brightly, sticking out her hand in Parker's direction. When he took it she worked hard not to cringe.

"The place is looking beautiful," Parker said. "Mike has done a terrific job."

"He tells me you've done a good job, too," Chris said. "I'll feel a lot safer knowing your equipment is at work and your people are listening for my call," she lied.

"That's our job," Parker said. "You making any new movies these days?"

Bastard, she thought; you know I can't see to do my work, and you're rubbing it in. "I have a new project in development right now, as a matter of fact."

"What is it?"

"Well, I can't talk about it until we've signed contracts, but if all goes well, I expect we'll start shooting early next year."

"Can't wait to see it," Parker said. "Excuse me, I think I'll get some champagne." He moved off toward the bar table.

Danny approached Larsen and handed him a fresh glass of champagne. "I've let down the stairs from the deck. When do we move?" he asked.

"Not yet; still too many people here." The party was an hour and a half old now, and he saw a few people approach Chris to thank her before leaving. "Soon, from the look of it."

"Yeah, once a few people leave everybody will get the idea.

They watched, and Danny was right; the rush to leave was on. Soon only a dozen or so people were left, including Moscowitz and Mel Parker.

Larsen handed his glass to Danny. "I'll go first," he said. "You follow when we're down to half a dozen people." Parker was not talking to Chris now, but he was at the bar, only a few steps away, pouring himself another glass of champagne.

Larsen approached Chris. "I'd better get going," he said, sure that Parker could hear him."

"Oh, can't you stay a while longer?" Chris asked plaintively. "The sunset is going to be marvelous."

"I'm sorry, but I've got to go to a meeting at the office; my boss insists. I should be through by ten or so, if you want to have a late dinner."

"Okay; I'll wait for you here."

Larsen shook Mike Moscowitz's hand, then left the house.

Danny wandered out onto the deck, looked to make sure he was alone, then lowered the stairs to the beach. On his way back in he stopped and chatted with the framer, Bud Carson.

Larsen got into the car, took the small receiver out
of his pocket, placed it on the seat beside him, and
turned it on. A babble of sound hit him, and he
turned down the instrument. Jim had been right;
this equipment wasn't good enough to distinguish
one or two among a lot of voices.

He started the car and, with some difficulty, maneu-
vered around a dark blue van parked behind him. He
had seen that van before somewhere; he made a mental note of the license plate number. He pulled out into
traffic and drove back toward Los Angeles.

Suddenly Danny's voice was loud and clear.

"Chris, I have to run to the drugstore in Malibu
Village; will you be all right for half an hour?"
Danny had made sure to stand near the living-room
bug.

Chris's voice was lost in the babble, but Larsen
didn't need to hear it. A couple of hundred yards
down the beach, he began looking for a break in the
houses so that he could go through to the beach.
There was none. Malibu property was too valuable
to allow for gaps between houses. Larsen knew he
was getting too far from the house; he began to
become alarmed.

He pulled over, stopped, and reached into the
glove compartment for the little Radio Shack CB
transmitter.

"Danny, it's Jon; do you read me?"

There was some crackling, and then Danny's
voice came back weakly. "Yeah, I'm here, Jon."

"Where are you?"

"Down the road a few hundred yards from the
house. I can't find a way to get down to the beach."

"I'm having the same problem. There's a restaurant down your way; see if you can get through that. Crawl out a window, if you have to."

"Over and out," Danny said.

Larsen pulled his car right up to the nearest house; he got out and rang the front doorbell. A man in a bathrobe came to the door, and Larsen flashed his badge.

"I'm a police officer; I need to get to the beach. May I go through your house?"

"Let's see some ID with a picture," the man said.

Larsen produced a plastic ID. He was now very worried that he had been gone too long.

The man examined it carefully and compared the photograph to Larsen's face. "You got a warrant to enter my house?"

Larsen shoved the man aside. "I haven't got time for this; I'm coming through."

"Hey, I'll call the cops," the man yelled after him.

"I'm the cops," Larsen said, finding the kitchen. There had to be a way out of here. He found a deck with a stair arrangement similar to Chris's, got the steps down, and ran down to the beach.

"Fucking cops!" the man yelled after him from the deck. "That was unconstitutional!"

Larsen ignored him and started to run.

58

C hris was talking with Jimmy, the plumbing contractor, and his wife, who had both had a lot of champagne and were very merry.

"Listen, I could tell you stories about my clients," Jimmy was saying. "People will say and do anything around a plumber; we're like cab drivers—people act like you're not even there, you know?"

"I can imagine," Chris said. She had been keeping an eye on Mel Parker's shape; he had never left the bar, and he seemed to be in conversation with another shape.

Mike Moscowitz appeared at her elbow. "Well, folks, it's getting time to call it a night," he said.

Chris felt for his arm and whispered into his ear. "Mike, don't let Parker leave; if he starts to go, tell him I want to talk to him about some more security stuff, then you go, too."

"You're sure?" Moscowitz asked.

"I'm sure." She turned to Jimmy and his wife. "Please excuse the whispering; just some last-minute business."

"No problem," Jimmy said. "Well, we'd better get going."

"I'll drive," his wife said.

"Whatever you say, sweetheart."

Moscowitz saw them to the door, then came back to Chris. "Mel," he called, "Chris wanted a word with you." He leaned into Chris. "You're sure?"

"I'm sure; don't worry."

She saw a shape approaching.

"Well, I'm off," Mike said. "I think we're all ready for your move tomorrow, Chris. Should we come and clean up the bottles and leftover food?"

"Don't worry about it, Mike; the caterers will be in tomorrow morning to clean up."

"Good night, then," Moscowitz said.

Chris heard the front door close behind him. Now she was alone with Mel Parker.

Down the beach, Danny was arguing with the restaurant manager. "All I want to do is get down to the beach," he said.

"I'm sorry, sir, but we have an agreement with our neighbors that we won't allow the public to get to the beach through our establishment. The good-will of our neighbors is very important to us; I'm sure you understand."

"I understand," Danny said. "But *you* don't understand. I *have* to get to the beach; someone's life may depend on it."

"Sir," the manager said, "I hear all sorts of excuses from people who want to get to the beach and peep into the stars' homes, but I just cannot allow it. Now if you'll go down the road another mile or so, there's the pier, and you can reach the beach from there."

"I don't have time for that," Danny said.

"Well, I'm sorry, but if you want to get onto Malibu Beach, you're going to have to take the time to go through a public area, and this is *not* a public area."

Danny rose to his full five feet five inches. "Mister," he said, "I'm going to the beach out your back door, and if I can't go around you, I'll go through you."

"Just try it, pal," the manager said.

Larsen tried to pace himself. He had started his run at least a mile from the house, and it had been a long time since he had run a mile. The tide was out, and he kept to the wet sand where the going was easier. As he jogged along he reached into his pocket for the receiver and switched it on. He heard Mike Moscowitz's voice clearly, saying good night. Chris was alone with Parker. Larsen picked up the pace a notch. Don't sprint, he told himself; if you do you'll never make it. He thought he could see the house up ahead.

"Anything I can do for you?" Parker asked.

Chris tried to keep her breathing normal. "I've been having a rather unusual security problem," she said. "I was wondering if you might have some ideas as to how to solve it."

"Probably," Parker replied. "Somebody been bothering you?"

"Sort of," she said. "Actually, he seems like the

sort of guy I might like to know, if the circumstances were a little different."

"If you want to know him better, then why do you need more security?"

"I think I may have given him the wrong impression. You see, early on I involved the police, when that may not have been the right thing to do."

"You mean your buddy Larsen?"

"Yes; and now I don't seem to be able to get rid of him."

"Would you like me to get rid of him for you?" Parker asked.

"How would you go about that?" she asked. She was standing where she had been told to; she hoped to God that Larsen could hear her, that he was on the deck.

"I could handle that for you," Parker said.

The lights suddenly went off in the house.

Down the beach, Larsen was a hundred yards from the house when he saw the lights go off. What the hell? Every light in the place had been on, so that the wives could see the whole house, and every light had gone off at once. Either the main breaker had popped, or someone had thrown the main switch. He was nearly winded now, but he tried to run faster.

"What happened?" Chris asked.

"Looks like the main breaker went," Parker said. "There's enough light from the sunset, though."

There wasn't enough light to suit Chris. Her eyes didn't adjust to changes in light as rapidly as they used to, and she was now virtually in the dark. She looked toward the windows; the sunset was a dim radiance surrounded by a deep gray.

"Can't you fix it?" she asked. "I can't see very well at this light level."

"I could," Parker said, "but I sort of like it like this."

"Please," she said, "please go and fix it."

"Oh, all right," Parker said. "I'll be right back." He walked away from her.

Chris stood trembling in the dark. She put her hands in her pockets and felt for the little pistol. It was there, warm from her body heat.

Then she was startled by a hand on her shoulder.

Larsen reached the house, panting, gasping for breath. He paused for a moment, resting his hands on his knees, then looked for the steps to the deck. They weren't there. Larsen looked up at the deck, panicked. Then he heard Chris's voice, loud and clear over the receiver. "You must be crazy," she said.

59

Larsen remembered that he had once before been in this situation, unable to reach the folding steps from below. Feeling his way in the dark under the deck, he looked for the gap where he had been able to reach the front of the house; it was now completely covered over with siding and shingles. He ran back onto the beach and looked both ways; as far as he could see, houses stretched into the distance. There were no breaks between them, and no access from the beach.

Chris was spun around by the hand on her shoulder.

"What are you doing?" she asked. The lights were still off, and she could barely distinguish a shape in front of her.

A voice whispered, "I thought it was time you and I were alone together."

The hair stood up on the back of her neck. "Maybe it is time, at that. Where have you been?"

"I've been here all along," the voice whispered.

"Why are you whispering now?" she asked. "Why can't you speak like a man?"

"I like to whisper," the voice said. "It's more intimate."

"Funny," she said, "you haven't been acting like a man who wants intimacy; in fact, I'd say you've been behaving like a man who's afraid of women."

Suddenly he took hold of her hair, and for the first time, he spoke in something like a normal voice. "You think I'm afraid of you, huh? I think I'll show you just how unafraid of you I am."

Chris spoke very loudly and distinctly. "You must be crazy!" she said.

He backhanded her, hard, across the face.

Chris struggled to get closer to him, but he was holding her at a distance by her hair. He slapped her again.

"Don't like to get close to a woman, huh?" she said, grabbing hold of his shirt. She tried to pull herself closer to him, but he was too strong for her. "Go ahead," she said, "take me in your arms."

He reached out and circled an arm around her waist, then he released her hair and put his other arm around her, pulling her tight against him, squeezing the breath out of her.

Chris found his face with one hand. "At last, you sonofabitch!" Chris screamed. She drew back with her other hand, made a fist, and, as hard as she could, jammed her thumb into his right eye. He screamed and stepped back from her. Chris went for the gun in her pocket.

Larsen heard a man scream, then four loud pops erupted from above, and Larsen didn't need the radio to hear them. He threw down the receiver, leapt at one of the pilings supporting the deck, and began shinnying up it. Splinters stabbed at his hands and legs, but he kept at it, moving slowly up the piling. There was a horizontal support a few feet above him; if he could grab that he could hoist himself onto it and then reach the floor of the deck. He kept climbing.

Something struck Chris's wrist, and the pistol flew from her hand. Hadn't she hit him with any of her shots? He grabbed her again, and she managed to get hold of his hair with her right hand. She made a fist of her left and jammed the thumb into his left eye. He screamed again, then jerked his head from her grasp and moved to one side to avoid another blow, putting himself between the sunset and Chris.

Now she could see his shape, silhouetted against the dying sun; she could see that his hands were at his face and that his feet were spread apart. "Now you're blinder than I am, aren't you, you son-ofabitch!" She took one step toward him and kicked upward with all her strength, screaming with the effort. Her foot caught him full in the crotch, and his hands left his face and grabbed at the new pain. Reaching out for him, Chris found his head. She grabbed his hair with both hands and pulled his face down to meet her rising knee, and she felt the blood seep through the silk pants she was wearing.

A howl of pain and anger rose from the man, and he staggered through the open sliding doors onto the deck, straightening up. As he did, she saw something bright in his hand. The man started toward her.

Larsen reached painfully up for the horizontal tim-
ber, and got a grip that allowed him to get both
hands on it. He hoisted himself up, got a knee on it,
then stood. His head was now at deck level; he saw
the shape of a man in the fading light, and he was
holding the biggest knife Larsen had ever seen. He
reached for his pistol, and at that moment another
shape rocketed out of the house and onto the deck,
colliding with the knife-wielding man and shoving
him forcefully back toward the railing.

The railing gave way from the weight of both of
them, and the two shapes, locked together, plummeted
toward the rocks twenty feet below them. Larsen put
the pistol on the deck and hoisted himself up. He
grabbed the weapon and ran toward the broken railing.

Chris dropped to her hands and knees and felt for
her pistol; something was going on, but she couldn't
tell what. Then she found the gun.

As Larsen reached the gap in the railing, a flash erupted inside the house, and he felt something hum past
his ear. He spun around. "No, Chris!" he shouted, "It's
Jon!" She was crouched in a firing position, as he had
taught her, the pistol held out in front of her with both
hands. She stopped shooting. "Easy," he said. "It's all
right now." He started toward her, then he was
stopped in his tracks by the sound of a gunshot behind
him. He turned and ran back toward the broken railing. As he did, another shot erupted, then another.

Larsen looked over the edge and, in the dim light,
saw a man with a gun standing, straddling another, who
was prone on the rocks. "Freeze! Police!" he shouted.

The man with the gun turned and looked up at the deck.

"Drop the weapon now, or I'll fire!" Larsen shouted.

"Jesus, Jon, it's me," a voice said.

"Danny?"

"You were expecting the cavalry?"

"Don't shoot anymore," Larsen said.

"I don't think I'll have to," Danny said.

"Stay right there; I'll be with you in a minute. Chris?" He went back into the house and gathered her in his arms.

"What happened?" Chris asked.

"It was Danny," Larsen replied. "He's taken care of Parker; it's all over." He held her at arm's length and looked at her. "Are you all right?"

"I want some light," she said.

"Stay right here." Larsen ran into the back hallway, found the main switchbox, and pulled the master switch. The lights came on, and he went back to the living room. "I'm going to go down to the beach and check on Danny," he said. "Don't go onto the deck; the railing's broken."

"I'll wait here," she said.

Larsen went out onto the deck, lowered the stairs, and ran down them. Danny and Parker were only a few feet in front of him. "Are you all right, Danny?" he asked as he reached the smaller man's side.

"I'm just fine," Danny said, pointing with his pistol. "He took the force of the fall."

"Did you have to shoot him?" Larsen asked quietly.

Danny turned and looked at him. "You're damn right I did."

"All right, listen to me; you ran out onto the deck and shot him there, understand?"

"What's the difference?"

"The difference between justifiable homicide and second-degree murder; the difference between no charges and twenty years in San Quentin. Do we understand each other?"

"Perfectly," Danny said. He looked down at the body at his feet. "I wish I could see him better."

"I can see him well enough to know that his mother wouldn't recognize him," Larsen said. "You put three into his face; he's a mess."

"I'm glad," Danny said. "I hope to God he was alive when I shot him."

"What took you so long to get here?" Larsen asked.

"I tried to get to the beach through the restaurant down the road, but the manager was a little tougher than I counted on. So I got in the car, and drove back here as fast as I could. I came through the front door, and I saw Parker on the deck with a knife."

"I saw the rest," Larsen said. "You were great, but remember what I said about where you shot him."

"I'll remember."

"I've got to go call this in," Larsen said. "Will you wait here, and if any neighbors turn up, keep them away from Parker?"

"Sure," Danny said, sitting down on a boulder. "You go ahead; Admirer and I will be just fine."

Larsen took the gun from Danny's hand and climbed back up the stairs. He went to Chris and took the pistol from her and put it in his pocket. "Parker's dead," he said. "It's finally all over." Then they were both startled by a man's voice.

"Will somebody tell me what the hell is going on?"

Larsen turned and looked toward the living-room door. Mel Parker was standing there, leaning against the doorjamb and rubbing the back of his neck.

CHAPTER

60

The house was full of people again. The local cops had brought in everything they had, and there were flashbulbs popping, ambulance lights flashing, and, of course, the blue lights of the squad cars out front. The only furniture in the house was some chairs rented for the party, and Danny Devere, composed and relaxed, sat on one facing a homicide detective.

"Now let me get this straight," the detective was saying.

"Would you like me to go through it again?"

"Please."

"I came back into the house through the front door in time to see this guy stagger out onto the deck—the sliding doors were open. When he straightened up he had a knife in his hand, and he was moving toward Chris. I ran between them and fired three times at the guy."

"How close to him were you?"

"I'm not sure; pretty close." He shrugged. "It all happened so fast."

"And where did you aim?"

"I didn't aim, exactly; I just pointed the gun at him and pulled the trigger three times. He went backward through the railing and landed on the beach."

Larsen broke off his conversation with another detective and approached. "I can confirm all that," he said. "I was climbing up to the deck from the beach, and I got my head above deck level just as he fired." He handed the detective Danny's gun. "Have you found out who he is yet?"

"They'll search the body for ID as soon as the medical examiner is finished with him."

As if on cue a man carrying a black bag entered the room from the deck. "Okay, he's all yours," he said.

"Cause of death?" the detective asked.

"You've got your choice of two: either the three bullets in the head, or the smashed skull on the rocks. One eye was shot through, and the other was ruptured by some injury."

"Which happened first?"

"Impossible to say; the head injury and the gunshots probably occurred within seconds of each other. The eye injury could have occurred either before or after."

"Thanks, Doc." The detective turned back to Larsen. "Okay, we've got the knife, and they're taking prints from it, but as far as I can see this was a clean kill. I'll file my report to state no further interest from this department."

"Thanks," Larsen said.

"By the way," the detective said, pointing across the room. "we've got four small-caliber slugs in the wall over there."

Larsen looked at the wall. He had forgotten about

the shots he'd heard. "Miss Callaway has a small-caliber handgun," he said.

"Nice grouping," the detective replied.

Another detective entered the house from the deck, holding a plastic bag that contained a wallet, some change, and a large clump of keys.

The questioning detective removed the wallet from the bag, holding only its corners, opened it, and extracted a driver's license. "James E. Carson," he said, then turned the license so that Larsen could see the photograph.

Larsen looked at the picture. "Bud Carson," he said. "He was the framing contractor on the house."

The detective fished out a business card. "Frameworks Unlimited," he said.

Larsen nodded. I had him down as Bud Carson Framers, he thought; that's why the gray van didn't show up under his name; it must be registered under his business.

"You look a little pale," the detective said to him.

"I feel a little pale," Larsen said, sinking into a chair next to Chris. "He wasn't who I was expecting."

"Who were you expecting?" the detective asked.

"That guy over there," Larsen said, pointing at Mel Parker, who was being questioned by another detective. "I've been following him, thinking that he was the stalker in this case. Seems I was very, very wrong."

"Don't take it too hard," the detective said. "It's happened to everybody at one time or another."

"Yeah, I guess," Larsen said.

Al Martinez from Beverly Hills Homicide walked into the house. "Hi, Jon," he said. "You rang?"

"Yeah," Larsen replied. "We have a new suspect

in the Helen Mendelssohn case. He's out on the beach, dead." He took the driver's license from the Malibu detective, holding it by its edges. "A Benedict Canyon address." He held the license so that Rivera could read it.

Rivera nodded. "Let's go take a look at the address," he said. "You can tell me what happened here on the way."

"Give me a minute," Larsen said. He turned to the Malibu detective. "You through with Mr. Devere and Ms. Callaway?"

"Yeah," the detective replied, "they can go. As soon as the body's off the beach we'll clear out of here."

As he spoke, two ambulance men came through the house carrying a stretcher holding a body bag.

Larsen turned to Danny. "Danny, will you take Chris back to my place and stay there with her until I get back?"

"Sure, Jon."

He gave Chris a little hug. "Go on home with Danny; there's nothing to worry about anymore. I just have to clean up some details."

"Jon," Chris said, "was Bud Carson Admirer?"

"Yes," Larsen said. "I expect to be able to prove it before morning." He looked across the room and saw that Mel Parker, holding an icepack against the back of his neck, had finished talking to the detective. Larsen crossed the room. "How're you feeling?" he asked.

"I'm okay," Parker replied, "just a little sore."

He pulled Parker away from the others. "Listen, I owe you an apology; I thought you were mixed up in something you weren't."

"Is that why you've been following me?" Parker asked.

"Yes."

"Well, you're not very good at it. Were you in my backyard, too?"

Larsen blushed. "I haven't got time to talk right now, but during this investigation it's been uncovered that you've started a security business under a false name. I won't even ask how you got by the fingerprinting, but the point is, it's known to the police who you are."

"Are you going to arrest me?"

Larsen shook his head. "It's only a misdemeanor, and I'm not inclined to press it—if you get out of the business."

"You mean shut it down?"

"I should think what you've built up is valuable enough to sell to another security business. Do that inside of, say, three months, and I don't think you'll hear from the police."

Parker shrugged. "Okay, that's fair."

"I'm sorry you got slugged; believe me, it could have been worse." He went back to the Malibu detective. "I'd like to borrow Carson's keys," he said. "We need to have a look at his home; he's a suspect in a Beverly Hills homicide."

"Okay," the detective said, handing Larsen the large key ring.

"I'll get them back to you tomorrow." He turned to Martinez. "Let's go," he said.

Larsen followed Martinez's car back to Beverly Hills and up Benedict Canyon. Martinez slowed to look at numbers, then turned into a driveway. Larsen pulled up beside him and switched off his engine, then both men got out of their cars. The house had a single light burning inside.

"This is an old place," Martinez said. "I'll bet it goes back to the twenties, when there weren't many houses up here."

"I'll be interested to know how a subcontractor in the construction business, and one as young as Carson, could afford it."

"I'm betting on inheritance," Martinez said. "Come on."

They rang the doorbell, but no one answered. While Martinez held a flashlight, Larsen matched a key from the ring to the front, door lock, and in a moment they were inside.

"Not bad," Martinez said. The house was nicely furnished, and it looked freshly painted. The two detectives walked through the house, careful not to disturb any evidence it might contain.

"It looks to me as though the place has recently been remodeled," Larsen said, pointing to some paint spatters on the newly refinished floor. "That could explain why Carson rented the Millman guest house for a while."

"Could be," Martinez agreed.

They continued their search of the house, finding nothing until they came to the large country kitchen. On the floor of a seating area was an Indian rug.

"I've got a photograph of this back at the office," Larsen said, fingering the rug. He walked to a bookcase in the room and found a volume of medical photographs, and when he leafed through it, he found the photograph he was looking for. "This is my man," he said.

"I hope the hell he's mine," Martinez replied. "Let's keep looking."

They combed the guest rooms, the basement, and the attic, and found nothing more.

"I wonder what's out back," Larsen said. "Let's take a look."

At the back door he flipped some switches and floodlights came on behind the house.

"Stables," Martinez said, pointing at the building behind the house. "I guess you used to be able to ride up here without worrying about traffic."

The two detectives got the door unlocked and entered the building, turning on lights as they went. The stalls were still there, but the rest of the place was an extensive workshop, with power tools and a workbench with many electrical tools. Larsen saw the briefcase toolbox that he had seen in the Millman guest house, and his police radio was lying on the workbench. His pistol would turn up, too, he was sure. While he looked through the circuit boards and switches, Martinez looked elsewhere.

"Uh, oh," Martinez said. "Come take a look at this." He was looking into one of the stalls.

Larsen walked over and looked. At the rear of the stall stood a large commercial-grade stainless-steel refrigerator. It was padlocked.

Larsen compared the lock to the keys, selected one, and turned it in the lock, which snapped open. He stepped back. "I think I'm going to let you open it," he said.

Martinez nodded and stepped forward. He lifted the lock off the hasp and set it on the floor, then took hold of the handles and opened both doors wide.

Larsen forced himself to look. The frozen faces of two women stared out at the detectives, their dead eyes still open, the heads sitting neatly on a steel shelf. The matching torsos were arranged on the floor of the freezer, along with the headless bodies of two dogs.

"For Christ's sake, close it," Larsen said.

CHAPTER

61

Larsen and Chris walked along Malibu Beach, hand in hand, the following afternoon. Danny was back at the house, unpacking boxes that had been delivered from stores that morning.

"So you see," Larsen was saying, "you are involved with one of the more stupid police detectives in the western hemisphere." He had told her everything, but only because he knew she would find out anyway.

"I'm glad you told me all of this, but it doesn't change my opinion of you in the least. I think it was most logical of you to suspect Mel Parker; after all, he did fit the bill. As far as I'm concerned, you saved my life."

"No," he said firmly, "I put your life in jeopardy; a half-pint gay hairdresser saved it."

"You did it together; Carson might never have been caught if it hadn't been for your trap. It worked, even if not exactly as you'd planned. Why are you beating up on yourself like this? You've solved not only your stalking case, but a triple homicide as well—a serial murderer, for God's sake. You should be very proud of yourself; I'm certainly proud of you."

They stopped at the bottom of the stairs to the deck, and he took her in his arms.

"I've been thinking about your very kind proposition," he said, "and I'm afraid I'm going to have to decline."

"I thought it was a pretty good offer," she said.

He shook his head. "If you want me, you're going to have to make an honest man of me."

"What if I become an honest-to-God movie star; can you live with that?"

"I'll force myself."

"Are we going to argue about money?"

"Probably, but hell, it's the nineties, isn't it? I guess I can learn to be a nineties man."

She put her hands on his cheeks. "I can nearly see you now," she said, "but I want a good clear look at you before I commit. After all, I can't be expected to marry a man I've never seen."

He kissed her. "Get well soon," he said.

Danny leaned over the patched deck railing. "Will you people stop fucking around and get up here? You expect me to do this all by myself?"

Chris laughed. "Be nice, or I won't let you be my maid of honor."

Danny smiled broadly. "Yeah?"

"Yeah," she replied.

"You can be the best man, too," Larsen said.

Danny affected a lisp. "Gee, that's always been my dream."

THE END
Santa Fe, New Mexico, March 22, 1993

•

Here is an excerpt from

IMPERFECT STRANGERS

Published by HarperCollins*Publishers*

CHAPTER

1

As the sun rose over Berkeley Square, the May sunshine drifted through the blinds in the Mount Street flat, two blocks west. The rays fell across the face of Peter Kinsolving, waking him as if they had been the bell of an alarm clock. He lay on his back, naked, and blinked a couple of times. Oriented, he turned to his right and moved toward the woman next to him. He shaped himself to her back and pressed his groin against her soft buttocks, and he felt the stirring come.

She gave a soft moan and responded, pushing against him. In a moment she was wet, and he entered her, moving slowly, enjoying the early morning moment.

The phone rang, the loud, insistent jangling that only an older British phone could make. He cursed under his breath, and without stopping the motion, reached across her and lifted the receiver.

"Hello?" he said hoarsely.

"Peter, it's Joan." She waited for him to respond.

He still did not stop moving. "Yes," he said, finally, then he became more alert. "What time is it in New York?"

"Nearly two A.M."

"What's wrong?"

"Daddy has had a stroke."

He stopped moving, wilting like a violet in hot sun. "How bad?"

"They don't know, yet, but at his age . . ."

Jock Bailley was ninety-one. "I'll get myself on a flight as soon as the office opens. Where is he?"

"Lenox Hill. I'm calling from there."

"I'll let the New York office know what flight I'm on."

"Albert will meet you."

"You all right?"

"Tired."

"You'd better go home and sleep. There's nothing you can do there."

"I suppose you're right. Laddie and Myra are here, anyway."

"You should all go home and sleep."

"I will. I can't speak for Laddie."

"See you this afternoon."

She hung up without saying good-bye.

Peter replaced the receiver. A little ball of apprehension had made a tight knot in his belly.

"*Peter*," the woman said accusingly. "You stopped."

Peter rolled onto his back. "Sorry, luv. I've just been put out of commission."

"Bad news?"

"Yes, bad news. Illness in the family."

"I'm sorry."

"Thanks. I'd better get dressed. Do you mind breakfasting at home? I have to go to New York."

"Certainly, dear," she said, rising and heading for the bathroom. "I'll just get a quick shower."

"Thanks." Peter stared at his ceiling and tried to put a good face on all this. Jock wasn't dead, yet. That was something, at least.

·   ·   ·

·

Peter took the lift down at eight o'clock and let himself into Cornwall & Company, the wine shop on the ground floor. He stood for a moment and watched the sunbeams cut little swaths through the dust in the air, which was in the process of gathering on the hundreds of bottles that lined the walls of the large shop.

He walked to the rear of the shop and climbed the old circular staircase to the offices above. He set his briefcase on the desk in his little office and sat down heavily. As he did, the door from the first-floor landing opened and Maeve O'Brien stepped into the offices.

"Maeve," he called out.

She came to his office door. "Yes, Mr. Kinsolving?"

"Would you get me a seat on a flight to New York? The earlier the better."

"Of course. I thought you were staying until next week, though."

"Old Mr. Bailley has had a stroke."

"Oh, I'm sorry to hear it. I'll call the airlines." She hung up her coat and went to her desk.

A few minutes later, Maeve was back. "You're on the eleven o'clock; it was the earliest. I'll pick up your ticket from American Express, across the street."

Peter suddenly couldn't tolerate the office anymore. "I'll pick it up myself. I could use a walk."

"As you wish."

He let himself out the front door of the shop, locking it behind him and walked slowly past the Connaught Hotel and toward Berkeley Square. Even if Jock was still alive, at his age he couldn't come out of this whole. What would happen if he couldn't communicate, couldn't make his wishes known? Oh, Jesus.

He circumnavigated Berkeley Square and started back up the south side of Mount Street, past the poulterer's and the antique shops, past the tobacconist and the chemist, past his tailor's. He remembered he had a fitting that morning. He stopped at the little American Express office as the manager was letting herself in.

"Good morning, Mr. Kinsolving," she said pleasantly.

"I'd like to pick up a ticket for New York," he said. "The reservation's already made."

"Certainly. I won't be a moment."

He stood outside the agency and watched the morning light fill the elegant street, with its pink granite buildings, lately sandblasted of the decades of London grime, looking new in the moist air. He loved this street. He could get almost anything done within the block—have a suit made, lunch at the Connaught or Scott's, pick up a packet of condoms from the Indian chemist, then forget to use them, be measured for a brace of shotguns at Purdy's on the corner, or select a case of good port at Cornwall & Company, his London base. It jarred him that he was leaving this to go back to New York before the appointed time. He didn't know what awaited him there, and he didn't want to guess.

After a passable airline lunch, he ordered a single malt whiskey, uncharacteristic for him at this hour. He wasn't sleepy, but he wanted to be. An announcement came that the movie was about to start. He flipped up the little screen on the arm of his seat and adjusted the headset.

As he did, someone came forward and took the empty seat next to him. "My seatmate snores," a man's voice said. "Hope you don't mind."

"Not at all," Peter replied, smiling politely, not bothering to glance at the man.

The titles came up on the screen, and Peter prepared to lose himself in whatever the movie might be. It turned out to be the Alfred Hitchcock classic, *Strangers on a Train*.

2

Peter folded away the screen and put away the headset, then accepted his third Scotch from the flight attendant. He turned to the man beside him out of automatic courtesy. "Join me?"

"Don't mind if I do," the man replied. "What is that you're drinking."

"Laphroaig."

"Oh, yes, the same for me, please."

Peter looked at his companion for the first time and found him to be very much like himself. Hardly identical in appearance, but about the same age, mid-forties, the same good clothes, good haircut, good teeth. His hair was sandy, going gray, as Peter's was dark, going gray. He noticed the three-button cuff at the end of the man's sleeve and knew that they went to the same shirtmaker. His accent was hard to place; something English in it, but not English; mid-Atlantic, maybe.

The man offered his hand. "I'm Alexander Martindale," he said. "Sandy will do."

"Peter Kinsolving." They shook hands.

"Not Pete, I hope."

"No. I had more than one fistfight over that as a kid. Never like it."

Sandy's drink arrived. "Your good health, Peter," he said, raising his glass.

"And yours, Sandy." Both men drank.

"God, that's good! You can taste the peat. Too many of them wouldn't do your liver any good, though."

"Certainly wouldn't," Peter replied. "Not unless you were laboring very hard in the vineyard, sweating it out."

"And what vineyard do you labor in, Peter?"

"Wine. I buy and sell it. You?"

"Art. I buy and sell it. In San Francisco."

"I'm in New York and London. I can't place your accent."

"California Brit, I guess," Sandy said. "Born in Liverpool, been out on the coast for twenty years."

"How's the art business?"

"Good. And wine?"

"Good and getting better. I'm glad to see the recession behind us. I've got a lot of good claret in the cellars I'd like to have sold two or three years ago."

"But you can get more for it with the extra age, can't you?"

"Yes, but it's less nerve-wracking to sell it young, keep it moving."

"Your clothes are English, but your accent isn't."

"Grew up in Connecticut. Lived in or around New York all my life."

"School?"

"Amherst."

"I was at Oxford, probably about the same time."

"I envy you the experience. I tried for a Rhodes Scholarship, but didn't make it."

"You're the right age for Vietnam."

"Missed it. Had a wife and child by the time I left New Haven."

"What did you do right out of university?" Sandy asked.

"Went into advertising, like my father."

"When did the wine trade come along?"

"Not for some time. It was liquor, at first. My wife's father has had a large distributorship since Prohibition ended."

"Sounds like he might have been in the business before it ended," Sandy said, smiling.

"Right. His family were distillers in Scotland. He was the second son, so they shipped him to Canada, to see if he could move some of their goods to a thirsty America."

"And did he?"

"Oh, yes, and the goods of a lot of other distillers, too. By the time he was twenty-one, he was driving fast motorboats down the Bay of Fundy to the coast between Boston and Portsmouth. He knew Meyer Lansky, Lucky Luciano, the lot of them. They convinced him he should stick to importing, rather than distributing. They had that well in hand."

"So, when Prohibition ended, he went legal?"

"That's right. His father died about that time, and his older brother inherited. But he had the distribution rights to the family brands, and he was well connected with other distillers, as a result of his recent activities. He poured his illicit profits into the business, and pretty soon he was leading the pack."

"And how long did he run the business?"

"Right up until yesterday. He had a stroke last night."

"That's a long run. How old was he?"

"Ninety-one."

"So you'll take over, now?"

"That remains to be seen," Peter sighed. "Old Jock

had a son and a daughter late in life. The son's in the business; I'm married to the daughter." He sighed again.

"You don't make it sound like the happiest of circumstances."

"I'm sorry. I didn't mean to whine."

"Oh, nothing like that, Peter, but I can see how that sort of family could be difficult to live in."

Peter pulled at the whiskey again and began to relax. He found he needed to talk, and he had the ear of a sympathetic stranger, someone he'd never see again after this flight.

"It was difficult at first," he said. "I married Joan the summer after my junior year at Amherst. She was at Mount Holyoke, and she was pregnant, if the truth be known, and I wanted to do the right thing."

"Were you in love with her?"

"Yes, and I was, oddly, very happy when she told me she was pregnant. Old Jock, her father, thought I was after his money, of course, so I made a point of not taking a penny from him. I worked two jobs my senior year, and we lived in a garage apartment. I don't think I've ever been happier."

"Why advertising? You said your father was in the business?"

"Yes, he was an old-timer at Young & Rubicam, and I joined the trainee program there. Did well, too. Jock had assumed I'd want a job with him, so I managed again not to meet his worst expectations. He liked that. Before long, he was insulted that I hadn't come to work for him, and he began to press me hard. When I thought I had played hard-to-get for long enough, I gave in. Since by that time, I was a successful account executive at Y&R, I thought he'd want me to take over his marketing." Peter laughed ruefully at the memory. "Let me tell you something, don't ever go to work for a Scotsman without a contract."

"I take it you did."

"I did. He put me to selling booze, and do you know what my territory was?"

"Not good?"

"The Bowery! One day I had a nice office and a secretary on Madison Avenue; the next, I was in and out of every gin joint from Eighth Street to Houston, in the regular company of what used to be called bums— that was before they became homeless."

"I don't guess you sold much single malt whiskey."

"Not much. Sixty percent of my sales were in cheap gin and rye. We weren't in the wine business in those days, so I didn't have to sell muscatel."

"Was it tough work?"

"I worked my ass off, and never made a squawk, either. Jock was waiting for that. Meantime, his son, John Junior, or Laddie, as he's always been called, was working the Upper East Side, lunching at 21 every day and getting his suits made at Dunhill's. If I'd showed up on the Bowery in a Dunhill suit, I wouldn't have lived through the first week. I worked in coveralls, out of a panel truck."

"I take it this didn't last forever."

"No. After two and a half years, Jock brought me uptown and put me in marketing—as *assistant* marketing manager, working for an old rummy who didn't know a third what I did about marketing and advertising."

"And how long did you take that particular form of abuse?"

"Not long. After about two weeks, I walked into Jock's office and, more or less, told him to go to hell. I told him I wouldn't work for him another day, that he didn't have sense enough to use talent where it would do some good."

"And what was his reaction?"

"I don't think anybody had ever talked to him that way before, but he took it surprisingly well. Cunningly, he asked if I had another offer somewhere. I told him the truth—I didn't, but I'd go out and make a job for myself. Advertising was in something of a depression at the time, and Jock knew it, but he knew I wasn't bluffing, either, so he surprised me."

"He gave you the marketing job?"

"No. He asked me what I'd like to do in the business."

"And what did you tell him?"

"I hadn't expected the question, so I didn't have a ready answer. Rather impulsively, I blurted out that I wanted to start a wine division. Jock didn't know anything about wine. I mean, he drank single malt Scotch with his meals. Not that I knew a hell of a lot about it, either, but I had the advantage of knowing more than Jock did, and to my surprise, he took me up on it. 'Okay,' he said, 'I'll give you a hundred thousand dollars of capital and a thousand square feet of warehouse space. Go start a wine division of Bailley & Son, and let me know how you do.'"

"That was quite an opportunity."

"I was flabbergasted, really. I walked out of his office in a daze. I don't think I slept for a week; I read every book about wine I could get my hands on, I visited every wine shop on the East Side, and I found an empty storefront on Madison Avenue and rented it. I invested most of my capital in California wines, and I took full-page ads in the *Times* and sold at steep discounts. It was my only way into the market, and it worked; I turned a twenty-thousand-dollar profit my first year, and I established some invaluable contacts with growers. The business grew rapidly.

"Then, three years ago, I heard from a friend that Cornwall & Company, an old established London shipper and retailer, was about to go on the block. The last Cornwall was on his deathbed, and he had not done a good job with the business when he was healthy. They had a golden reputation and a severe cash-flow problem, and I persuaded Jock to go for it. I bought it from the widow a week after Cornwall died, and it's been the most fun I ever had."

"That's great," Sandy said. "What happens now?"

Peter finished his drink and signaled for another. "I don't know. If Jock had stayed healthy for another month, I'd have been a major stockholder in Bailey & Son."

"You mean you're not?"

"I own about three percent of the stock, but Jock was finally ready to do the right thing. The success of Cornwall finally convinced him that I was indispensible, I think, and he made me some extravagant promises."

"Which now, he may not be able to keep."

Peter started on the new drink. "Right. I don't know why I'm telling you all this."

"Can I make a guess about something? The marriage to Joan isn't what it once was."

"Hasn't been for, I don't know, twelve, fifteen years."

"And Jock has a grandson?"

"Our boy, Angus."

"Is he in the business?"

"No, he opted for medicine. He's a resident in cardiology at Lenox Hill Hospital."

"Is Joan in the business?"

"Not up to now," Peter replied.

"Suppose Jock dies tomorrow? What will Joan do?"

"She and her brother, Laddie, will inherit Bailey & Son. Except for my three percent, of course," he said ruefully. "And then I think it's likely that Joan will divorce me."

"Ahhhhh," Sandy moaned softly. "She's got you

between a stone and a very firm surface, hasn't she?"

"She has."

"Well, you're not alone, Peter. I've been building my gallery for eighteen years, and it's become a regular cash cow. However, my wife of fifteen years has just announced her intention to divorce me and marry a painter that I made into a giant of the art world."

"I'm sorry, Sandy, that's a tough break."

"Tougher than you know. California is a community-property state."

Peter let out a short, ironic laugh. "Believe me, if New York were a community-property state, *I'd* divorce *Joan*."

"It gets worse," Sandy said. "Her new husband, the painter, will take most of my good artists with him, once the divorce and settlement are final. She'll take half the business, then, together, they'll gut my half."

The captain came onto the loudspeaker system and announced their approach into Kennedy Airport.

"Peter," Sandy said, "did you enjoy the movie?"

"*Strangers on a Train?* Loved it. I must have seen it half a dozen times."

"Tell me, what went wrong with Bruno's plan for him to murder Guy's wife and for Guy to murder Bruno's father?"

Peter thought for a moment. "Two things, I think; first of all, Guy didn't take Bruno's proposal seriously until it was too late, and second, and most important, Bruno was crazy."

"What do you think would have happened if Guy *had* taken Bruno's proposal seriously, and if Bruno *hadn't* been crazy?"

"Well, I think they would have pulled off two perfect murders." Peter stopped talking and looked at Sandy with new, if somewhat drunken awareness.

"Peter, do you think I'm crazy?" Sandy asked.

"I don't believe you are," Peter replied.

"Do you think I'm a serious person?"

Peter looked at Sandy for a long time. "I believe you are," he said, finally.

The airplane touched down and taxied to the gate before anyone spoke again.

Sandy stood up and stretched. "Perhaps we should talk again," he said.

"Perhaps we should," said Peter.

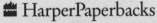